Further Praise for *The Universal Donor*

"Nova is himself a sort of 'universal donor.' His books are for everybody." —Scott Bradfield, *New York Times Book Review*

"Intellectual pulp fiction. The masters of noir are obvious influences on Nova; his prose races with a fast pulse."
—Jocelyn McClurg, *Hartford Courant*

"In the novels of Craig Nova, something always happens—hearts are broken, shots are fired, flames are lit and roads are traveled. *The Universal Donor* is a hard-edged look at the struggle and moral conflicts within one man's heart, used as a reflection of the human race as a whole."
—Dorman T. Shindler, *Denver Post*

"A neat compression of Raymond Chandler and Michael Crichton (Philip Marlowe goes to medical school) leavened with a bit of David Mamet."
—Rex Roberts, *Washington Times*

"One of America's most accomplished—and underappreciated—novelists. . . . [The fate of Virginia] is something you'll discover only if you plunge into the dangerous, blood-tinged world of this darkly hypnotic novel."
—Alan Cheuse, *Dallas Morning News*

THE
UNIVERSAL
DONOR

THE
UNIVERSAL
DONOR

CRAIG NOVA

W. W. NORTON & COMPANY

New York · London

Book design by Melodie Wertelet

Library of Congress Cataloguing-in-Publication Data
Nova, Craig.
The universal donor / Craig Nova.
p.   cm.

I. Title.
PS3564.O86U55   1997
813'.54 – dc21   96-37997   CIP

ISBN 0-393-31845-1

W. W. Norton & Company, Inc.
500 Fifth Avenue, New York, N.Y. 10110
http://www.wwnorton.com

W. W. Norton & Company Ltd.
10 Coptic Street, London WC1A 1PU

1 2 3 4 5 6 7 8 9 0

FOR WOLF KAHN

ACKNOWLEDGMENTS

I would like to thank the many people who made their knowledge and expertise available to me when I was writing this book. In particular, I would like to convey my gratitude to the following physicians. If there are any medical errors in this book, they are mine, and if there is an accuracy in the description of the case portrayed here, it is theirs. – CN

Dr. David Albright   Dr. John Bookwalter

Dr. David Fagelson   Dr. Peter Gibbons

Dr. Michael Gregg   Dr. Herschel Raney

Dr. Franz Reichsman   Dr. Chris Thompson

He discovereth deep things out of darkness,
and bringeth out to light the shadow of death.

[Job 12:22.12]

THE
UNIVERSAL
DONOR

D R. TERRY MCKECHNIE stood at the sink in his kitchen and looked out the window. It was seven-thirty in the evening. From his window he saw Los Angeles, or he saw those parts south of Sunset that stretched away toward the ocean. After dark, the lights made a yellow clutter that was beautiful, yet oddly alarming, as though it concealed a threat. Terry got a glass of water and thought about the hospital. More patients had drug-resistant tuberculosis than before. New diseases from the tropics were appearing in the city, and many of these were particularly vicious. Vicious diseases, of course, were nothing new. After all, plague had even broken out in Los Angeles, in the twenties. A couple of hundred people had died. What really left Terry staring at the lights with dread was the number of gunshot wounds he was seeing. The high-velocity rounds were particularly destructive, and he was seeing more of those cases. The gunshots were bad, but there were some other cases, too, that left him standing here and looking out the window. He'd seen one the night before.

1

As Terry stood there he realized that his state of mind was something new. He had gone through the same process as most physicians, a kind of hardening that was necessary to go on being a doctor, but recently this toughness had become insufficient. In its absence, he had moments like this, which left him wondering just where he was headed. Terry touched the Xanax in his pocket, a sample that had been left at the hospital by a drug salesman.

The water tasted of chlorine, which, from Terry's point of view, wasn't such a bad thing. A friend of his, an epidemiologist, liked to remind Terry that bacteria of different species were able to exchange genetic material. As a physician, Terry liked to think that he was able to keep one jump ahead of the mutants with new antibiotics, although at times he wasn't sure about this.

Terry came from a long line of physicians and surgeons. In his grandfather's house, which was on Hollywood Boulevard not far from where Terry lived now, the talk had always been of medicine, of sutures and instruments, of incisions (Rocky-Davis, McBurney, and Battle), of one's percentage in correct diagnosis. Terry's grandfather maintained that if you were always a hundred percent correct in operating for appendicitis and never found an appendix that wasn't inflamed, someone was going to die. It was better to find some appendixes that weren't inflamed than to miss one that was. Eighty percent correct was the figure he thought was right.

On the day Terry received his acceptance to the UCLA Medical School, he drove from Westwood (where, as an undergraduate, he had an apartment) to his father's house out in the Valley. His father had been a radiologist. Terry's father looked at the letter, and said, "Well, we better get over to your grandfather's," and then they got into his car, a good, serviceable station wagon (unlike the primer-gray Porsche that Terry drove). They went over the hill and pulled up in front of Terry's grandfather's house, which was built against the hillside, a series of enormous white blocks topped with terra-cotta tile. Terry's grandfather's name was Jack McKechnie, but everyone called him Iron Jack.

Iron Jack had quit his practice, although he still treated a few of his old patients, and when Terry and Terry's father had entered the study, which now served as an examination room, Iron Jack was checking Ben Halloway's prostate. This was the Ben of Ben's Supermarkets. Ben was curled up on his side, knees pulled up to his chest, pants around his ankles. Iron Jack wore a plastic glove and his eyes had the faraway look of any physician who is checking a prostate. Terry's father held up the letter for *his* father to read. Ben grunted. Iron Jack said, "Yes. That's all right. Everything's fine," being as economical with words, now, as he was in his surgical technique, summing up both the medical school acceptance and Ben's prostate at the same time. They had champagne in the kitchen, where Terry's father (who was now in a nursing home) and Iron Jack (who was now dead) and Ben (who, when Terry saw him now said he wished he was dead, the way his joints were killing him) stood next to one another as they drank. Between sips Terry's grandfather discussed surgical technique. A Battle incision gave the best exposure. A Rocky-Davis was made in the skin line, and left the smallest scar. He said that he had treated some gunshot wounds, bad wounds, by clamping the arteries from the heart in such a way as to divert blood to just the head and the heart. "It buys a little time," he said.

Terry wondered why it is that medicine seems to run through families, like a streak of white that some people have in their hair. And when he was preparing for medical school he often wondered where the ability to endure medicine existed, or just where on the genetic material a physician was marked, the strands of

DNA twisting around each other like a banister going around a spiral staircase.

In medical school, Terry attended a lecture where he had learned that one of the best questions to ask a patient, when trying to diagnose alcoholism, is "Can you remember your first drink?" A real drunk will answer this with an uncanny clarity, recalling the clothes he wore, the time of day, the people he was with, the odors that had been in the air (especially the scent of perfume), the way in which the light around him had been enhanced by warmth and brightness. Terry understood this perfectly, not in the context of alcoholism, but of the moment when he had discovered he was a universal donor. He could still remember precisely what he had been doing when he had found out. He had been standing in a biology laboratory, the light of the fall afternoon coming through the windows. The panes of glass were dusty, and this made the light into a whitish haze. Terry stood next to a young woman whose cotton blouse had been dried on a clothesline, and the fabric had the scent of the open air. She had been leaning over the counter, where she was working, the fragrance of her hair mixing with that misty light. It made him feel that much more attracted to medicine because it really was in his blood after all. And in a way that he found difficult to describe, the knowledge gave him hope.

Now Terry was in his middle thirties. He stood at the sink drinking water and thought about the case he had seen the night before. He turned and looked at the refrigerator, where a magnet held a wedding invitation to the door. It was from a classmate of Terry's from medical school. Rick Bartlett. Rick once had a landlady who used to get up in the middle of the night and turn off the electricity for an hour to save money, and to beat her at her game Rick used to set his electric clock an hour ahead. And, of course, sometimes the landlady slept all the way through the night, and Rick got up an hour early for nothing. In medical school, losing an hour's sleep was a serious matter. Terry and Rick started to become friends when Terry said, "Get a windup clock." Rick had talked about becoming a surgeon, even a neurosurgeon, but in the end he had become a dermatologist. Regular hours and good pay is how Rick had explained it, blushing as he did so. Easy practice. All you need, said Rick, are Valium and cortisone and to remember the basics: if it's wet, make it dry, and if it's dry, make it wet. Terry hadn't seen him in years. He looked at the invitation: the printing was good, engraved, textured when you touched it.

Terry hadn't been getting out enough. He knew it was a bad sign when he went out and couldn't talk to people who weren't physicians, but he took comfort in the fact that it was a fairly new phenomenon. When he was alone, the weight of a bad case, which previously he had been able to ignore, now seemed to combine with a general longing for an antidote to those moments when he stood at the window and drank that chlorine-tainted water. He stood there, looking at the lights from the city, the coolness and gaudy intensity of them seeming like malice itself. In the silence of the house, in which regret so perfectly mingled with desire, he reached into his pocket for the Xanax. He took half of it, estimating the rate of absorption, and then he thought, Screw it, and took the other half. Sometimes he stood at the kitchen sink until the lights seemed warmer and more appealing and even romantic. Anyway, he guessed he'd go to the wedding.

Terry practiced internal medicine, but recently he had been spending two nights a week at the hospital. One of the emergency medicine physicians had died and while the hospital looked for a replacement, the medical staff was dividing up the work. Everything took more time now than it used to: there were federal regulations to follow, hiring practices to observe, and, of course, a number of committees to consult. The hiring process had dragged on for months. Terry didn't think much was going to change.

The hospital was situated south of Westwood, and it took cases from neighborhoods that were well-off and those that weren't. Usually, the gunshot cases started coming in at around eleven o'clock. Terry supposed that this was because it took a couple of hours of hard drinking in the evening to bring people to the point of using a gun. On weekends the gunshot wounds started coming earlier, although Terry usually had a little warning because the ambulance called ahead. The worst cases were those that just came in the door. No warning. There had been one of those the night before.

In California, in the spring, the storms build steadily: at first there is nothing more than a mist in the sky, but each morning is a little more gray than the one before. It continues like this, day by day, the soft hues of the sky slowly becoming darker and filled, too, with a hint of foreboding that can be relieved only by rain. It was in the building stage right now. Terry had driven to work glancing at the sky.

A young man had arrived at about nine o'clock. Everything about him, the T-shirt he wore, the jeans, the running shoes, his jacket, suggested someone who could tell, down to a minute, what was cool and what wasn't. He probably wanted to get a tattoo, but hadn't been able to decide about the right one. A flower? A nude woman? A diamond in the small of his back? . . . (Terry was seeing a lot of geometrical tattoos these days.) His friends had simply brought him in, through the doors that opened with a swish, all of them running up to the triage desk. There were three friends. The young man they carried was having convulsions.

He had long red hair and freckles. His name, Terry learned later, was Sam Peterson. He had been riding around in a friend's car. They hadn't been able to find anything to drink or smoke, and so the young man had gone into a convenience store and bought a can of butane.

His heart had already stopped. Terry looked around for the cardiac equipment, but it was down the hall. While he went to get it, a nurse stayed with the young man. A woman was in the next cubicle, by the defibrillator: she had come to the hospital after taking a handful of Tylenol. She looked at Terry with a mixture of shame and defiance as he came in and grabbed the machine and pushed it out into the hall and from there into the room where Sam Peterson was, the nurse hammering on his chest, and saying, "Oh, shit. Oh, shit." They put the paddles on his chest, which was pale and thin and looked as though it had never seen the sun. The young man jumped when the electricity hit him: the suddenness of it reminded Terry of Frankenstein's monster coming to life. There was a brutality in it, too, as if the mechanism of life had become spiteful.

The heart started again, and Terry and the nurse and an anesthesiologist stood there. Terry still held the paddles. He listened for the heart. It was going all right. The anesthesiologist intubated the young man. They could control the oxygen better that way. The throat was swollen and it wasn't easy to get the tube in. Terry realized that he had been clenching his jaw, and thinking, Don't die. Don't die.

At that moment Terry heard a noise, a reassertion of ordinary sound, footsteps in the hall, the squeak of a curtain on an overhead runner, the odd rattles of a stainless steel IV stand, the distant sound of the television in the waiting room, the clicking of computer keys, all coming back as though whatever had been happening wasn't a matter of terror but something that simply filtered the sound.

Terry noticed some pink froth coming out of the tube that had been down the young man's throat. The lining of the lung, where gases are actually exchanged, is only two cells wide, and Terry realized, as he saw that froth, that the butane was breaking it down. He first thought about the possibility of the boy drowning in his own blood, but that was before he thought about acidosis — the buildup of acid in the blood. The heart stopped. They had a monitor attached to him, and Terry watched it. He could do nothing about the heart because the shocks only worked if there was enough oxygen in the blood. The anesthesiologist and Terry stood there and watched while the young man died.

Anyway, in the morning, after Terry had finished his shift, he stood in front of the hospital for a while, and just at dawn he had seen the sky filled with a diffused and yet aureate glow. A few stars were still visible, too, in the west. It hadn't rained and the clouds had disappeared. Then he got into his car and drove home, touching the sample of Xanax in his pocket. He didn't take it right away. He was tired enough to sleep on his own for now.

In the evening, he woke and went into the kitchen, where, through the window, he saw the clutter of the city. His face was a little numb, as though he were wearing a plastic mask. Along with this, he had another sensation, which was the presence of something that seemed to suffuse the landscape with . . . an impulse toward . . . he didn't know precisely what, a loving inevitability, he supposed, between himself and another human being. He swallowed the bitter water. Just how was he connected to the young man, anyway? Terry had wanted to keep him alive. This desire was something he could depend upon. It was the purest thing he had ever experienced. And what, if anything, had been torn, or ruptured, when the patient died? It was the summation of such moments, the continual addition of that sense of separation, that left Terry with the impulse toward some particular human being: he didn't know who she was exactly, but he was sure, if only by the effect of her absence, that she existed.

Terry stood in the kitchen. The thing that he saw on the icebox was the invitation to the wedding.

THE MORNING Virginia Lee was bitten in earnest, by a taipan, she stood in the clean lab with the snake moving up her arm. It did this by swinging from one fang to the other. Mostly, this is something that a cobra does, although other snakes have been known to do it. Virginia removed the taipan, feeling the smooth, actually pleasant touch of its skin, and the strength of its movement, which suggested a spring-loaded mechanism. Virginia put the snake back in the box from which she had taken it. She closed the lid. Other specimens were in boxes along the walls, brown snakes, some Asian snakes, and death adders, too. Virginia had been mystified that anything as dangerous as a brown snake could have such an unassuming name. A taipan didn't sound as bad as a death adder, but it was far worse.

Virginia's hands were covered with small scars, white, half-moons and round shapes that were the color of mother-of-pearl. The scars came from the many times she had been bitten by snakes. She was a tall woman, close to thirty, slender, with blond hair that was a metallic color. Her lips, which were full, were the color of raspberries. Her eyes were a particular green, like a leaf with the sun behind it.

The taipan was a brownish snake with neat rows of scales. Near the head and along its side, it had some markings that were the color of nicotine. Its head was pointed and sleek, and the snake seemed to have an expression of intense, yet unfriendly, curiosity.

Sometimes, a person who has been bitten begins to see the world through a yellow cloud. Virginia wasn't sure whether the taipan produced such a toxin. She wondered if the fact that she didn't know was an indication that she was already getting hazy. Virginia knew most venomous snakes produced a combination of toxins: some caused bleeding pathologies, while others paralyzed skeletal muscles, and some interfered with the blood's ability to carry oxygen. She looked at her arm to see if her skin had started turning blue.

She supposed that the snake had been hungry, which is another way of saying that it had been cranky. Some snakes in the lab seemed to have a palpable moodiness one could predict and, to some extent, depend upon. Mostly, the snakes were easier to handle after they'd eaten. Virginia liked to watch them when they were in a mood that required that they be handled with extreme care. At these times the snakes were alert, and moved with a liquid grace. They did not slither. They flowed. These days, venom of the taipan brought $219 a gram, although the venom from a brown snake was bringing $1,550.

The antivenom was kept in a refrigerator by the door of the lab. It was white, and it had a neat red cross on it that reminded Virginia of military ambulances. She opened the door and found the vials for the antivenom she needed. There were two of them. One was filled with a clear liquid, but the other seemed to have been exposed to air. This vial was only partially filled, and the substance inside wasn't clear and obviously medicinal, but brownish and apparently spoiled. Virginia wondered how regular the rotation of the supplies had been. The bottles weren't dated.

Virginia hoped she hadn't been envenomed. Certainly, though, she didn't have a lot of time if she had been, not more than an hour, but she was sure that she could get to the hospital by then. She didn't trust the other people in the lab to do the right thing, or to stay out of the way. The best course, or so she supposed, was to say nothing. She picked up the two vials of antivenom and went out, passing the receptionist, going through the automatic doors and into the parking lot. She'd drive to the hospital. She trusted a doctor there, or at least she wanted to be with him now. That was the critical thing.

It was a clear day, and the light fell with all the force of tropical rain. Was she beginning to see the world through a hazy, urine-colored mist? Did the venom work that fast? She had a headache, but she wasn't sure that it had been caused by the venom, although she knew a headache was one of the early symptoms. Along with irritability. In front of her, the cars were arranged in neat rows, but the colors were mixed together with a kind of disorder. The sun shone on the chrome as an elongated and silver star.

Virginia kept trying to determine if the light was turning yellow. Like old newsprint, she thought. As though trying to save something that was slipping through her fingers, she thought of those moments when the light had been beautiful, not so much because of the light itself as much as what it was able to reveal. She hoped that beauty had some therapeutic effect.

She remembered the cabin that her grandfather had built in the Sierras. The cabin was made of logs from nearby trees, and it had two stories, and a chimney made of round stones. Her grandfather had been an engineer, although in his heart he had wanted to be a prospector. He spent his life poring over the documents of early Spanish settlers for a reference to a mine in this part of the Sierras. He was convinced a number of them had been here, and that the clue to their whereabouts was in old deeds. Her grandfather had sat in the chair, the one with broad wooden arms and a seat covered with wool, and told her stories about Spanish gold mines, which he knew were there because he had seen nuggets the size of walnuts, and just when she thought he was a crazy old man, he had taken her hand and dropped into it a nugget that was the size of a walnut. It was heavy on her palm and bright in the light from the hissing Coleman lamps, the sheen of the gold almost liquid and somehow ominous, if only as a reminder of the treachery and obsession that had gone into obtaining such nuggets. He offered it as a proof of truthfulness and of his love for her.

One time she had stayed alone in the cabin. She had fallen asleep on the sofa, which she had made up as a bed. She didn't sleep for long. The sun came in the window and lay across the foot of the bed in a yellow triangle. The light made the cabin warm, and Virginia kicked off the blankets and lay there, in just a T-shirt, seeing the shape of her legs, the sheen on her calves, the sunlight as it fell into the hair between her legs.

Soon, though, it got cloudy, the color of the sky becoming a series of shades of purple on deeper purple. Lightning filled the room with a purple strobe, and the thunder came with the two-toned quality of something being ripped before it explodes. Along with the sound she saw a shower of light, just small flecks, which emerged with a crackle. This, she supposed, was heat lightning. It seemed to come down the chimney, or just appeared in the room with an electric presence. The bright flecks were almost like the color and shape of those that come off a sparkler. She lay in the static electricity, which had a faint scent, like the one that surrounds a generator. The thunderstorm kept on moving, and the sunlight appeared again, although now, as it came in the window, it seemed tinged with a little green, as though somehow the aspect of the damp shadows under the pines and oaks had been able to tint the light, too. The air had the fresh scent of grass and bark, and the water that dripped from the eaves seemed particularly silver, each drop as round as a bubble. She lay in the sunshine. Outside, she heard some birds, and in the breeze she heard the susurrus of the pine needles around the house. The sounds and the light, the air and the piney scent, combined in a moment of exquisite promise.

Now she got on the freeway, and began to think that this wasn't a good idea because it was crowded. The cars came to a halt, one behind the other. She put her hand on the horn and almost began to blow it, but she knew this would do no good. Around her the other drivers stared straight ahead, all wearing dark glasses and looking like the attendants at the Styx who had been dressed up to pass in the modern world. She swallowed, although it was getting a little harder to do so. The paralysis began in the cranial nerves and would reveal itself in the muscles in her face. She guessed that the yellow tint to the air was just pollution, and she tried to comfort herself with that.

For a while she thought that her heart was beating very quickly, but she hoped it was just the throb of the idling car. The exit she wanted was only a few hundred yards away, and she thought that maybe she could get out and start walking, but what would happen if she didn't make it? How long would she be left at the side of the road? In Los Angeles these days, no one wanted trouble.

She put the car into neutral and tried to think clearly. There was no agreement about using a tourniquet. What it boiled down to was that a tourniquet was probably useful for venom with neurotoxins, which were those that caused paralysis, but probably not such a good idea for those that dissolve tissue. Virginia thought the taipan had some of both. She looked out across the hood of the car next to her: the landscape beyond it shimmered, as though the hood of the car had been as hot as a stove. The movement suggested something unstoppable. Virginia thought that anything to slow things down would help, and she took off her shoes and her panty hose and twisted them into an awkward rope that she tied into a loop and slipped over her arm. She took a flashlight from the glove box, which she used to twist the noose tighter. She guessed that it should make a firm pressure.

The cars sat there, filling the air with heat and fumes. Now that she could definitely feel her pulse, throbbing under the nylon, it seemed much faster than she thought it should be. She tried to comfort herself with the notion that it was fear, not snake venom, that made her heart beat like that.

The difficulty was trying to find the right amount of pressure for the nylon, just enough to dilute the venom so as to keep it from lysing the flesh, but not so much as to release the paralytic toxins. She let a little pressure off, if only to stop feeling that high, fluttering beat. Up ahead the cars began to move, although they seemed to go only about thirty yards before stopping again. She swallowed, which was even more difficult than before. Some people who had been bitten by Australian and New Guinean snakes had lost consciousness suddenly, and those who had survived described the sensation of being struck by a heavy object. She went back to waiting, watching the cars. Up ahead someone lost patience and began honking his horn, and the repeated bleating seemed to be the sound of futility itself. Virginia opened the door and started to get out, doing so with all the airy impulse of panic, but she knew that running would be the worst thing in the world to do, and then, as if having gotten through a bad moment, she sat down again to wait.

She turned on her signal, the clicking of it seeming idiotic, but there wasn't anything else to do. The cars moved ahead enough for her to get to the off ramp, which was crowded, too. She had to wait before making a turn. The air moved with a glassine undulation, at once clear and obscuring those objects she saw. She counted slowly, one, two, three, four, five, piling up the numbers as a way to fight panic, but they didn't do any good because they were nothing but ciphers. She tried to think of anything that was ordinary and part of everyday matters. Had she paid her income tax on time? Did she think all of the deductions would be allowed? Could she remember the wording of the IRS guidelines? Up ahead the cars had stopped, the air above them trembling with gases.

What about romance, then? she thought. That had to be better than the IRS. She thought about it for a moment, the delicious sense of letting go becoming almost indistinguishable from panic, as did any memory of circumstances in which things were out of control. There was nothing she wanted less, right now, than surrendering to some powerful emotion or desire. She looked around and saw that yellow cloud. Her pulse was obvious under the tightened stocking, and she became frightened about keeping the venom confined. The cars began to move, and she got down to the end of the ramp and turned toward the hospital.

It was a new building, made of brick, and from the front it looked like a pyramid, the steps on the sides going up one story at a time. Virginia guessed this was good architecture for a hospital built in a place that was waiting for the Big One, the earthquake that was taking centuries to unleash. A parking lot was in front of it, surrounded by a fence topped with razor wire. Across the street from the parking lot there was a brick annex, on which someone had taken a can of spray paint and written, "Yo gonna die." Someone else had come along and, in another color, a bright red next to the original yellow, had added "Soon." Virginia glanced at the spray-painted words and stopped in front of the entrance. It looked a little yellow.

TERRY HAD SEEN a few snakebite cases. The closest thing he had ever seen to an exotic snakebite was a couple of years previously when a herpetologist in Griffith Park Zoo had been bitten by an Indian cobra. It wasn't a king Cobra, but was still a very venomous snake. And then there was a man, a burglar, who had been bitten by a rattlesnake when he had reached underneath the front porch of a house, feeling around for what he hoped would be the door key. He told Terry that all he really wanted was the stereo and computer that he had seen through the window. A nice IBM. His arm had turned a number of shades of purple and red, was swollen to twice its normal size, and was encrusted here and there where the tissue had broken down and had started to bleed. Not that many people die of rattlesnake bites, though. Terry was more concerned with gunshot wounds. Or drug-resistant tuberculosis.

When Virginia arrived at the hospital she stopped at the entrance and got out of her car, not bothering to close the door or turn off the engine. She approached the building not so much like a runner coming out of the starting blocks, but with the sudden lurch of a drunk. There were a couple of people in the waiting room, and they turned to watch, their expressions limited by their own worries. Virginia walked to the triage desk. Her skin was pale. In one hand she had the panty hose and flashlight. She said she had been bitten by a snake, an exotic one. She had antivenom. She held it up for them to see. Was Terry McKechnie there? In a voice that was not as loud as she would have liked, she called out, "Terry! Terry!"

He came out and saw her holding out her arm. "Right here," she said.

They went into one of the examination rooms. She sat down on the table, crumpling the paper covering, still holding out her arm. A nurse came in and took her blood pressure. Virginia kept looking directly at Terry, and when the nurse went out, she said, "Are you going to help me?"

Terry took her arm and looked closely at the skin. She had only a small scratch, as though someone had nicked her with a nail. He wasn't even sure that it had been made by the snake. Maybe she had brushed up against something, a splinter, a bit of wire in the lab where she worked. As he looked at her arm, she kept staring at him. "You know what I'm thinking?" she said.

"I bet you're plenty scared," he said.

"That's what I'm feeling," she said. "I'm thinking how much I love you. Do you know that?"

"Yes," he said. "Everything is going to be all right."

"I bet you say that all day," she said. "Have you ever treated a snakebite? A real one?"

"I've seen a couple," he said. "What kind of snake was it?"

"A taipan," she said.

"How bad a snake is that?" he said.

"A bad one," she said.

"What makes it that way?" he said.

"The venom has more than one toxin," she said. "It has a lot of them. Neurotoxins. Hemolytic toxins. Mylotic. I don't know a lot. It was a snake I'd never handled before. I'd read a little. Not much. But that's not the real problem."

"What?" he said. He looked right at her.

"The real problem is that this particular snake seemed to be a little different from other taipans. The guy who caught it thought it might be a different species. That might mean it has different toxins, although I guess they'd be somewhat similar to the ones we usually see. Anyway, that's one of the things we were trying to find out about it."

"Where was it from?" he said.

"New Guinea," she said.

She held out the vials of antivenom, one full and clear, the other half empty and brown. Terry looked at them, trying to remember what he knew about exotic snakebites. The one thing he didn't know was what happened when antivenom broke down. Were there toxins in it? What happened when you gave out-of-date antivenom? One thing was certain: antivenom didn't have a long shelf life. Couple of months. It was expensive, too, and he guessed that the lab where Virginia worked would want to get as much time as possible out of each new purchase.

Terry went into his office and dialed the number of the local poison control center, but the physician, a woman with a very pleasant voice, didn't know much about snakes from New Guinea. She said it was a good idea to give the antivenom early. What did early mean? asked Terry. Within a couple of hours, the sooner the better. She didn't think that the antivenom broke down into something that would hurt the person who took it, but she wasn't sure about this particular antivenom.

Terry wrote down a list of preparalytic symptoms to watch for. It was a good idea, he was told, to call a medical herpetologist. He could find one at Stanford. The poison control center gave him a number and he called. The line was busy. He tried again. He turned on the computer and ran Grateful Med, but he found nothing there: lots of articles, plenty of abstracts, but nothing that told him anything. He dialed the number again, closing his eyes while the call went through, squeezing the telephone and hearing the sound, the repeated throb and tone, throb and tone, having the aspect of something at once cute and mean-spirited. He thought of Virginia as she lay in the sunlight in his bedroom, the color of her skin highlighted by it, and if he got very close, he could see a sparkle in the minute texture of the flesh. Then he stood up and went back into the room where she waited now. As he stood there, she told him she was going to throw up, and he held a wastebasket for her, and when she was done, he washed her face, and thought, All right. That's one thing I was supposed to watch for. He wished for a clear, definite progression, but he knew that it wouldn't work that way.

"The paralysis begins in the cranial nerves, doesn't it?" she said.

"I think so," he said. "Do you feel any numbness in your face? Any difficulty in swallowing?"

"It's hard to say," she said. "Maybe it's just beginning."

She looked pale, almost blue, and she was sweating, too.

"Are you allergic to anything," he said, "like horses?"

"Yes," she said. "A little bit, I think. I get a little sneezy around them. My eyes water."

He turned to look at her now. Antivenom was made from

horse serum, and the use of it with someone who was allergic to horses could be almost as bad as a snakebite.

She looked around the room. "Why is the light so bright?" she said. "Can't you turn it off?"

"I've got to leave it on," he said.

"Why do you have to do that?" she said. "I've got a headache. You can't believe how it hammers. It feels like someone has got something wrapped around my head. Oh, stop it, please stop it. Why won't you help me?"

"Tell me about the light," he said.

"It looks yellow," she said. "Piss-colored."

He stood there, trying to think. Was being allergic to horses, just by being around them, to their dander, was that the same as being allergic to the serum? He went back and redialed, waited, hearing the busy signal. What could the man possibly be talking about? He had a number at UCLA, too, and he tried that now, but he got a departmental secretary who said that the doctor he wanted to talk to was at a conference in Singapore.

Terry came back in. Virginia's blood pressure had fallen a little.

"The sooner you use it the better," she said.

"Listen," he said. "Here's what we're going to do. I'm going to scratch your skin with a little antivenom. Just a little. If you're going to have a reaction to it, it should show up with the scratch."

"Maybe you should just use it," she said. "The sooner you use it the better."

Terry felt along her arm and into her armpit to see if there was any swelling. The venom spread through the lymph system. He turned toward the antivenom, but the difficulty was which one to test, the half spoiled one or the one that was still in a vial that hadn't been exposed to the air?

"I wish you'd turn off that light. It looks broken, like glass that's all shattered."

Terry looked at her face. Was she just exhausted or did she have some lack of expression, a slackness around the eyes?

"Can you swallow?" he said. "Try."

"Yes," she said. "It's a little hard."

He made two scratches on her arm, one with the seemingly spoiled stuff, one with the antivenom that looked all right. He didn't think it would be very long, a couple of minutes maybe. He stayed there. He didn't think he could stand to hear the busy telephone again. He thought about MedLine and the other computer search engines. Those were for people who had all the time in the world. The trouble was that a lot of exotic snakebites were idiosyncratic. Certainly he had heard of cases where everything seemed to be fine, and then the patient crashed: renal failure, shock, hemorrhage in the brain. He knew that twenty percent of people who died from a bad bite had bleeding in the brain.

"I don't even know how it happened," she said. "It happened so fast. That's what everyone always says when something goes wrong, but that's the way it was. You can't believe how quickly these things can happen. I wasn't being careless. I really wasn't. Do you think there's going to be any bleeding?"

"I don't know," he said.

"Ah," she said. "I'm not going to scream. That's what I'm telling myself."

"Scream if you want to. The problem is that you never know what the dose of venom is. That's always an unknown."

He looked at her arm, and although he wanted to touch the scratches to see if there was any swelling, he didn't, if only because he didn't want to make them red, or do anything that might make the reaction unclear.

"You know what I keep thinking about?" she said.

"No," he said.

"I had a beautiful dream," she said. "Last night. I saw a man, totally white, like Ivory soap, and he was very muscular in his chest, and his arms melded into white wings. He was flying around, turning flips, and diving into the foam of the ocean. He was very white."

"It sounds reassuring," he said.

"I don't know. I guess it depends on your point of view," she said. "How long do we have to wait?"

"Not long," he said.

She waited for a second. "It's getting harder to swallow."

"Uh-huh," he said. "Do you have any tingling in your face?"

She shook her head. "Don't desert me," she said. "Please. I couldn't bear that. All right?"

Virginia had a slight swelling along the scratches. Not quite reddish, and not really raised. It was so slight as to be almost unnoticeable, and for a moment Terry thought he was making it up.

"What do you think?" she said.

"I don't know," he said.

"Fuck," she said. "Why can't I have something a little definite? Just once."

He guessed this was fear mixed with the irritability caused by the venom. What he wanted to do was to take a moment and say, I love you. Do you know how scared I am? I didn't think such fear could exist. He wasn't sure whether this would help her or not. Probably it wouldn't, so he stood there. The nurse took Virginia's blood pressure. It was rising, although he knew that later, when the shock started, it would fall. Her pulse was going up. Certainly it would be a good idea to talk to the guy in Palo Alto, but he knew, too, that the sooner he used the antivenom the better. He felt a kind of moral terror sweep over him: Just how bad had he been for her anyway? And was he getting ready to do something here that was harmful? Wasn't that the first thing, to do no harm?

She put her head back and covered her eyes. "That light," she said. "I can't take it much more."

"All right," he said. "I can treat the allergic reaction to horse serum."

"OK," she said. "There isn't much choice."

Even then he was thinking, What synergy is there with the venom and the allergic reaction? If the scratch test was vague, does a larger dose cross a threshold? He went back into his office and called the guy in Palo Alto. He got through this time, but a secretary answered the phone. Terry left his phone number and went back in to set up the antivenom in an IV drip, and he watched the steady, almost clocklike progression as the fluid came out of the bag and into the tube that ran down to Virginia's arm.

"I feel faint. Real shitty. I'm going to be sick," she said.

A nurse had left a clean plastic wastebasket in the corner of the cubicle and he held it out for her. He guessed he'd load her up with steroids for the allergic reaction, and give her some adrenaline, too, for the shock. He called the nurse to get the steroids, and she told him he had a telephone call. Some guy in Palo Alto.

The man in Palo Alto was trying to be calm and businesslike. He spoke with an accent, one that Terry had heard before, one that came from an eastern school. Groton, Terry supposed. Still, even though the man tried to speak slowly, he had something in his voice that Terry didn't like. After a second it became clear to Terry. The guy's voice, the tone of it, suggested relief at not being in Terry's shoes. If you only knew, thought Terry.

The man in Palo Alto agreed that Terry had taken the right course, at least he had started to. He asked Terry if he had given Virginia the adrenaline yet.

"No," said Terry.

The man in Palo Alto sighed. "That's good," he said. "I wouldn't give it to her. Not unless she's getting sour. Not until you think she's going to die."

"Why's that?" said Terry.

"The venom is going to cause some bleeding," said the man in Palo Alto. "Or it might. It's hard to say. But if she starts bleeding, it could be in the brain. The adrenaline will raise the blood pressure. That'll make the bleeding in the brain worse."

"All right," said Terry.

"You can call again," said the man in Palo Alto. He waited a minute more. Then he said, "You'll probably want to."

For a moment neither said anything, and Terry had the notion that the man in Palo Alto felt guilty about wanting to hang up, just as Terry didn't quite want to let go. Was there something else he should know?

"Let me give you another number," said the man in Palo Alto. "There's someone else you should talk to."

"Who's that?" said Terry.

"A man in Australia. Angus Bouton. That's his name."

Terry looked at his watch: it was four A.M. in Australia. He'd try in a little while. He wrote down the number and put it in his pocket.

"OK," he said.

"Bouton knows all there is to know about these bites. Call him if you need more help."

Another physician was on duty, an internist, whose name was Mary Bell. She came in now and looked at Virginia, then went over to Terry. Terry asked her if she knew anything about exotic snakebites, and Bell shook her head. She said, "Have you talked to someone who knows about this stuff?"

"Yes," said Terry.

"What did he say?" she said.

Terry shrugged.

"You don't look so good."

"No," said Terry. "I probably don't."

He talked the situation over with her, and she listened carefully. Then she said, "All right. If that's the way it is. At least we know what to look for."

"Uh-huh," said Terry.

"It's too bad," said Bell. "She'd just gotten married, too."

"Yeah," said Terry.

"Her husband is on his way," said Bell. "You want me to talk to him when he gets here?"

"No," said Terry. "I'll talk to him."

About a half hour later, Terry found Virginia's husband in the waiting room. Terry hadn't seen him since the afternoon, a few months previously, when Rick and Virginia had gotten married. Rick was a dark-haired man who managed to make being tall seem awkward. He had always been shy about his height, and when Terry thought about medical school he remembered Rick slouching against doors and walls. His eyes were dark, almost black, as shiny as licorice.

"Well," said Rick. "What's the verdict?"

"I don't know," said Terry. "Not really."

They went back to Terry's office and sat down. Rick had become a dermatologist because, in medical school, he noticed that the only group that was always at the lunch table on time in the cafeteria were dermatologists. Terry tried to describe what the difficulties were, although he didn't tell Rick everything. He mentioned maybe a third of what was on his mind. The truth was that Rick understood the medical difficulties in only a general way because his practice didn't involve really sick people. If he saw a bad case, such as an aggressive cancer, he referred the patient to someone else. Also, many things had changed since the two of them had been in medical school together. Diagnosis had been the art that they'd all learned there, although now it wasn't so important. The tests were very good, and a missed diagnosis was a rare thing.

"That sounds pretty bad," said Rick.

Terry thought, He really doesn't understand.

"She's pretty sick," said Terry.

"Is she going to be admitted to your care?" said Rick.

"Is there someone else you want?" said Terry.

"No," said Rick. "It's funny, she's been asking about you a lot recently. Like, what you were like in medical school."

"Oh," said Terry. "Is that right?"

"Yeah," said Rick. "Is there any trouble in having her admitted to your care?"

Terry shrugged and looked around the room. The walls were a cream color, off-white, and some books sat on the shelves. It wasn't much of an office, really. Then he thought of how often he had advised other doctors to get out of a case if it was difficult, or somehow beyond them: just having someone take a fresh look was useful. In bad cases, physicians ended up chasing each new event rather than seeing the entire scale of what they were facing. Secretly, though, he had always had a mild contempt for physicians who did this, although he had never articulated it to himself until now. Along with it came the fear that such contempt was a variety of justification for what he was going to try to do. After all, the critical care people were waiting to take the case from him. All he had to do was step back.

"What about the critical care guys?" said Rick. "Are they going to take the case from you?"

"I don't know," said Terry. "I'll talk to them. And the medical director. They'll be there no matter what. Especially if things get difficult."

"Difficult," said Rick. "That's one way of putting it."

Terry said they were going to put a tube into her throat to help her breathing. Rick wanted to know if Terry was going to do it, or if they were going to get an anesthesiologist. Terry said he'd get the anesthesiologist to do it, if that made Rick feel better.

"Yes," said Rick. "I guess. I only had to do it once. I couldn't get the damn thing in."

Part of what Terry didn't say was that some snake toxins damaged the blood's ability to carry oxygen, so it wasn't just a matter of getting oxygen into the lungs. Terry didn't know if this venom had that toxin, and neither did the guy in Palo Alto. They'd have to wait and see. Anyway, Terry ordered more antivenom, thinking that they would probably go through a lot of it.

Every half hour or so he went into Virginia's room, upstairs, where she was hooked up to a monitor. She seemed to be breathing all right and the blood gases seemed to be in about the right place. She couldn't talk because of the tube, although she had a metal clipboard on which she wrote occasional messages in a loopy scrawl. Terry knew that it was possible that she could lose consciousness, and that it could happen fast, too.

Terry spent the night in the room adjacent to the physicians' lounge. The bed was made up with hospital sheets that smelled of chlorine and were stiff with starch. He got into it, but all he could do was smell the chlorine in the dark, which suggested the attempt to cover something up, as though a reassuring scent was all that was needed. He got up and tried to read for a while, but that wasn't good either. He walked along one of the halls upstairs, hearing the linoleum squeak under his shoes.

He went outside to the parking lot and got into his car. Now that he had time he wanted to be clear about just what was scaring him. More than anything else, he guessed it was that the effect of the venom and the effect of the allergic reaction to the antivenom could be about the same. The crash that came with an allergic reaction could take as little as ten heartbeats: the blood pressure could come down that fast. What would he be treating, shock heart from the venom or the allergic reaction? As he drove north, he looked at the hills. A few planes crossed the sky. Aviators loved the morning, before the air turned turbulent from the heat. Then Terry felt a suction, an inevitable advancement of a medical condition, one step leading to another, in which the possibilities were limited, each new limitation bringing Terry closer to the spot where he really didn't want to be: a position in which there really wasn't any good decision, just one that wasn't as bad as another. He'd watch for a rash. Any wheezing. Maybe he'd have a little warning.

And these were the possibilities before Virginia started to bleed. He suspected that was coming, but he was hoping it wouldn't. Maybe there wouldn't be any bleeding. Maybe they'd have a little luck. But just in case, he had asked the lab to match her blood so he'd be ready to do something about it if she started to hemorrhage. Above him the hills appeared as a dark shape, like something under a tarp. He hadn't been able to tell her he loved her, and as he drove up the street toward his house, he wished he had. Terry stopped the car and got out. Now the silence, the shapes of the trees, the dark houses, suggested a gulf of some kind. He wished he had been able to tell her.

VIRGINIA FOUND IT DIFFICULT to think clearly, although at moments she knew precisely where she was and what had happened to her. Later, though, she felt the dimness of the room descend over her like a dark gas. The effect of the venom overwhelmed her, although even in the queasiness and the knowledge that something was terribly wrong, she wanted a clear idea of just how she had come to this particular place.

When she was lucid, she guessed that the bite, and some other trouble, too (which she didn't want to name, but which she let herself feel as a shadow of her attempt to love someone), had something to do with an automobile accident that took place a year before in Berkeley, California.

The accident had taken place at the corner of University and Shattuck. It was spring in Berkeley, and the afternoons were warm and filled with a hint of the Mediterranean. The entire vista was filled with pastels, warm yellows and pinks, and lime greens, and brownish hillsides that could have been in Italy.

Mostly, she had driven a series of secondhand cars with bald tires and with the stuffing coming out of the seats, old Volkswagens and Fords and Chevrolets which left a cloud of black smoke in the air like some genie of uncertain intent. The year she finished her studies, receiving a Ph.D. in zoology with a specialty in venomous snakes, her uncle had given her a car, a fire engine red, four-wheel-drive Jeep. Her uncle lived in Colorado, and he sent her a note that said, "Congratulations. There's a car waiting for you at the Jeep dealership on University Avenue. I don't want my niece driving around in some wreck like every other new Ph.D. who's top-heavy on knowledge and light in the transportation department."

She had been driving down University when another car, trying to make a left-hand turn, had simply driven into the new Jeep. It collided with the left front fender, making a bang, as if someone had hit an oil drum with a baseball bat, and the headlights broke with a tinkle. The radiator hissed. Virginia got out, not hurt as far as she could tell, although her legs and hands were trembling. Other cars went by, some backed up behind her, and she was disoriented and embarrassed. Along the sidewalk people turned to stare. The steam from her car smelled of antifreeze. She noticed that some birds sat on a telephone wire across the street, all of them turned the same way. Even then she was curious as to why she was trembling so much, and she guessed it wasn't just the noise and the suddenness with which she had been made into a spectacle in the street, but something else altogether, the malicious arrival of the unexpected. It had been waiting, or so it seemed to her as she stood there in the steam, to jump out at her.

She looked at the driver of the other car, and thought, A crypto-hippie. He didn't exist in the old style, but as a second- or third-generation flower child, a man about her age who was, as nearly as she could tell, a mirror image of the changes that had taken place in the country, which is to say that while the hippies from years ago had been interested in peace and free love, he was more interested in money.

He had dark hair. As she stood there, still trembling, wishing that the hissing would stop, that she could get away from this mess, she realized that he looked more European than American. He was a little taller than she, and he was wearing a blue shirt and a pair of gray pants, and as he appeared out of the steam and the broken glass, the two cars locked together like mechanical beasts fighting over territory, he seemed to have arrived by legerdemain, or by some other theatrical stunt.

"I'm sorry," he said. "It's totally my fault."

She now walked around to the front of her car and looked at the fender. It was pushed in a little, but she thought she'd be able to drive it. His car was dented, too, but not so badly as hers. Hers was newer, more plastic and less metal.

"Are you hurt?" he said.

"I don't think so."

"Well, thank God. What do you think it would take to square it?" the young man said. He opened his wallet. He had a stack of hundred-dollar bills.

"I don't know," she said.

"A thousand?"

She looked at the car.

"Well," he said. "We can talk that over. Let's drive these cars out of here. My apartment is right here. We can park in the lot."

"Are you hurt?" she said.

He stopped and looked at her. "Me?" he said. "No, I'm all right."

Her car now seemed forever reduced, in a way she didn't like to think about, and her hopes along with it. She had been planning to get a job working outside. Some studies were being done with western snakes. Anything would be better than a lab someplace, gathering venom, although she guessed that was important to do. Some preparations, such as Captopril, which lowered blood pressure, were made from the venom of the Brazilian viper. Another drug was a muscle relaxant. Did it come from mambas? She couldn't remember. She didn't like the feeling of being in the damaged car, which seemed like hope come to grief. She pulled into the parking lot.

The apartment building was an old one, squarish and pink. There were trees along the street, and leaves formed lacy shadows on the sidewalk. Virginia found herself thinking of some underthings she had bought but never worn because they had seemed too daring. Why had she bought them anyway?

"I guess we've got to report this," she said to the driver of the other car.

"Do we really need to have the cops involved?" he said.

She turned to look at him. He seemed too self-assured, someone who thought he was above rules and regulations. Virginia was a moral woman, and she took rules and regulations seriously: she would never cheat on her income tax, and if she discovered that anyone had given her the wrong change, in her favor, she would make an effort to return the money that wasn't hers. She told the truth, particularly in matters where people depended on her. She was, in fact, a woman to whom people instinctively turned: she inspired enormous trust. Now, though, she stood in the parking lot, looking at this man and finding that, for an instant, the notion of rules and regulations, of a correct way of doing things, had, or so it seemed right then, all come at a price. She wanted a moment to think, to slow things down.

"Why not?" she said.

"My insurance expired when I was out of the country," he said.

"Where did you go?" she said.

"Oh," he said. "Here and there. Europe. Have you been to Europe?"

She hadn't, and she didn't want to admit it, because it seemed to be giving ground somehow. Instead, she shrugged and said, "That was a new car."

"I'm sorry. But we can fix it. Why don't we do this? Why don't I buy the car from you and you can go buy another one?"

He spoke quite sincerely. She thought of the stack of hundred-dollar bills in his pocket.

"Come on," he said. "Come up for a moment."

"I better stay here," she said.

"OK," he said. "I'll make some coffee and bring it down."

He turned and went upstairs. Virginia was still shaking, but she nevertheless gravitated toward the man who had hit her car. She stood there, trying to summon up a good, trustworthy anger, but her effort had about it all the irritation of artifice. She found herself trying to explain the fact that she was soothed by him. What was behind it? She guessed that it had something to do with his friendliness, and the fact that whatever she wanted to do was fine, or so he seemed to be saying.

Virginia stood in the parking lot, looking at the two cars, the bright red Jeep still steaming. Wasn't it rude of her to have refused to come upstairs? After all, the man had admitted that the entire thing was his fault, offered to pay for the damage. In fact, his behavior had been exemplary, even charming. And what about her? She had been shrewish and ungraceful. Was the piece of machinery more important than her manners, her dignity?

She went out to the sidewalk and into the building. There, in the hall, the vernal light was tinted gold as the lines of sunlight streamed through the window, the flecks in it making infinitely small flashes, as though the dust was made out of glitter. She went upstairs, following the scent of coffee, which was strong and bitter.

At the door of the apartment she hesitated. Wasn't she supposed to be standoffish with someone who had hit her car? Wasn't there a battle line to be drawn? Maybe there would be a lawsuit. Was coming here something that could be used against her? Was accepting coffee agreeing to some resolution? She even imagined a lawyer grilling her about her motives for entering his apartment. Just what had she intended by it?

He was in the kitchen. She could hear reassuring domestic sounds, the banging of silverware, the opening of a cabinet, the clinking of good china cups on the counter. Virginia considered how different the sound of this kitchen was from her own, where the man she lived with liked percolator coffee that came in a can.

She looked into the living room and saw two couches with big pillows. Some prints hung on the wall. She glanced at one, a nude, in which a woman's nipple was painted a fertile pink. For some reason, she wanted to be precise about the color, if only to avoid thinking about the soft and enticing image. What was the color of the skin, of the nipple, of the small triangle of brownish pubic hair, and what was it in the paint, what glow seemed to imbue it all?

She walked into the kitchen.

"Oh," he said. "So you decided to come in. Good."

The kitchen cabinet doors were made out of wire so that what was on the shelves could be seen. A round table stood in the middle of the room. Virginia thought of what it would be like here in the morning with the warmth of the room mixing with the aroma of coffee and sweet rolls and the scent of flowers on the table (pink ones, the same color as in the painting). What kinds of things did people share, a man and a woman, say, in such a place? What piercingly intimate thoughts or dreams?

She took the cup of coffee he offered her. It was good and strong.

"You know," he said. "After that accident, I think I'm going to have a little brandy in mine."

He took a bottle of brandy from a high shelf, a green bottle, and poured some into his glass. She watched the flow of the brandy, and wondered how he could drink so early. It was barely afternoon, wasn't it? She had always associated drinking something like brandy in the afternoon with the forbidden.

She wondered what the man she lived with, whose name was Peter (not Pete: he was very strict about that) would think of her now, in this warm kitchen, with her smashed car downstairs, having a drink in the afternoon. Peter was blond, crew cut, a student of computer science. He got up early, ran, did his work, and lived by a set of rules that, while never articulated, seemed to be a somewhat elaborate version of the Boy Scout code. He liked to cook, and was good at it, and he had a sense of humor, although it was a little tart. When they got into bed, it was with a regimented quality as well, as though they were obeying rules here, too. Once, after they had been through this sexual routine, she started giggling, and although she would dismiss it as a mood and wouldn't dream of saying another word about it, nevertheless what had occurred to her was that more than anything else these occasions struck her as being a little like a very polite Ping-Pong game. Or, at least, as regular and about as satisfying. She couldn't say to him, I want you to be a little rougher . . . I want you to reach with your fingers and . . . I want to be marked somehow, if only in the heart, by some secret knowledge, by something we could never even mention to someone else.

"Yes," she said when he offered her some brandy. "Please." She held out her cup.

Even then she suspected that the danger here wasn't so much that he might hurt her, but something else, something unnameable, just a suspicion, a fear that she was somehow reducing her usual life to a phantom of itself. It was becoming unreal, losing its grip on her. She wasn't sure if she liked the notion of that, of being without moorings.

He sat there, with his head down, one hand to the side of his face. It was a gesture of some gentleness and concern, something that seemed essentially good. She looked up and saw a handgun on the icebox. Or so she thought it was. A wooden crate with pigeonholes in it sat on top of the icebox, and it looked like one of the pigeonholes held a pistol. The butt seemed to be made of wood that was textured with small pyramids. She looked away. Surely this was more of her bad nerves after the accident. Her hands were shaking and she couldn't tell whether it was from the accident, or the unknown possibilities that suddenly presented themselves. She glanced into the living room where she faced the print of the nude woman. The woman was reclining, her arms behind her head.

"You don't even know my name," he said. "It's Joe Egan."

He held out his hand, and she took it, feeling the warm, dry palm.

"It's nice to meet you," she said. She blushed. He looked away.

"Listen," she said. "I don't know about not going to the police. I've got to think about it."

"Of course," he said. "Sure."

She went downstairs, remembering the taste of the brandy, which lingered in her mouth like a kiss.

The car didn't drive so easily as before. The front end shimmied, and when she put on the brakes, it pulled to one side. The car was overheating. She wished that the accident hadn't happened, that she was just going along with her life, as usual, but even then she had the suspicion that if this accident hadn't happened, something else would have: this notion left her uneasy.

She parked the car and got out and walked along the avenue, stopping from time to time to look in a shop window. She saw only herself in the reflection of the glass, but even there she could see that she had never looked better. Her face glowed, was at once moist and yet warm. And her features seemed to be set a little differently.

She went into a restaurant and walked to the rear, where there was a women's room. She went in and closed the door, locking it behind her, and there she turned and looked at herself in the mirror. Her eyes and her skin, which had always been smooth, and her expression, too, were clearly changed in some way. She could see the effect of . . . well, she didn't know what to call it precisely, but certainly part of it was a blush of vitality. And a hint of shock, too, as though she had seen an unexpected pornographic image.

She put down the lid of the toilet and sat there, trying to sort out what was happening. More than anything else she didn't want to succumb to vanity. Just the possibility of such influence made her harden her resolve to think things over and to be careful. She had to admit that not only did she look good and alive and radiant, but that she looked fertile, too.

She went out to the avenue and started walking back to her car, somehow hoping that when she got there, she'd find it without damage. She passed the restaurants, bookstores, and New Age hippies selling tourist junk.

At home, Peter said he had almost bought something on impulse.

"What did you almost buy?"

"A Ping-Pong table," he said. "But there was no place to put it."

"A Ping-Pong table?"

"Yeah," he said. "Don't you like Ping-Pong?"

She told him about the accident, and they went downstairs and looked at the car. He kneeled down in front of the fender with an air of taking care of a sick animal, a lamb, maybe. She knew that he was trying to show that he cared about her, but she wished he wouldn't fawn over the car.

"Well, the guy has insurance, doesn't he?"

"Well, yes," she said.

"What does that mean?" he said.

"He's got money," she said.

"So what?" he said. "Do you want me to handle this?"

She looked at him. "No," she said. "I'll take care of it."

"Sure?" he said.

"Yes," she said.

Peter went for a run. When he came back, he seemed more cheerful, as though he had accomplished something. Joe Egan called when Peter was in the shower.

"Hi," said Egan. "How are you?"

"All right," she said.

"I just wanted to say that I was sorry about the accident today," he said.

"It's all right," she said, although she was thinking, No. No. It's not all right at all. Twenty-four hours ago I was certain about things, so unshakable about what I was doing that I could even afford a mild contempt for myself, and now . . . now, she realized, now I've been waiting for you to call.

"I want to see you," he said.

"Well," she said. "Maybe. I don't know."

"How about tonight?" he said.

She looked toward the bathroom: she could smell Dial soap. She knew what it meant when he used Dial soap.

"No," she said. "I don't think I can get away."

"How about tomorrow?" he said.

"Well," she said. "Maybe."

"When?" he said. "In the morning?"

"All right," she said, sighing.

He mentioned a place on Telegraph Avenue. She said she knew it, and they agreed on a time. Peter came in wearing a towel around his waist. He asked her how she was feeling.

"How am I?" she said.

"Uh-huh," he said. "You feeling all right?"

He threw back the covers and lay down on the bare sheet, legs spread a little. She sat down next to him and undressed slowly.

"You sure you're feeling all right?"

"Fine," she said.

She smelled the Dial soap, the scent of it seeming safe and predictable, and when she felt him touch her, she tried to imagine something dangerous, a gangster who would come into a room and take off his coat and hang it on a chair, exposing his shoulder holster, with its straps across his back and the pistol in it, which he would hang on a chair, too. In the dark, with Peter next to her, his breath coming in reassuring sighs, she felt ashamed. She had never done that before, never denied the presence of someone she was sleeping with by imagining a scene so silly and cheap. She lay there in the dark, feeling again and again, with the same regularity as the lingering sensation she had after a day on a sailboat, the sudden thump of the cars banging into one another and the almost musical tinkle of the broken glass.

Virginia and Joe Egan were both early. She had showered with Dial soap and had put on a blue shirt and tan skirt, realizing that she wanted to look scrubbed and innocent, as though that could compensate for what she was thinking. She knew that she didn't want Egan to be good, or decent, or even trustworthy.

They both had coffee. His hands were shaking a little, and when she noticed, he looked at her and smiled. He knew, he said, that she had probably gotten a funny idea about him. For instance, had she seen the gun in the kitchen?

"Yes," she said.

"I should have put it away."

"Why do you need it?"

"Well," he said. "That's what I wanted to talk to you about."

He said that he wasn't sure how to explain to her why he was going to speak to her so honestly. She had to believe that it was honest, or the entire point would be lost. Of course, he had done some things that were illegal. It had started when he had had a business, importing used car parts into India from Europe. He drove the parts in a truck. That's how it had started, and of course, one thing led to another. She had no idea what kind of people he spent time with. They were vile, really, and they cared only about money, or making a display of themselves. The horrible thing is that he found it difficult to meet anyone who wasn't like this. He even wondered if he had driven his car into hers just for the sake of meeting her.

"What can you tell about the person in the other car?" she said.

He shrugged.

"Maybe more than you'd think," he said.

It was important to him to be able to spend a little time with her. He didn't know how much time he had, really. Sometimes he had the impression that there wasn't a lot of it. After he said this, he sat quietly in the warm room, surrounded by the scents of baking bread and pastries. He didn't mean to presume anything. Not the smallest thing. No impertinence was intended. All he wanted her to know is that he had been places, right here in Berkeley, or in Oakland, that were appalling. It was hard to suggest to her what he had seen, and, for that matter, he didn't want to. It was important that she allow him those hours with her when he could have the illusion of getting away from those things. He said there was nothing romantic about gangsters, or almost nothing, and even when they had nicknames like Bucket o' Blood, if you understood it, the name was anything but an amusing curiosity.

They each had a pastry, an apple tart, and she sat there, tasting the cinnamon and sugar, and looking at him. How could she say that the last thing in the world she wanted was goodness? Was he going to write poems for her? She preferred to recall the moment when she thought she had seen a pistol in the kitchen. Still, she was touched by his sincerity. He really meant what he said. The odd thing was that all of this made her more sure of her own desires, her own fascination with the dangerous and unpredictable: wasn't it there, in the face of possible disaster, that one learned just what one was really made out of after all? In an instant she saw that things had changed: it was up to her. He would go along with what she wanted to do.

They both ate the sweet pastry, the almost jellied apple. She put her hand across the table and took his, knowing that the gesture sealed some promise between them.

At home, she was reading a paper on the extermination of grizzly bears in California when the police came to the door. She looked up when she heard the knock, and as she got up to answer it, she was infuriated with herself for looking so proper, so like a schoolteacher, with her short cropped hair, her blue jeans and T-shirt, her sweater on top of it, her frumpy handbag (on the table), her scrubbed good looks. The way in which she had been living seemed to her somehow cowardly and sterile at the same time, and that the safe man she lived with, the steady academic progression, the regular and even predictable advancement of her life, all carried with them a variety of deadly confinement.

One of the policemen had white hair and blue eyes and he wore a sport coat with stretched-out pockets. His partner was a younger man in running shoes, blue jeans, a blue shirt with a yellow tie, and a jacket that had come from some expensive shop. Or maybe not. Maybe it was an imitation of an expensive jacket. It was hard to tell.

She invited them in. They sat down.

The policeman with white hair looked a little sick. Perhaps it had come from walking into one too many strange apartments, but now he sat there, looking at Virginia with an expression that was compounded by fatigue and illness and which didn't imply curiosity at all. He introduced himself as Walter Bennet. He had shown her his badge, but he knew that she had forgotten the name almost immediately. His partner, who identified himself as John Marshall, looked around the room.

Bennet was thin, and the lines on his forehead and around his mouth suggested a perpetual expression of having been correct, although this wasn't a matter of pleasure because mostly, over the years, what he had been right about had to do with the number of times someone had lied to him.

"You were in an accident recently, weren't you?" Bennet said.

"Yes," said Virginia.

"Did you report it?"

"No," said Virginia.

"You know," said Bennet, "you're supposed to report accidents to the police."

"I thought if no one was hurt it wasn't such a big deal," said Virginia.

"You've got to report the accidents," said Bennet. "That's what the law says."

"Well," said Virginia. "I'm sorry."

"Uh-huh," said Bennet.

"A lot of people are pretty casual about the law," Marshall said.

Bennet looked right at her. Was she casual about the law? "You know," he said. "We have a certain amount of discretion about filing charges."

"I can imagine," said Virginia.

"Uh-huh," said Marshall.

"What do you know about the man who hit you?" said Bennet.

"Well, we kind of hit each other," said Virginia. "It was rush hour and . . ."

"That's not what we asked you," said Bennet.

"Had you ever seen him before?" said Marshall.

"No," said Virginia.

Marshall didn't say anything.

"Have you been to his apartment?" said Bennet.

"Yes," said Virginia.

"See?" said Bennet to Marshall. "What did I tell you?" He turned to Virginia, and said, "You know, we want to be cooperative. About your not reporting the accident."

"Of course," said Virginia, not knowing what she really meant.

"We've been interested in this guy for a while," said Marshall.

"For what?" said Virginia.

"This and that," said Bennet. He said it with a flatness of tone which suggested crimes too large to mention easily. She was reminded of a doctor who might say a patient was pretty sick when in fact the patient had cancer. "So we'd like a little help."

"Like what?" said Virginia.

Bennet shrugged. "It wouldn't be any big deal," he said.

"We've got grounds for cooperation," said Marshall. "You've got trouble reporting an accident."

"One hand washes the other," said Bennet. He looked out the window when he said it.

"That's right," said Marshall.

"I've never heard that expression," said Virginia.

"No?" said Marshall.

"You scratch my back, and I'll scratch yours," said Bennet. "Have you heard that?"

"Yes," said Virginia.

"Now we're getting someplace," said Bennet. "You know what being a cop is really all about? It's communicating. Sometimes you can get across easily. Sometimes it takes more effort."

"Some people don't understand finesse," said Marshall.

"She understands," said Bennet. "It's nice dealing with someone who's smart."

"I haven't done anything wrong," said Virginia.

Marshall and Bennet didn't say anything. All three of them sat there, Bennet looking down now, his hands hanging between his knees as though he'd just let something valuable slip between his fingers. Bennet cleared his throat.

"Who knows what you've done? We haven't looked in your car yet."

"There could be all kinds of things there," said Marshall.

"Like what?" she said.

"Contraband," said Marshall.

"What we want to ask you to do is to go over to Egan's apartment from time to time," said Marshall.

"And do what?" said Virginia.

"Just keep your eyes open. You're smart."

"There are some things we're interested in," said Bennet.

"Maybe I'll just take my chances with the traffic violation," said Virginia.

"Maybe it's more than that," said Bennet, looking out the window again. "Like we said, maybe we'll find something in your car when we search it. All kinds of things turn up in cars."

"It's your decision," said Marshall.

"What should I be looking for?" said Virginia. "At Egan's?"

"The obvious," said Marshall.

"Well," said Virginia. "I don't know."

"We understand," said Marshall.

"Sure," said Bennet.

"We'll come around again. You can let us know. Think it over."

"I'd think it over, if I were you," said Marshall.

They went to the door and said good-bye. Virginia closed it and listened to their steps as they went down the stairwell. She sat down. Just how should she go about thinking about it?

The body shop was on University, and it was a dark, large place in which cars were being repaired, their fenders covered with gray primer very much like the color of a python's skin, and the automobiles that were about to be painted had their windshields and headlights masked with yellow tape and newspaper. The air smelled of resins and paint. Virginia waited on a bench, wanting to have a written estimate, if only so she'd have a reason to walk down to Egan's apartment.

"About twelve hundred dollars," said the body man. "That's what it's going to cost to fix your car. Twelve hundred and change."

He passed over a pink piece of paper with the figures. She reached out and took it, got into her car, and drove to Egan's apartment. There, in the hall, she climbed the stairs, smelling the scent of curry and saffron and incense, too, which she supposed was meant to cover up the smell of pot. She decided that now, at least, she was going to get to the bottom of things. She put her hand out and took the smooth banister, and as she climbed she realized that the possibility of treachery had come into her life, too. She was appalled by it, and yet, at the same time, its existence somehow made her feel a little stronger than before. Or perhaps *stronger* wasn't quite the word. A little more real. She stood before his door, waiting, uncertain about what was really going on. Was it just a fling, some impulse that she was going to follow through with and nothing more, or was she standing on a threshold, beyond which she could look into her own heart and find a horrifying depth, an ability that was at once exciting and damning?

"Oh," he said, when he opened the door. "Hi. Come in."

She came in and sat down at the edge of one of the sofas, her bag in her lap, with both hands on it. What she wanted to do was to relax, to be as comfortable here as possible, but instead she sat with her hands clasped while she despised herself for being so ignorant of who she really was. Why was this necessary after all? Why couldn't she just sit back calmly? Wasn't that the graceful thing to do?

She looked at him, into his eyes, which were blue with deeper, almost purple flecks in them. She held out the estimate. He looked at it and got up and went into the other room and brought back a pile of money, hundred-dollar bills, which he counted out in front of her, putting them down with a quick, practiced regularity that implied a long intimacy with large amounts of cash.

"Here," he said.

She still held the slip for the estimate, the thing flimsy and pink and with purple writing on it. Through a doorway, she could see a bed, a large one covered with only a white sheet, the sunlight falling on it in bright trapezoids from the window.

The money sat there as though it validated something. After all, if he had that much cash, everything he had said might be true, just as it made the interest of the police more legitimate as well. As much as she was frightened, she found that this room had a quality that kept opening beyond her, that kept beckoning, not because it was decent, but because it was exciting. And even then she tried to determine where the excitement came from. Her thinly denied sense of romance, or the hope that here, at least, anything was possible? To reassure herself, she reminded herself that she could easily be a spy, but the thought left her somehow more intrigued than before. Did she have a license to do whatever she felt like because two detectives had come to her apartment? Was it more pleasurable to be absolved of one's actions in advance? It seemed awkward that her impulse should be validated, or encouraged by the police.

"Well," he said. "That should do it."

"Yes," she said.

"Aren't you going to take it?"

She picked up the money and put it in her bag.

He went into the kitchen, and she heard a cabinet being opened. He came back in with a bottle of brandy and two small

49

juice glasses. He poured out two drinks, and passed one over. She took a sip, feeling the warmth of it in her mouth and the long, slow burn in her chest as she swallowed. She looked out the window and heard the traffic of the ordinary world.

"Have you ever had someone inform on you?" she said.

"No," he said.

Occasionally, as she sat there, she had the sensation that she could escape the odd gravitational tug of the apartment. She wanted to leave, but even as she imagined getting up and going into the hall and closing the door, she knew that if she did so something would vanish from her life.

She wanted to be committed to the moment. While the possibility of betrayal, and the sense of stepping outside her usual life had brought her this far, all she wanted now was to be frank. She wanted to stand in front of him, whispering, removing her clothes, saying things that she had only heard rumors of. . . . And even then the possibility of betrayal lingered: it seemed to add another, deeper sense of freedom. For one horrific moment, she realized that she could inform on him to justify coming here. Was she really capable of such a thing, as though doing something like that could absolve her of her actions? Just what license did she have as a spy?

"You have no idea how often I go places to do business and sit in a room, thinking of how people are getting ready to . . . well, do me no good," he said.

"What makes you so sure I'm different?" she said. She took another sip of brandy. She could just catch a glimpse of herself in the mirror on the opposite wall. She had never looked so good.

The phone rang, and he answered it and walked into the hall, trailing a long cord, where he spoke quietly for a while. She could hear the raspy voice, but she couldn't make out the words. She had never been more alone.

She sat there, feeling her hands tremble, and thought she might be approaching a breakdown. She had always assumed that when such things came, they did so with a sudden onset of hysterics, and now it occurred to her that maybe the opposite was true, that such a breakdown could come on the heels of something exquisitely pleasurable.

She was standing by the door, holding her handbag, when he came back. He held the phone in one hand, the cord snaking its way behind him, back into the hall.

"I need a little time to think," she said.

"OK," he said. "Sure." He turned and put the phone down.

"Everything is going a little fast," she said.

"Sometimes I like that," he said. "It's like riding a motorcycle. Have you ever been on a bike?"

"No," she said.

He shrugged. "Well," he said. "OK. Fine."

She went out the door. He closed it. She stood in the hall, already feeling that she was making a mistake, that her entire problem was one of being too careful, too frightened, of thinking too much. No, she hadn't been on a motorcycle. Maybe on the way home she'd go to a motorcycle showroom and . . .

But she didn't. She went back to what had always been a regular life. She did her work, cooked dinner every other night, listened to Peter as he complained about a program he was trying to write, and as she did so, she found herself straining, waiting for the phone to ring, gritting her teeth when it did. What would happen if Egan went on a trip, back to Europe, to South America? What would she be left with then? Everything around her, the prints on the wall of her apartment, the clothes that hung in the closet, the furniture, the enormous TV that Peter had gotten on sale, the movies they watched on the VCR, all seemed dependable and yet oppressive, too. The familiar things now seemed like props for a routine, and what had been part of domestic security now seemed like evidence of confinement. How could something as mundane as a cheap coffee table look monstrous? When Peter asked her what was wrong, his voice was claustrophobic and repetitive, like the recorded voice of a doll. Two weeks went by. Peter became sullen. She apologized when she wanted to scream.

One morning when she was alone, she took a long bath. She told herself that she would dress comfortably, although she picked a clinging top, something she told herself she'd seen a woman in a French movie wear. She primped in front of the mirror, and walked downstairs, carrying a bag, swinging it back and forth. She walked down to the south side, where Egan lived, and went upstairs and knocked on the door. She waited. No sound came from the other side of the door. She turned away, not knowing what to do exactly, feeling somehow that she had waited too long and that she had missed her chance. She guessed she would go home and try to pretend she hadn't come here.

He met her as she was going down the stairs. He said hi, and they turned around, not saying a word, and went back to his apartment door, which he opened, pushing it in with his shoulder.

"Let's go lie down," she said.

They went down the hall into the bedroom, where the light streamed onto the white sheets and left them tinted with gold. The small orange tree in the corner filled the room with the scent of its leaves, at once dusty and fragrant. A couple of small oranges hung from it, each as bright as the tip of a soldering iron in the green depths beneath the leaves. Outside a car went by, the tires rough on the pavement.

She reached over and held one of the small oranges to her nose. "I've always liked the scent of oranges," she said. She sat down.

He said that he had always liked the scent of the oranges, too. It was why he had the tree. He had been intrigued by the tart scent, the stark odor of the leaves. She stretched out, into the sunlight, feeling the warm caress of it. He said that there were oranges in Spain that were wonderful. Had she ever had one? He used to buy them when he was on business in Europe and passed through Spain. He'd sit at the side of the road, in his truck, taking one from a bag and peeling it, splitting the orange into sections, seeing the color, almost red. They were juicy. He could still feel the touch of them in his mouth, so sweet and yet a little tart. He ran his hand under her blouse. She heard the sound of the cars outside.

"I can trust you, can't I?" he said.

"Of course."

Wasn't this what was always said?

She concentrated on the scent of oranges. It seemed that the odor made palpable some maddeningly elusive thing, such as the attractions of a man who was so different from her. He stood and awkwardly removed his clothes, the muscles slithering under the skin of his naked back. She wondered at how delicious it was to drop what she had always believed about herself (a woman who was restrained and sexually shallow, who had used sex as a seal upon domestic arrangements), although she knew that no matter what she discarded, she wanted to make sure she discarded it only here. She wanted to be able to walk out of this place and return to her usual disguise. Even now she could have simply stood up and put on her clothes and walked away, but the sunlight, so permeated with the mixture of vitality and danger, seemed to lie across her like some infinitely pleasurable fabric, warm and silky.

Someone knocked on the door. It was steady, repeated, and

seemed insistent if a little matter-of-fact. Egan closed his eyes, and said, "Maybe they'll go away. Just wait a moment. I'm so tired of being alert. Always alert." He put his hands over her ears. He looked at her eyes, and he was still looking at her when they heard the door as it was ripped off its hinges. The door squeaked, then it made a cracking noise, and finally it splintered.

He still looked at her.

"No," she said. "I had nothing to do with this. The police came to see me —"

"Did they?" he said.

"Yes," she said. "But I didn't agree to anything."

He looked at her again, trying to decide.

"You would have," he said. "If you had been given enough time."

He stood and went to the door, and into the hall. White dust, from the plaster, covered the floor. The police had put a jack against the opposite wall, outside the apartment, and had used it, with a piece of four-by-four, to break the door out of the frame. He turned back to look at her again. After all, he had wanted only something decent. He looked as though he were getting ready to die.

Marshall and Bennet, and some other men, who had guns, came through the doorway and over the plaster dust and the debris of splinters and larger pieces of door. The dust looked like flour. Marshall was wearing the same yellow tie and same blue shirt. Virginia began to get dressed, but she turned to Marshall, and said, "Am I under arrest?"

"No," said Marshall. "We don't want you. Go home."

She buttoned her blouse and put on her shoes and walked through the door, finding it somehow appropriate that it was shattered into a hundred pieces. She ran down the stairs, shaking, believing that she had had her fling, her infatuation, although she knew by the time she had gotten to the street that she had been teased and that, in fact, she had discovered nothing at all, aside from the possibility that she and Egan had been cheated. In fact, she wondered who had been corrupted the most, Egan by goodness, or her by her own impulse toward . . . well, excitement. Egan was going to jail, but, of course, that wasn't her fault, was it? She wasn't entirely sure. When she had left Egan's apartment, he had screamed, "Don't come to see me when I'm locked up. Please. I couldn't stand to have you see me there. Promise me you won't come. Promise." He had gone on screaming when she went down the stairs.

She came in the door to her apartment and found that in an instant she and Peter were arguing. She had been late, hadn't she? They had planned to go out. How could she be so egotistical as to keep him waiting the way she did? Time meant one thing to him and another to her. They couldn't even talk to one another. Wasn't that right? Just what the hell had she been doing? In the kitchen, she started breaking the glasses that she and Peter had gotten at a gas station, which gave its customers redeemable stamps, and they had collected the glasses and used them and felt thrifty and grown-up, when in fact, she now realized, they had been just penny-pinching and cheap. He stood there, listening to the sound of the glass breaking, each crash seeming to reflect something he had believed but which had turned out to be untrue. They had both been nicked by the breaking glass, on the hands and the face, and they stood there, the glass like ice on the floor, the two of them bleeding, looking at each other with disbelief.

"All right," he said. "That's it."

"Yes," she said. "I guess it is."

S o Virginia continued to try to trace the path along which she had traveled, and which had brought her to this hospital room: it wasn't just the facts themselves that she was concerned about, but their implications. Anyway, after she had finished school, she had come to Los Angeles to take a job at a laboratory.

She had driven from Berkeley and checked into a motel on Ventura Boulevard while she looked for a place to live. On her first morning in town she had gone out to breakfast at a Bob's Big Boy. In the classified section of the *Los Angeles Times,* she had found an ad that said, "Bottom half of hillside house. View. Privacy. Furnished." Virginia circled it with a red felt-tipped pen she had bought for the purpose, and then had a sip of coffee as she sat at a counter. Outside she could see a plastic statue of Big Boy, a fat creature who seemed perfectly to combine gluttony and innocence and a sexual neutrality, as though he had been castrated. She went back to her paper, to thinking that she was starting over. While she was old enough now to doubt the ability of new starts to straighten everything out, she nevertheless found that, much to her surprise, she was able to detect in herself some reserve of hope that she hadn't known was there.

Her job started in a week. She was living out of a suitcase in the motel, and she tried to keep things ordered, neatly putting the take-out food boxes into the bag they came in. Now she looked outside, watching the passing cars. She had gotten drunk the night before, sitting in that room by herself, watching TV with the sound off. Her hands were a little unsteady, and the prospect of looking at an apartment carried a weight with it.

The apartment was in a house in the hills above the Hollywood reservoir, and, while she couldn't actually see the water, she liked the idea that it was there. The apartment had a living room, bedroom, and a small kitchen. She had her own entrance, although a door connected her rooms to those upstairs. She moved her things in, took a shower, and looked at the map to decide the best way to get to work. The first night she was there, she heard the people upstairs, a man and woman in their late thirties, watching a pornographic videotape. The sound track had a repetitive, oddly insistent quality (like a recording of profound failure), and she sat there, looking at the city, telling herself everything was fine, listening to the sound until she couldn't stand it anymore and got up and went outside, where she could smell the eucalyptus trees. She came back inside, and after a while she took a glass and put it to the door, listening to the sound: she tried to imagine what was on the screen, and then she stopped and sat down. What, after all, was more lonely than pornography?

She even laughed at herself as she thought she should write a country-and-western song called, "Here I Am Again, Offering More and Asking for Less." In fact, as she sat there, it seemed to her that her loneliness had a pornographic quality itself, and that just sitting there was an admission of an unrealized and constant desire. She thought about staying up all night so that she could see the sunrise, the bright mist of it spreading over the city in the shape of a hemisphere, the air cool and containing only a residue of the smog from the day before.

She guessed she was ready to make some compromises. After all, that was the grown-up way. She didn't expect passion, or anything like that. She was going to be realistic. She had her work in which, after all, she was continually pursuing the mysteries, if not the beauties, of the natural world. That was something, and she should be grateful for it. The expectations of love or romance were somewhat adolescent, weren't they, if not outright silly? She remembered the sound of the pornographic movie, and thought, well, silly or not, she would put her expectations aside so as to be able to live with the silence of this room.

In the morning she woke and lay in the sunshine that came in through the window: in California, in the late summer, the sunshine is so clear as to call attention to itself, and every detail — the molding around a window, the shape of a leaf, the texture of bark, the arrangement of houses on a hill — is uncannily visible. Virginia lay there, feeling the heat of it on her leg. She got up and went outside to a chaise longue on a small patch of grass beyond her door. Before taking a shower or having coffee or anything at all, she lay in the sun in her bathing suit, simply letting the hot, comforting caress lay over her.

During the day she cleaned the apartment, getting down on her hands and knees and working around the molding in the corners with a toothpick and using the strongest, most toxic cleaner in the oven, and from time to time she went to the window or stood in the door to the small backyard and looked at the light, the yellow quality of it now more pronounced than in the morning.

She found herself going to the library and taking down a book from the shelf, *The Properties of Light,* and flipping through the pages, reading about wavelengths and photons, and the excitability of atoms, and looking at pictures in which the light broke into a rainbow. She went to UCLA and sat in on a physics lecture, and she went to the museums to look at paintings, the impressionists mostly, although some of the old masters, too. She could define just what the fascination was: the light suggested order, and a private sense of beauty which was somehow suffused with romantic possibilities, too. The light was a secret code of some kind, a way of having access to those deep feelings that one tries to dismiss as impossible, but which one nevertheless wants to acknowledge. She liked to walk through orange groves, up near the coast, and to see the deep green shadows in the trees, the glowing balls of oranges, the dust in the air between the trees, all of which were scented with that citrus odor. Or she went to the beach and lay in the sun, able to apprehend the light as a glowing presence that shone through her eyelids with a hot private color. She liked to think of the mountains where the light came through the pines in a rush of green tinted air, or the coast, when the light was almost golden, just at sunset, as it receded through the vaporous air.

Virginia didn't have much in the way of housewares because she had left most of that in Berkeley with Peter, and the notion of going out to the hardware store and buying what she needed, pots and pans, glasses, silverware, spatulas, a garlic press, left her with the sensation of a generic life, one that made her a little uneasy because the new things, ripped out of shrink-wrapped plastic, betrayed a failure, or at least an anonymity that she had to struggle against.

The swap meet was on a ten-acre field, just north of Los

Angeles, and Virginia had found out about it from her landlords, who had picked up some good videotapes ("even some pretty kinky ones") at these places, and "reasonable, too." It was afternoon when Virginia arrived among the clutter of vaguely nomadic cars and vans and station wagons.

It occurred to her as she bought a spatula, one with a green, chipped wooden handle, or a mixing bowl with a stripe around the top, or a knife with a worn blade, that she was manufacturing a past with these things that could easily have come out of the kitchen of a loving mother or father, maybe even a rural couple.

A tall man was just ahead of her, and he went along under the temporary blue or green awnings from one accumulation of things to the next. When she was looking at him, he turned back and glanced away, although a little later he saw her again and smiled. When she passed him, he said, "Find anything?"

"Well, a couple of things," she said.

"Look at this," he said.

He held up a mug in the shape of Calvin Coolidge. "Do you think it's a good likeness?"

"I don't know," she said. What did Coolidge look like? She couldn't remember. "Are you a historian?"

"Me?" he said. "Hell no. I'm a dermatologist." He looked at the things she carried. "What's all that?" he said.

"I just moved to Los Angeles," she said.

"Well, it's a hard town," he said. "Make no mistake about that."

"That's what I've heard," she said as she took her bag of utensils, the spatula and grater and can opener, and started to walk away, but he stopped her, and said, "Wait. Here. Take this. Welcome to LA." He held out the mug of Calvin Coolidge.

"All right," she said. "Thanks."

"There's a stand up here that sells coffee," he said. "You want a cup? My treat. Come on."

They walked between the aisles of junk, stepping over a peavey, a seed spreader, some LPs (Rachmaninoff, Elvis, Johnny Mathis, all consigned to the dung heap of camp and recycled objects), and as they went, Virginia had the sense of how easy this man was to be with: it was his basic charm. He had few, if any, rough edges. They drank coffee together, and he asked about her job, and she told him, even showing him the scars on her hands where she had been bitten.

She began seeing him regularly. They went to dinner at Japanese and Taiwanese and Spanish restaurants, and they drove up the coast, or into the mountains, all of it done with an instinct for comfort and with the air of long-term association. It was as though they had been married for years. It seemed to Virginia that a romantic compromise with this man would be the adult thing to do, and, after all, everything about him suggested accommodation. She was amazed that he wasn't already married, and when she asked him about it he said he guessed he hadn't really inspired passion in anyone, or commitment. He shrugged. In the springtime, he asked her if she'd marry him. She said she'd think it over.

It is difficult to say why it is, precisely, that anyone marries anyone else, or to suggest what attraction and practical considerations, too, finally make one agree that the moment has finally come after all. Rick was tall and ugly, but he was dependable, and that, in its own way, was seductive, too. He wasn't humorless, although it took awhile to understand just when he was making a joke. For instance, he'd say about dermatology that "the best thing about it is that the patient never gets well and never dies."

She wanted to make the right decision. She even thought that it might be a good idea to sit down with a piece of paper and make a list of qualities that she could bring to a marriage, and to scale each one of them, and then to do the same thing with Rick, but it occurred to her that this manner of thinking was precisely what was wrong with the world, and that if she was going to marry someone, it should be, even under these circumstances, with a leap of faith. Even so, she thought that she could bring loyalty and concern and decency to the marriage, and these things were important to her. She wanted to have children, although now they existed as an abstraction, which, she supposed, would make itself more real as time went on. For herself, she wanted safety and protection from the silence of the place where she lived now, just as she wanted to be protected from the impulses that she had had in Berkeley and which had ended with the police coming through the door. She had begun to believe that there were currents in human affairs, and that once you chose a course, you stepped into a stream over which you had little control. She was terrified of such a moment. She decided that the best thing would be to make her peace. She was twenty-nine years old and had learned her lesson. Making the decision gave her a peculiar sense of order, as though she had balanced her checkbook and everything had come out right. In her heart, she thought that this was the right thing to do: she was abandoning vanity and sentimentality, and she was coming to terms with what was usually referred to as the "real world." What could be more worthwhile and praise-worthy?

Virginia and Rick got together at a small restaurant in Laurel Canyon. She was right on time, and so was he. They reached the door at almost the same instant. She believed that such small details as arriving at the same time could, after a while, become the stuff of compatibility. They sat down at a table next to a large plant. They had a glass of wine, and he said, "Well, what's the verdict?"

"Let's wait a minute," she said. "It's nice just sitting here."

"What does that mean?" he said. "That it won't be so nice in a couple of minutes?"

"I'd just like to wait," she said. "Maybe I'm still thinking."

The room had five or six tables with white cloths. Patrons ate plates of salads and light pasta and drank white wine: it all had a claustrophobic ease to it. The place didn't seem dead really, but not vital, either, as though life here was confined to a small arena in which the ragged edges had been carefully removed. She turned and looked at Rick.

"All right," she said.

"All right, what?" he said.

"We'll do it, if you want to."

"That's good," said Rick. "That's wonderful."

"I'll do my best," she said. "I really will."

"Of course," he said. "I will, too." He sat back. "Well," he said.

"It'll be fine," she said.

"Sure. Of course. I don't know what to say. I guess I'm more nervous than I thought," he said.

She looked across the room where the people ate pasta in light sauces and drank wine out of odd looking glasses. Outside, on the canyon road, the sports cars went by.

So they began in earnest. It became apparent to both of them that having made the decision was only the first step. There were a lot of other steps, and one of them was finding people with whom they could be friends, not separately, but as a couple. It was difficult to explain, and in fact both of them approached this more with instinct than theory, but what it boiled down to was this: the people they saw together formed a validation of the marriage, and gave it its style, or its elegance and comfort, and most importantly, established a sense of just where they stood. Both of them felt the desire to appear in the best light, not just individually, but as a couple. Virginia hated to admit it, and she was ashamed that such considerations came into her life, but nevertheless she knew they were interested in something like a pecking order among the people they knew. She guessed it was a way of keeping doubt in check.

Now, when they saw an old friend, Virginia and Rick had new standards. If, for instance, someone told silly jokes, or made a comment that was ugly, the impact of it was amplified by Virginia's and Rick's perception that such behavior diminished them as a couple. They were keenly alert to the possibility of being sullied. Quietly, slowly, they began to eliminate old acquaintances. Of course, Virginia was exasperated when new people turned out to be worse than the friends they had already discarded. She thought all of this was somehow bogus, and that they were going through it to disguise their doubts. This indictment was unstated but nevertheless mutual, and, to come to terms with it, Rick said, as though unveiling a secret weapon he had been saving for a critical moment, "There's someone I'd like you to meet."

"Who's that?" said Virginia.

"An old friend from medical school," said Rick. "Terry McKechnie."

What Rick remembered most about Terry, aside from the meticulousness with which he did his work, was his old Porsche, a speedster, that was constantly breaking down, but which, from time to time, still ran pretty well. Sometimes Terry used to come by Rick's apartment and pick him up. They drove northwest on the Ventura Freeway, and Terry opened it up. They raced through the flat land, where here and there an orange grove still existed, and the blue San Gabriel Mountains stood in the distance. At the heart of these trips was the full rush of possibility, of youth, of romance, and they went along in the warm air, which seemed to surround them with an almost palpable promise. They fled the confines of medical school, the demands of organic chemistry, the rigidity and theatrics of their professors, and just about everything else that seemed inescapable. The car's movement was at once carefree and profoundly pleasurable, or satisfying. The other cars slipped behind them, and the landscape continued to slide backward in a way that becomes possible only at a hundred and ten miles an hour.

Once, when they were out toward West Lake, Terry glanced in the rearview mirror, and said, "We've got a cop chasing us."

"Well," said Rick, "pull over."

"I don't know," said Terry.

"What's that supposed to mean?" said Rick.

"Maybe things aren't so hopeless," said Terry.

"This isn't medicine," said Rick. "This is a cop."

"What's the difference?" said Terry. He sped up, and pulled off at the next exit, barely slowing down in time to make the turn at the bottom of the ramp. He started again, the cop in pursuit now. This was agricultural land, flat and dark, just waiting to be turned into condominiums.

"What the fuck are you doing?" said Rick.

"Wait," said Terry.

They went along a straight stretch, and then Terry turned into the driveway of a two-story farmhouse, which had about it the air of doom; it wouldn't be long until the real estate developers were there in force, if they hadn't appeared already. A windbreak of eucalyptus trees stood on one side of the place. Terry pulled up and got out and ran up to the house. Rick ran with him, although he kept turning to glance over his shoulder, into the cloud of dust that drifted along the driveway. Through the glass panes in the kitchen door, they saw a man and a woman at the table eating corned beef and cabbage. Each of them was drinking a glass of beer. Dabs of mustard, as bright as paint, sat on their plates.

Terry went in, and said to the man, "You're choking."

The man put down his napkin. He stretched out on the floor.

The cop pulled into the driveway and got out, running up to the house. He had his gun drawn. Terry guessed it was made from stainless steel. Maybe they were having problems with their guns rusting. The cop was breathing hard when he came in the door, and Terry said, "I'm a medical student. This man is choking." Then he reached down and put his arms around the man on the floor and gave him the Heimlich maneuver. The man gasped and started breathing again. The cop stood there for a second, and said, "All right. OK," and turned around and went outside, and when he was gone, the man who had been on the floor said, "I'm telling you, Terry. This is the last time. I mean it."

When Rick had said that he was going to become a dermatologist, Terry didn't come around so much anymore. Rick liked to remember those times when they had driven the freeway all the way out to the rolling hills, especially in springtime, when they were misty green with new grass. After a while he heard that Terry had sold the car. He'd bought a new Subaru, which was just the thing for a medical student to have.

Even though Rick hadn't seen Terry for years, he thought of him now as someone who might be reassuring. Rick suspected that there was some connection between Terry's impulse to practice real medicine and his desirability now. This left Rick a little uneasy, as though Terry's indictment of him years ago had somehow turned out to be well founded, and angry at himself for turning to the man who had disapproved of him, or so it seemed, so many years ago. But Rick put such considerations aside, and told himself how pleasant it would be to see an old friend. In fact, as he looked up Terry's number nostalgia mixed so perfectly with his current difficulties that he dialed the number with a glowing anticipation. He invited Terry for a day's sailing on a little sloop that Rick kept at a marina south of Los Angeles.

The morning of their meeting was foggy, and the mist near the water was tinted green, as though it had picked up something from the glassy chop beneath. Soon, though, the sun, a disc of platinum foil, broke through, and the mist evaporated, leaving the sky so fresh that it turned the color of a blue sheet drying on a line.

Virginia stood on the dock with a basket lunch. She had packed pâté and cold chicken, food that was easy to eat. She hoped it would be all right. It would be nice to hit it off with one of Rick's old friends. That would make everything a little easier. She had napkins and wineglasses, and two bottles of white wine on ice. She and Rick waited. Virginia turned from time to time to look at the ocean, which seemed to exist with a tug or an ache that she didn't quite understand.

She had thought that getting married and making a life was a fairly straightforward proposition, but now she found that it was a web of difficulties, which increased her sense of claustrophobia. She had supposed that marrying Rick would make life easier, if only because they were both trying to make the best of what each had to offer. Instead, she found that the reverse was true: because they had a lot to compensate for, and because the marriage didn't flow from one motive (such as being in love), the preparations required more work, or more thinking, as though in the absence of love, some other guiding and yet elusive principle was needed. At work, she put in long hours, gathering venom, planning projects that she might be able to get her company to fund, always trying to find some beauty in the complexity of the natural world, in the flow of electrons, in the generation of energy, in the intricacy of natural selection, in the beauty with which speciation took place. Now, she stood and looked at the greenish chop beyond the dock: here and there, in the glassy shape of the water, there was a film of gold.

Then she turned to the hills. They were cluttered with houses. From time to time a seagull, as white as Ivory soap, floated by. She stood, wondering again if the things she had packed for lunch were right.

A car turned off the main road and came along to the end of the dock and stopped. A man got out. He walked down a gangplank, came up to her, put out his hand, and said, "You must be Virginia."

"Hey," said Rick. "I'm glad you could come."

"It's been awhile," said Terry. "Hasn't it?"

Terry turned back to Virginia. "Well, it's very nice to meet you," he said.

"We thought it would be good to get in touch with old friends," said Rick.

Virginia blushed.

They got into the boat and sailed along the breakwater, which was a long, narrow strip covered by a slag of crushed rock: it looked like a rampart built in anticipation of the onslaught of some unseen thing. The waves broke against it in a green and white pattern, their backs marked with stress lines that revealed themselves like streaks in glass. The foam was as white as a wedding dress.

Rick said that whales went up and down the coast at this time of the year, and he had seen them in the channel between the mainland and Catalina. Their backs were black and gray, seemingly scarred where they had been injured somehow, maybe in fights with other whales. When they appeared, they broke the surface like enormous black inner tubes that turned slowly.

The boat passed the end of the breakwater and entered the channel. Virginia looked out for whales, thinking of their dark and streaked and scarred shapes suddenly appearing from the depths with all the unstoppable power of lies, say, that are finally being exposed for what they are. She tried to imagine the shape of the whale's back. Was it shiny like wet rubber and did barnacles grow on it? She guessed that birds flew alongside the whales, or at least she thought there should be birds to feed on the small sea snails that clung to the whale's back.

The line for the jib was fouled, and Virginia climbed out of the cockpit, passing Terry as she did, and crawled out on the deck. She was wearing tight white jeans. She got the line untangled and came back, where she and Terry stood and looked at the blue-gray sky and the greenish sea, which ran together at the sharp horizon. It was like a line that divided things neatly into two halves.

"I always wanted to see a whale," said Terry.

"Me, too," said Virginia.

"Maybe it's just some romantic idea," said Terry. "But then I get ideas like that from time to time. I do my best not to give in to them."

"Well," said Virginia, "I know what you mean."

"But, still, a whale is another matter."

"I've even dreamed of them," said Virginia. "I see them appearing, hundreds of them, their backs slick."

"Are they coming after you in your dream?" said Terry.

She looked at him carefully, as though she were considering an important decision. "No," she said. "I'm usually going after them somehow. But I never get there. It reminds me of work. I'm always going after some secret or other that never seems to be there for me."

"Me, too," said Terry.

"Do you find a lot of secrets?" said Virginia.

"I don't know," said Terry. "Sometimes . . . but . . ."

Terry stopped now, if only because he didn't want to bring anything serious to this: after all, it was supposed to be a pleasant occasion and he was determined to be up to it.

"But?" said Virginia, still looking at him closely. "But there's always something that eludes you, right? You keep thinking it's right there, and you get closer, and then you find that you don't know anywhere near as much as you thought. Sometimes I take it personally when I can't know or don't know something. Do you ever feel that way? It comes on me late sometimes, when I can't sleep."

"What do you do then?" said Terry.

"Oh," she said. "Wouldn't you like to know?"

She smiled at him. Terry turned away to look at the ocean.

"Yes," said Terry. "I guess I would. Do you take something to sleep?"

"No," she said. "I think about the most beautiful things I've ever seen. I have a list. I go through it from the top."

"Tell me one," said Terry.

She blushed. "No," she said. "I couldn't."

"Why not?" said Terry.

She blushed again. "It's pretty private."

"Oh," he said. "I'm sorry. I didn't mean to pry."

"It's all right," she said. She smiled again. "No harm done."

"Well," he said, "maybe we'll see a whale. They always remind me of something forbidden."

"Really?" said Virginia.

"Or maybe just something sudden and alive," said Terry.

"Or maybe something that can just cause trouble, right?" said Virginia.

"Well," said Terry, "I guess there's all kinds of trouble. There's good trouble and there's bad trouble."

"How can you tell the difference?" said Virginia.

"I guess you have to wait awhile," said Terry.

"Probably," said Virginia. "More's the pity, too, because then it's too late to know which is which."

"What are you two talking about?" said Rick.

"Whales," said Virginia.

"Oh," said Rick.

"You don't sound too excited by them," said Terry.

"I can take them or leave them," said Rick.

"Oh?" said Virginia. "Terry and I feel a little differently about them, don't we?"

"They're just big, dumb creatures," said Rick.

Terry looked out at the greenish chop. The hull pounded steadily, repetitively, and the water hushed along the side of the boat.

"And they're doomed," said Rick. "The Japanese are going to get every last one of them. A computerized ship, with a cannon that shoots harpoons. That's the wave of the future."

"Is it?" said Terry.

"The future has it's own pace," said Rick. "There's not a thing you can do."

"Maybe they're tougher than you think," said Terry.

"Listen," said Rick. "It's a beautiful day. We're all out for a sail. Sufficient unto the day is the evil thereof. If I were you, I'd open some wine."

"Well," said Terry, "I'd like to see one."

"Do you think birds follow them around?" said Virginia.

"You two have got a conspiracy going," said Rick. "I can tell."

"Are we conspiring together?" asked Terry.

Virginia turned toward the ocean, putting her face into the breeze. "I'm just trying to do what's best," said Virginia. "Is there anything wrong with that?"

"What?" said Rick. "What did she say?"

"She doesn't want to be frightened by a whale," said Terry.

"Yes," said Virginia, "I guess that's right, isn't it."

"You don't have to worry," said Rick. "The Japanese are going to get them."

"I'm not so sure I like that," said Virginia.

"What?" said Rick. "I can't hear in the wind."

"Maybe we'll see one," said Terry. "You know, it'll just appear. Swimming along. They're all going south, down to some bay in Mexico."

"What do they do when they get there?" said Virginia.

"The usual thing," said Terry.

She turned back into the wind.

"Hey, Terry," said Rick. "Open the wine. There's a corkscrew in the basket, OK?"

"Sure," said Terry. He turned to Virginia. "Would you like some, too?"

"Not right now," she said.

Terry opened the wine and found the glasses, poured, and watched the clear wine take on the tint of the ocean. He passed one glass over to Rick, and he poured a little for himself.

"She seems upset," said Rick. "I can tell."

"Maybe she's thinking about her work," said Terry.

Rick looked over at him and smiled.

"Jesus, it's good to see you," said Rick. "What times we had in medical school. In the middle of it, I didn't think it was ever going to end. You remember Wilson?"

"Wilson?" said Terry. "You mean the guy who washed his hands all the time?"

"Yeah," said Rick. "Who was it who took all the soap out of all the bathrooms?"

"Probably Pearce," said Terry. "That was the kind of thing he liked to do."

"Well, yeah," said Rick. "But you remember when Wilson couldn't wash his hands, and he kept going from one floor to another? They hauled him off right after that, didn't they?"

"Yeah," said Terry.

"Well, medicine isn't for everyone," said Rick. He took a sip of wine. "What's Pearce doing?"

"He's a urologist," said Terry.

"No kidding?" said Rick. He took another sip of his wine. "Are you seeing any unusual cases?"

"Some kids are huffing butane," said Terry. "I'm seeing some of that. And gunshot wounds. I'm seeing a lot of those."

"You should have gone into dermatology," said Rick.

"Well," said Terry. "I don't know."

"Sometimes I think I should have got into orthopedics. Now, there's a growing field. What do you think those guys are getting for a hip replacement? Guess."

"I don't know," said Terry.

"Take a guess," said Rick. "It'll make you green."

Terry stood up.

"Come on," said Rick. "What have you got against orthopedics?"

"Nothing. Some of my best friends are orthopedic surgeons."

"What do they say about it?" said Rick.

"One of them told me that if you were an orthopedic surgeon, and you didn't have at least three malpractice suits going, you weren't working hard enough."

Rick raised an eyebrow. "No shit," he said.

Terry looked at Virginia. "Hey," he said. "Have you seen one?"

Virginia shook her head.

"Come on," said Terry. "Have a little wine with us. Rick's going to start talking about the stock market soon. I can tell."

"Well," said Rick. "I got a tip. What would you say to a biodegradable, disposable diaper . . . ?"

Terry poured Virginia a little wine and passed it over to her.

"Listen," said Rick. "Don't knock money. It beats a lot of things."

"Virginia and I like whales," said Terry.

"But at a distance," said Virginia. "Getting close is a luxury I can't afford."

"Oh, come on," said Rick. "You two are hopeless. The Japanese are going to get them all. Come on." He looked at Virginia. "I'm just kidding. Don't be upset."

"I'm not upset," she said. "I was just thinking there are things that you keep hoping for, and one day you realize that you've been hoping for it for years, but you haven't even really put it into words. Isn't that odd?"

"Listen," said Rick. "I didn't mean anything. I'm sorry."

"Maybe we should have something to eat," said Terry.

"Yes," said Rick. "Let's do that."

"All right," said Virginia. "That's a good idea."

She opened the basket and passed out plates on which she put a piece of chicken, a bit of pâté, and a little salad. She had brought the salad in a Ziploc bag and she poured in a little dressing and shook it. They ate the picnic, hearing the wash of the boat, and feeling the slight pounding as the hull hit the small chop.

"You know, the way you two talk about whales, you make them sound like fanatics," said Rick. "You know, uncompromising."

"Well, that sounds like the IRS or something," said Terry.

"There's nothing romantic about the IRS," said Virginia.

"Virginia got audited last year," said Rick. "They didn't get a thing on her. She's a straight arrow."

"Wait until they take a look at you," said Virginia.

"Not *me*," said Rick. "It's going to be *us* after we get married."

Virginia turned to Terry. "What do you do to relax? You know, after a hard day at the hospital. Or when you're upset?"

Terry thought, How can I say, Well, I take a Xanax, or something else the drug salesmen leave around. I'm getting to be an expert about the rate of absorption. He wanted to say something frank and truthful, but he didn't know what to say exactly, since this entire occasion was ceremonial rather than anything else. So he smiled, and said, "The usual."

Virginia turned and looked across the surface of the Pacific. As the sun rose the green ocean seemed a little dusty, the sunlight penetrating it in rays. The surface of the water was marked by a streak of sunlight, broken up into facets. The hollows of the chop looked as though they were covered with silver paper, or maybe a film of some space-age material, like Mylar.

"What's that?" said Virginia, pointing over the water.

"I don't see anything," said Rick.

"Over there," said Virginia.

"I don't think it's anything," Rick said. "You know you can go on looking for something and just make yourself miserable. You know that, don't you?"

"Yes," said Virginia.

"I think I see something," said Terry. "You're not going to believe this. But I think something is really out there. And not too far away, either."

The whale was a hundred yards from the boat, its back sliding along with a continual motion, its skin dark and streaked, covered with gray scars. It appeared not suddenly but slowly, in an orderly fashion and with a scale that was different from most other living things, as though for creatures its size, time ran at a different velocity. Rick put the boat on a new tack, one that went toward the whale.

"What are you doing?" said Virginia.

"I thought you wanted to see one," said Rick.

"We don't have to play around," said Virginia. "We really don't."

"We can get a little closer," said Rick.

"It's not a good idea to corner things," said Virginia. "Creatures don't like to be trapped."

"This one's got the whole ocean. It's not trapped."

"I'm not so sure it feels that way," said Virginia.

"What about you, Terry?" said Rick. "What do you think?"

"I wouldn't mess with it," said Terry. "Frankly, I'd leave it alone."

"Tell me why I should do that?" said Rick.

"There are some things you shouldn't get in the way of," said Terry.

"Is that right?" said Rick. "Well, I think there's not much to be afraid of. You can control most things, if you're smart. The only thing that creature is interested in is food. Any fool can see that."

"There are other things aside from food," said Terry.

Terry thought of the cool ease with which the whales moved

south, breaking through the surface of the ocean from time to time. Maybe that felt pretty good. Then he thought of what it was like to come home now to an empty house, especially after a hard shift at the hospital. This afternoon, though, he was determined just to have a nice time, and to be polite. Being pleasant was a variety of resistance to those late nights after things had gone wrong, and no matter how much of an illusion such pleasantness might seem later, right now it left him with a momentary feeling of strength.

Virginia saw Terry against the light that stretched out on the water: it surrounded him with a silver nimbus in the mist, and he appeared there, with the moisture in his hair, as a figure outlined against that streak on the water, which was at once silver and liquid, and flowing toward the horizon. He glanced back at her, the light in the chop behind him seeming to shatter as he moved.

The whale appeared again, although it must have turned, because it was now only a few feet from the bow. It surfaced, just showing its back with that same slow, and yet unstoppable motion, the scars suggesting a significant, but yet unknown event.

"Jesus," said Rick, who pushed the tiller toward the sail to come about. As he did so he still looked at the whale, and he was half standing as the boom swung across the cockpit, hitting him on the back of the head. He put one hand up as he tripped over the gunwale and went into the water, only a few feet from the whale. Virginia saw him, defined by a tub-shaped splash of water, and for an instant he simply disappeared from sight, along that long, steadily moving and scarred shape that seemed to be smeared with light.

"Do you know anything about sailing?" said Terry.

"Not much," said Virginia.

"Me neither," said Terry. "Jesus."

He picked up a life jacket and threw it into the water, near where Rick had surfaced. Terry pulled the tiller, making the boat jibe, and it turned back toward Rick. Beyond him, the whale continued to show itself, the boat going toward it. Virginia took the tiller and Terry reached down and put his arm over the gunwale so that Rick could grab it. They could smell the fishy, mudflat-like odor of the whale, and the boat heaved in the small wake that came off it. Rick reached through the chop and grabbed Terry's arm. His grip was hard and cold. Virginia put the boat into the wind, and the sail luffed with a constant, maddening sound.

The sail went on luffing, and she saw Terry surrounded by light as he kneeled in the cockpit over Rick. The whale appeared one more time, the smear of the sun on its back running down into the long silver streak of light on the water and even into the silver nimbus that surrounded Terry. They got a blanket for Rick.

"Maybe I'd like a little wine," said Rick.

Virginia looked back now, her hands shaking: the first thing she had thought, when Rick had gone in, was, Thank God. She was appalled that she could have thought such a thing, and she sat down, thinking, What made me think that? What? How could I have thought such a thing? My God, what am I coming to? She turned and looked at Terry, who smiled, and said, "Looks like your groom is going to make it to the wedding after all."

"Yes," said Virginia. "Yes."

"I'm sorry I was being such an ass," said Rick. "Do you forgive me?"

"Of course," said Virginia. "What's to forgive? I'm just glad you're safe."

"Why don't you tell me how to get the boat under way," said Terry. "You take it easy."

In the distance, they saw the mainland, the brownish and low hills touched here and there with the clutter of houses.

VIRGINIA WAS MARRIED at a church in Antelope Valley, California. The church was a small white building with clapboard siding and a steeple that was so fine and narrow that it looked like an illustration of a mathematical principle. On the day of the wedding the sky was a pale blue in which a few puffs of clouds floated, moving with the constant pressure of a wind that carried the scent of wildflowers and grasses.

Virginia was driven to the church by her father and her mother, in their Buick. As she sat in the back seat, she watched the spring landscape. The hills were green and rolling, and here and there a tree was visible against the sky. It was the landscape, more than anything else, that suggested freedom and cleanliness, only untainted feelings.

"It's all for the best," said her father.

"What?" said Virginia.

"Marriage," he said.

The fields went by, the slow undulations of them green, although this minty hue was fresh and fragile, a thin disguise for the brown grass of summer.

"Look at the wildflowers," said Virginia.

"I've seen them," said her father.

The patches of wildflowers showed in irregular shapes on the otherwise green hills. Virginia rolled down the window to smell the spring air.

"You'll get mussed," said her mother.

"Will I?" said Virginia.

The car came over a hill and by the new grass on both sides of the road, which had been so recently resurfaced that it still smelled of oil and tar. Below, sheltered against the side of the hill, was the church. There were cars around it, like creatures that had come to feed.

"Well, it's a beautiful day for it," said her father.

He pulled up in front of the church. His wife put his boutonniere into his buttonhole.

"There," she said, giving him a pat.

The guests had gone into the church, although a few were still arriving. Mostly the people were friends of Rick's and Virginia's parents, although a number of guests were people she had known at Berkeley, and they showed up in blue jackets and white shirts and light pants, their young faces, their bright ties, their stylish haircuts, all mixing harmoniously with the brightness and pleasantness and promise, too, of the verdant hillsides. Virginia got out of the car, stepping from the shade into the bright sunshine, which seemed to be filled with the smell of flowers.

The church was at an intersection and, aside from the churchyard, there wasn't anything else around: it was isolated on the rolling hills, and when a worshiper, or a member of a wedding party, looked away from the church, the most striking detail of the landscape was the scale of the sky. The church's isolation and the enormous sky made Virginia turn and look down the road before going in, as though to see just where it was she had come from, but, as she hesitated, her father at her side, standing up straighter than he had in years, and clearing his throat in anticipation of giving her away, she saw in the distance, at the end of the road, a car approaching at a high rate of speed.

It came over one hill and disappeared into a swale, a sleight-of-hand trick, and then it emerged again, with not only the on-ward rush, but a small movement from side to side, too, as though gliding a little in the silvery pool of heat on the road. The car disappeared into a small dip in the road and came over the last rise and pulled up in front of the church, the hot engine ticking after the driver switched it off.

Terry got out of the car and stood in a cloud of dust from the shoulder of the road that blew around him like mist.

"I'm not too late, am I?" he said to Virginia.

"No," she said.

He smiled.

"Are you a doctor, too?" said Virginia's mother.

"Yes," said Terry. He glanced at Mrs. Lee. "Yes." He turned to Virginia. He thought about embracing her, but somehow it didn't seem right. She put out her hand. He took it and smiled again. Maybe it was the smile. She looked toward the church and at the sky, which seemed to her to reveal the intensity that the physical world brought to the living. She looked back at him and thought, Oh, no. No. It's just nerves. Nerves are bound to do things like this, at the last moment, aren't they? Isn't this the usual thing when standing on the steps of the church? Oh, no. Not now.

"Well," said her father. "Are you ready?"

"Good luck," said Terry. He went up the steps and into the church.

"Virginia?" said her father.

"Yes," she said. "All right."

They went up the steps of the church, which were gray and which creaked knowingly, or so it seemed to Virginia. She wondered how many others had stood there and heard that same creak, which as far as Virginia was concerned made the same chill as if she had heard a stair creak at two o'clock in the morning in a house that she had presumed to be otherwise deserted. She looked over her shoulder at the road that stretched away into the distance where it was absorbed by the rolling hills, the grass, the sky, and by a silver and undulant shimmer where the heat had collected in the road. They went in.

The people in the church turned to face her, and she blushed. Under the bouquet she carried, she felt a sensation in the tips of her fingers where they had touched his. He now stood at the back of the church, near the aisle. She looked away and started walking, but the suspicion that perhaps she was making a mistake surrounded her with all the delicate claustrophobia of the veil that she had pulled down and through which she saw the faces that had turned to watch. She found herself looking at the somewhat ugly but still cheerful man who she had decided would be her salvation and her protection, and who, as he stood there, smiled complacently, as though everything she had ever worried about had now been obliterated. His lips looked cool and a little wet.

The reception was held in a house that was rented out for such occasions. It was a red brick building, two stories high, and it had an orchard behind it and a field on one side, where the wedding tent had been set up. Wild roses grew in front of the building, and now their blossoms were clean and white.

At the reception, Virginia had a glass of champagne. Her husband asked her if she was happy and she replied that she was, deliriously so. He winked at her, as though he had a salacious notion to take up with her later in the afternoon. Was this going to be an occasion for which some special effort was going to be made? They danced. Terry came up to her and shook her hand.

They were alone for a moment. The guests stood around them, the men in blue coats and white pants and bright ties, the women in cheerful dresses that were covered with flowers, and, over all, there was the odor of champagne mixed with a number of expensive perfumes. A waiter came by with a tray of champagne, and Terry and Virginia each took a glass. The champagne was very dry, and had a slight cast to it, like a patch of yellow wildflowers on a distant hillside. Virginia took a sip. It was amazing, really, how much privacy you can have in a crowd. Then she looked at Terry again, and immediately turned away, thinking, Oh, no. No. When she was sure of her voice, she said, "I'm glad you could come."

"It was lovely," he said.

"Was it?" she said.

"Yes," he said. "Are you going away for a while?"

"Just a weekend," she said. "My parents have a cabin. We're going there."

"Uh-huh," he said.

He looked around now with the air of a man who was about to do something he shouldn't. Or maybe this was just a notion based on the fact that it was possible that there was something wrong with the two of them just standing together. She tried to calm down. After all, getting married was upsetting. There were bound to be some surprises, especially on the wedding day. Everyone is tired by then. How often had she smiled when she hadn't wanted to in the last few days? Her face was a little numb with the effort. She reached out and touched Terry's hand, doing so without thinking. It seemed, for an instant, like the most natural thing in the world.

"Is anything wrong?" he said.

"No," she said. "I guess not. What could be wrong?"

"Have another drink," he said. "That will buck you up."

He smiled and finished what was in his glass.

"Have you ever thrown a wineglass into a fireplace?" he said. "You see that in those old movies. I always thought it was sappy but somehow romantic. Wouldn't you like to throw a champagne glass against a wall?"

Those green hills and that blue and white sky were beyond him, and the slight breeze ruffled his hair. For a second, she had the sensation that the earth was tipping one way and another. What would it be like if she fainted? She felt sweat along her brow, and as she tried to get a grip on herself, still feeling the lingering touch of his skin on her fingers, she wondered what it is she would say to him, or just what, if she had the chance, she would be able to understand if she could speak freely? In the scent of flowers and champagne, and along with the sweetness and vaguely erotic odor of perfume, there seemed to be unexpected promise. What she wanted to do was to start talking, to say, You see, you see? She wanted to say, I am operating on the theory that you have to live without certain things, like love, and that you have to be tough to do that, and there are times when I weaken. I took a chance once, and ended up with the police breaking through the door. In my heart, I am confused. But I feel this lack of conviction is a flaw, and that I am insufficient. What I wouldn't give for a moment in which everything made sense. She thought the most important thing was not to panic. Not now. She took a breath and looked around. Yes, she thought, I'd like to break a champagne glass against the wall. Yes.

"I'm sorry," she said. "I guess I'm not feeling very well. Don't say anything. Please. Rick would be upset. Everyone would be upset. It would spoil the party."

She listened to her own words while she looked around. She thought of the car Terry had driven, the speed of it suggesting a stream of chrome and metal, but its approach through those mint hills implied pleasure, as though, for an instant anyway, it was clear that he was unencumbered by the mistakes that came from fear or mishandled longing. Then she dismissed this as the effect of anxiety and champagne.

"Why don't we walk over here," he said. "Give yourself a minute."

They went to the edge of the field and walked along the grass. A brick outbuilding was a little ways ahead of them, and at the back of it some wild roses grew, the blooms piling up there in delicate clouds, which had a shape like those white puffs that dragged across the sky with an unstoppable inertia. At the corner of the building there was a trellis with a doorway, around which roses climbed. Virginia went through it. The trellis and the roses screened them from the party, although they could still hear it, the musicians now playing a song that hung in the air with the same delicate quality as the perfume.

Virginia leaned against the wall. The roses were on her right, the billows of them seeming to trace the shape of her dress. At least, here, she wouldn't fall down. She tried to think how often a bride had felt like this. Almost always, she supposed. She looked at Terry, who stood in his jacket, his head turned toward the field, patient, polite. What she wanted, she realized, was to be able to begin talking, to explain that she thought that every impulse she had had toward doing the right thing was just an excuse, and that in her worst notion of herself, she had to admit that she had been a coward and that she was paying the price for it. Certainly, cowardice had a price. It attracted everything you didn't really want. You tried to appease your fears and somehow you ended up confined, having given away a central thing. She wanted him to understand that precisely. Maybe she would scream at the top of her lungs, and, in fact, she felt the first catch in her chest, the first deliberate taking of breath. Did he think she was a coward? She stopped and felt her hands tremble. Well, of course she was upset. Of course.

For an instant, the green hills, the flowers, the sky, the white shirts and bright ties and jackets of the men who stood on the lawn drinking champagne all seemed too much. She began to talk, but she stammered. Under the slowly dragging clouds, in the scent of the roses, she felt him take her hand. She leaned forward. Her dress, with its underthings, made a cloud around them. Her lips brushed his as he came closer. Had she stumbled, or just leaned forward? Either, of course, would have been all right, but why did they have to remain that way, their lips just touching, as though the touch was the only thing that held them here at all? They were both appalled. And because they were going to have to pay for it, they seemed to hesitate for an instant. It wasn't long, just enough for them to realize that they were hesitating, which, after all, was probably the worst thing to know. It implied a world of uncertainty. He straightened up, and she pulled away, her hand to her lips, on which the sensation lingered.

He looked toward the crowd of people. She wanted to say it hadn't been anything. Just one of those things. They were all so excited and mixed up, and so much had been going on. She had been caught off guard, just after she had made up her mind about marriage. She'd had a nasty turn. Perhaps it had been the champagne. She didn't drink that much.

He looked back toward the house. A little laughter now mixed in with the music, although it seemed anxious rather than hearty. It was obvious that, more than anything else, he wanted to do the right thing: how could he best handle the moment? Pretend that nothing had happened at all, to shrug it off as the usual thing. Why couldn't they do that then? Why did they stand there, stricken in some profound way? And what about his feelings in the matter? After all, how could he have managed to be a party to something like this, without having his own desperate impulses made obvious? He looked back at her and smiled, and said, "I understand."

"Do you?" she said.

He nodded. He reached over and picked one of the roses and held it out for her. She touched his hand, pulled the rose closer to her nose, and then dropped it, the flower disappearing into the clouds of material of her white dress.

"Come on," he said. "Let's go back."

She stood away from the wall now, the back of her dress smudged with red from the brick. She swallowed, still trying to tell herself that nothing had happened to her. And, as they started through the arbor, passing through the clouds of blooms, it was the scent of the white blooms that seemed to emerge, with the beguiling hint of a damp and fruitful beauty.

They walked up the slight hill, seeing the grass move in the breeze. As they went, she wanted to talk to him more than ever. They came up to the members of the wedding party, and a waiter appeared with another tray of champagne. Virginia took a glass with an unsteady hand, glad for the dry taste, and more sure than ever that, really, the entire thing had just been a matter of losing her nerve, and that everything would be fine. She turned to face her husband, who was talking with a doctor, an older man with whom Rick had been considering forming a practice.

From time to time, at some distance, she saw Terry. She

drank more champagne and looked across the hills, on which the shapes of isolated trees made the forces behind them momentarily palpable. She turned away. Surely she was far too trapped to even consider the yearning of living things.

Then she thought she was being vile to herself, that she was torturing herself for having made her peace, and that all of this, the panic, the stolen kiss, the desperation, was simply a matter of being mean-spirited to her own desire to live an ordinary, regularly conducted life.

"How are you feeling?" said Rick.

"Fine," she said.

"I'm glad to see you were talking to Terry," he said.

"Yes," she said.

"The ladies always loved him in medical school."

"He seems shy," she said.

"Terry?" he said. "Shy? You've got to be kidding."

Now, in the scent of the champagne and perfume, in the sweet odor of grasses, she found that she was tired. If she could, she would have sat down on the ground and leaned against a tree. When she saw Terry on the other side of the open grass where the party was held, it was with the sensation of being close to the cool implacable power that was at the heart of the events that confined human beings: it was palpable enough to have the cool touch of the breeze that blew around her. She was glad for the champagne.

After a while, she and Rick laughed until they cried. They got into their car and drove to the cabin in the Sierras. In the morning Virginia awoke and made him coffee and eggs and ham, her hands shaking as she found that now she wanted to say almost nothing. Her smile made her face feel numb, as though she had been out in the cold.

But even then, as they drove back toward Los Angeles on

Sunday evening, her wedding dress not so neatly packed in a suitcase in the back of the car, she began to think that it would be all right simply to talk to the man. And when she came home from work, in the early evening and before Rick was there, she thought about how she would do it: she could pick up the phone and make the call, and sometimes she stood in the bedroom, the receiver in her hand, one finger on the plastic button that silences the dial tone, and she began to speak, out loud, to hear what she would sound like. And what did she want to sound like? Would it be any better if she was able to convey an impeccable innocence, or an interest so cool as to leave him thinking that she was merely afflicted with a desire to talk without any other imperative at all?

They met in a hotel restaurant not far from his hospital. It was a new hotel that tried to suggest European comfort in its soft lighting, its carpets, the furniture, the chandeliers, the wood of the reception desk, the shine of the marble floors, the white table-cloths, on which small vases of flowers sat (which she held to her nose while she waited for him).

She told herself that it wasn't such a bad thing, his being late, if only because she'd have time to gather her thoughts. As she sat there, hoping nothing definite had been decided, she suspected that everything was already advancing with a locomotion that was as smooth as a waiter's approach, his shoes sighing on the carpet, and that events moved along with the silken hush of air, just at skin temperature, which came out of the invisible air-conditioning ducts. Things might be smooth, she supposed, but that wasn't necessarily reassuring. She sat, her hands shaking under the white tablecloth.

He came in and sat down, pulling out his chair, moving it with a graceful economy, which would have seemed abrupt if he had been anyone else. A waiter appeared at his elbow. Terry asked for a drink. Virginia put her fingertips together in her lap, where he couldn't see them. When she reached to take a sip of her drink, she almost knocked it over, and she imagined the clear fluid seeping in a widening stain across the tablecloth, falling into her lap, making her dark silk skirt even darker.

Still, she began. As she spoke, as the words came into the diminished sounds made by the men and women at the tables around her, she felt less hazy about who she really was. She didn't think she had been lying to herself before, just confused. Everything had been such a muddle, every impulse had been so obscure. Wasn't that right? As she looked at him, she felt that everything made sense once she had the chance to talk freely. No judging. Just understanding.

So she sat there, her fingers trembling, and talked. He listened. From time to time he looked at his watch, if only with surprise at the amount of time that had passed. Then she wondered if perhaps she had made another mistake in coming here, in putting him in a compromising position. He had agreed only to be polite. Was that possible?

She picked up one of the small flowers in the vase. It was a miniature iris, and the petals quivered in her hands. The lines of color, a deep purple, were set off against a splash of the brightest yellow she had ever seen. The beauty of it was clear. No equivocation. But even so, she continued to tremble, not knowing what to do, now more convinced than ever that her response to him was not just an attack of nerves, or anything like that. In fact, her nerves had been responsible for her inability to do anything about it until now. So she remained silent, looked around. A piano played in another room. The smooth air moved across the back of her legs as he said, "I've taken a room here. Let's have a bottle of champagne sent upstairs."

TWO DAYS BEFORE the wedding, Terry woke at three o'clock in the morning. He opened his eyes and looked at the ceiling, which the city lights tinted pink, an almost pretty color, but one that could suddenly change into something ominous. Then he sat up and put his feet on the floor and his head in his hands. He started to think about a patient.

The patient's name was Frank Sims. Sims's cancer had metastasized into the brain as well as other places, and Terry didn't think Sims had a lot of time left. As he sat there, he thought it was important to go down to the hospital. There wasn't much he could do, but there was always some small unexpected detail that might need attention. The nurses were excellent. It wasn't a matter of fear on Terry's part so much as an unspecified longing.

As he drove, he thought about the fact that Sims was under the impression that he was traveling now. Sims said he had gone places where no one else had ever been before, such as to a planet in the constellation Capricornus. Sims liked to describe it in some detail. Terry tried to concentrate on driving the car, on putting on his turn signal, on changing lanes or on making a smooth and orderly exit off the freeway. Few cars were out, but they didn't come in clusters. Mostly they were alone in the dark, quietly purposeful, their isolation defined by their lights. Still, it was nice to have no traffic, or the stink of daytime air. He pulled into the parking lot, trying to ignore the words "Yo gonna die soon" on the brick wall.

Terry had a cup of coffee in the cafeteria, where the odor of medicine and institutional food mixed together to suggest disease. He supposed it was chicken soup he smelled, and he thought of the times when he had come into this room, after midnight, to have a cup of that watery stuff. It was at that hour, in the stink of the stale soup and the silence of the hospital corridors, that he thought there was some hint of those things that were beyond anyone's ability to change. It was in that silence that he sat, drinking the coffee, trying to understand why he was here. After a while he went upstairs.

The halls were quiet. It seemed that he could smell the soup even up here. He stood in front of the door to Sims's room. It was pretty dim inside, although there was a light in a recessed panel above the bed. Terry stood next to the bed. Sims's legs were thin under the thermal blanket, like two posts. His eyes were open, and although he didn't turn to Terry, he said, "Thanks for coming."

"You can't sleep?" said Terry.

"No. Not really," said Sims.

A bag of fluid containing morphine hung from a stand at the side of the bed. Terry watched the silver drips as they fell into the tube running down toward Sims's arm.

"Are you uncomfortable?" said Terry.

"Yes," said Sims.

"Maybe I can do something about that," said Terry.

"All right," said Sims. "But just wait a minute."

"Sure," said Terry.

"I've traveled a long ways," said Sims.

"I know," said Terry.

"It was hard to get here. A lot of time alone. Some people aren't cut out for the loneliness of this kind of travel. But it gives you time to think when you get this far away. But the loneliness is hard. The landscape is beautiful here, though."

"Is it?" said Terry.

"Sure. The planet is a small one, and it has two moons. They glide by, and in the distance you can see part of the planet's blue and green rings. The blue is just the color of an iris. It's in the constellation Capricornus."

Terry didn't know much astronomy, and now he strained, trying to remember the little that he had ever learned. He closed his eyes trying to visualize a map of the stars.

"That's close to Sagittarius, isn't it?" said Terry.

"Yes. They're close. During the day, I gather specimens. There are flowers that are perfectly black with yellow centers, and small creatures, too. I am classifying them. Class, order, species. I get to name them."

"Yes," said Terry. "I guess that's right."

"You want to hear a name?"

"Sure," said Terry.

"There are purple flowers here. I call them dihedrals. It sounds nice. And there are some yellow and white ones, as big as teacups, that I call a Wild Sims."

He strained now as he breathed. The sound of it was like someone trying to get relief by exhaling. It reminded Terry of someone with emphysema trying to blow out the candles on a birthday cake.

"We have problems like anyone else in this job. Getting paid on time. Oh. There. You can see the moons. I'm so far from home. That's why they pay you so well, being out here, naming the plants and animals. The seas are green here, and trees the color of licorice. Whole other ways of living. There are creatures here that are just spiny puffs, like a dandelion. They're smart."

He breathed a little harder.

"Do you want to hear what my ship looks like?" said Sims.

"If you want to tell me," said Terry.

"What can compare with hardware, anyway?"

"Sure," said Terry.

"It has navigational devices. They are quite accurate. At any moment I can find the course home. Even at these distances it is accurate to within a tenth of a mile. I have a keyboard and a rubber ball. I can steer by pressing on the ball. Usually I travel from star to star. I do it with a crosshair sight, like on a rifle. The knobs are made of rubber, and the consoles are stainless steel. I spray it with some stuff in a bottle to make it shine."

He turned to look at Terry. "Can I go now?" he said.

"Yes," said Terry. "It's all right."

"I need your help," said Sims. "Please. I can't go unless you help me." He reached over and picked up Terry's hand.

"All right," said Terry.

"It's hard to breathe. It's like there's a cinder block on my chest. I just want to get rid of that weight. Even out here, at this distance, there still seem to be these problems."

Terry listened. Outside the hall was silent. He went out and passed the nurses' station. One of the nurses looked up.

"Mr. Sims isn't very comfortable," said Terry.

"Yes," said one of them. "We've given him the dosage in the orders."

"I know," said Terry. "But I'm going to increase the morphine drip. I'm going to run it pretty fast."

The nurse looked at him. "I guess that's best," she said.

Terry went back into Sims's room. He opened the stopcock.

"There," said Terry. "That should help."

"Yes," said Sims. "I feel better. There are some things I have to do. Reports to write. Letters home."

Terry looked out the window. An airplane passed by, its lights blinking on and off. It was almost morning. Outside shapes began to emerge from the darkness, houses, buildings, trees, the ordinary stuff of the world. After a while Terry covered Sims up, and went out into the hall.

The next day, as Terry arrived at the wedding, he heard the music in the church and thought of Sims's voice. For an instant, he saw the double moon moving across a greenish sky.

He thought of a couple of other cases, too. A couple of months ago a woman came to the hospital with her child, who had a high fever and was dehydrated and having convulsions. She was scared. Terry was able to treat the child, and to do so quickly. The convulsions stopped. The fever went down. The woman took Terry's hand and shook it when she left. She did so with great formality, but with real feeling, too.

But she came back a few weeks later. She had a round, beautiful face, so symmetrical that it made him stare. Terry was told that a woman carrying a child was in the waiting room and that she would speak only to him. Terry glanced into the waiting room. She stood up and came toward him, holding her baby. "Oh," she said. "I'm glad to see you. I'm so glad to see you."

Still, she wouldn't let Terry see the child, which she had wrapped in a blanket and which she held cradled in her left hand.

"Why don't we go inside?" said Terry.

"Oh, yes," she said. "Let's go in. You'll help us, won't you?"

In the examining room, she started singing, rocking back and forth, holding the baby. She gave the baby to Terry. He guessed it had been dead about twelve hours. She went on singing, looking at him, saying, "Won't you sing? I want you to sing for my baby. Please. Sing."

She came over and got Terry to sway a little as she sang. She said she'd come to see Terry because he had saved her baby before. What was he going to do now? Terry wasn't going to stop singing, was he? The child was light and cold. Terry had a lousy voice, and he had always been embarrassed by it, but the least he could do was sing.

He could still feel the weight of the dead child in his hands, just as he could almost hear the sound of his voice as he had tried to sing with its mother. On the way north, after leaving the clutter of the city behind, the hills had the faint, short-lived green tint that existed in early spring. The scent of the grass permeated the car with the pungent air of promise. Terry thought that the miasma of the hospital still clung to him. He apprehended it as the lingering sensation of that weight in his hands and the memory of his voice as he had tried to sing. He found that if he drove a little faster, he could get away from it, though only for a little while, as if he could leave behind whatever he was trying to get away from, but it eventually caught up to him. At first he was only going sixty-five on the back roads, through the foothills, but then it was seventy and seventy-five, until he came to the straightaway before the church, the speed there recalling for Terry that constant, unrelieved longing for someone else. He slowed down and stopped. He got out and took Virginia's hand. It was cool. The scent of roses was in the air.

At the reception he found that she was standing in front of him. She kept staring at him. Of course, he didn't want to look back. After all, he didn't want to be impertinent. Maybe he had treated her medically. He tried to remember. He thought that he was going to be sick, that he needed to sit down, but instead he looked at her and said, "Is anything wrong?" They walked across that grass, with the green, almost lime, tint, over to the arbor where the roses were piled up, filling the air with an almost tactile sensation, like the memory of a caress.

The mounds of roses surrounded them, her dress billowing, hazy and airy, misty. He watched her face as she leaned back against the wall, her head gently tapping the bricks. In that moment, the nights when he came home to an empty house, all seemed to disappear as she leaned forward and stumbled, her lips brushing his, the two of them hesitating, just touching, the mounds of white wedding dress and the mounds of flowers combining with the touch of her lips and the scent in the air. She looked at him with terror, and they pulled away, both of them determined to believe now that nothing had happened, nothing at all, nothing had passed between them. The entire thing had just been an awkward moment.

He walked among the other guests on the lawn, his terror (that any such thing could happen to him, particularly on the day of the wedding of an old friend) mixing with a barely acknowledged delight, which seemed to buoy him. He started drinking champagne, hoping for relief from the moment, or, worse, from its implications, and when he got into his car and started the long drive home, he found that he did so slowly, carefully, telling himself that the entire encounter was an aberration, that he had to get a grip on himself: he was grown-up, a physician. Was he going to let something as ordinary as a little longing get in the way of his obligations? He assumed that he would do absolutely nothing about the kiss, the touch, or the expression on her face. It was all a mistake. Wasn't it gauche even to notice someone else's mistake? He decided that the best thing was to forget the entire matter. This, after all, was the sensible approach. He felt better already, didn't he? There were times when he was aware of some tug, which seemed to have the continual hold of gravity. Well, it would pass. He sat in his empty house, and after a while he got up and went into the bathroom and opened the medicine chest. He took a whole Xanax. He spent his days thinking things over, each day seeming to be a little easier than before, and everything was fine, just fine, until he came home and found a message on the answering machine. Virginia's voice didn't hesitate, didn't pause. Maybe she had written down what she wanted to say and had read it. She said she had been thinking things over and wanted to talk. Was he available? They could meet somewhere. Terry could pick the place.

TERRY WAS STILL THINKING about what to do when the riot started, in the evening, about six o'clock. From his kitchen window Terry saw scattered fires, and in the dusk the reddish smoke rose like the billows from a Fourth of July glowworm. At the base of the smoke he saw flames, which, from a distance, appeared as irregular lines that were the color of filament in a toaster. As he stood there, he thought about the cases a riot sent to the hospital, lacerations, head injuries, gunshot and knife wounds, trauma associated with rape. Some burns, too. Then he thought about the message on the machine as he looked at the flames. Just what was he going to do, anyway? Was he going to call her? Something in her voice, a tone, a frankness, left no doubt about . . . well, he didn't want to put a word on it, preferring to think in general terms.

But he wanted to know what was right. In the emptiness of the house, he thought of what the dead child had left him with, which was a sense of isolation so definite he could apprehend it in the shadows that ran from the end of the sofa to the floor, making a dark triangle, or in the gray shape that came from the bottom edge of a picture frame, like a shade that had been pulled down. The edge of every shadow hinted at the boundary between light and darkness, between what one knew and what one hoped for. Of course, he wanted to hear the slight breathiness of Virginia's voice. He got up and replayed the message.

Right and wrong had always been part of his desire to become a physician. From the time Terry was eight or nine or ten years old, he had been curious about the Hippocratic oath. In the beginning, when Terry's grandfather asked him what he thought it meant, Terry had said, "It says you will not be a liar. You will not say one thing and believe another." His grandfather looked down at him. They were in his study (with the medical journals, that still meant something, in shelves on the wall . . . now, of course, everything is computerized). His grandfather had said, "No. It is not about lying. There is no oath for hypocrites, although there probably should be. I will ask you another time."

The next year came around and he asked again, standing in his study and looking at the city, saying, "Well, what does the Hippocratic oath mean?" Terry, who had gotten a copy of it from the library, answered, "The first thing is to do no wrong."

His grandfather stood at the window of his study, his hands behind his back. He hesitated, saying nothing, his eyes on the city, which lay beneath the evening's fog. Then he said, "I want you to remember something. The first thing is to do no *harm*. The second thing is to do no wrong."

Now Terry looked out his own window and saw his neighbor walking toward the house. He was a tall man with gray hair worn in a crew cut. His name was George and he liked to play double solitaire.

"Well?" he said. "How about it?"

"All right," Terry said.

They sat down at the table where they usually played and laid out a hand, and each started going through his cards. Three at a time. The air was tainted with the smell of burned roofing material, or maybe it was a stink that came from burning stucco.

"Have you got any Alka-Seltzer?" said George.

"That stuff's no good for you," Terry said. "It's like putting Drano down the pipes."

"I don't feel so good," he said.

"I'll bet you went down to that Thai restaurant, down there on La Brea. Don't you ever learn about that place? You were there, weren't you?"

"Yeah," said George. "They have a special. You get those little seafood rolls in that transparent white stuff."

"Uh-huh," Terry said. He reached out and put his hand on George's forehead. It was clammy. He looked a little gray.

"I feel sick to my stomach," he said.

"Anything else?"

"No," said George, although he looked away.

"Do you have pains in your chest?" Terry said. "What kind of pain?"

"It feels a little tight." George shrugged.

"Pull up your shirt," Terry said.

"Oh, come on," said George.

Terry had a stethoscope in the bedroom, and he went in there to get it, passing through the shadows. He heard George in the bathroom, throwing up. Terry picked up the telephone and called the hospital ambulance. The dispatcher wanted to know precisely where he was, and when Terry gave him the address, the dispatcher said he wasn't sure the ambulance could get through.

There was too much no-man's-land to cross. Terry could try the Valley, he said, but Terry knew that the Valley wasn't going to send an ambulance over the ridge. They'd tell him to try the other side. Well, what was he going to do? He thought of Virginia's voice on the machine, and he had the impulse to listen to it again, just to be sure.

"I'll drive you," Terry said. "Come on."

"Where are we going?" said George. "We don't have to go anyplace. I feel better now. Let's finish the game."

"Don't be difficult."

"I'm not being difficult. You're the one who's being difficult." He looked around the room as though he could find a place to hide.

"Is the pain getting worse?" Terry said.

"No," he said.

George opened the car door and got in and sat there as if he were resigned to visiting someone he disliked, and in that second before the engine started, the silence and darkness of the car seemed to rush up toward them as an embrace, which vanished as soon as Terry turned the key.

The road downhill curved one way and another, making it impossible to see more than a couple of hundred yards ahead. It was quiet in the car, and Terry tried to tell if George's breath was labored. He liked to keep some drugs in the house, but he didn't have any morphine and now he wished he had kept some around. Once, he gave a patient some morphine, and she had said, "You know what it's like? The warmest caress in the world." As they continued downhill, Terry thought about this. What was he going to do? He shook his head. Better just to get to the hospital. That was going to be enough, wasn't it?

Even before they came to the bottom, they could see a glow beyond the trees and the small ridges of the hill: it looked as if a bomb had gone off, although the flash was constant, brilliant, and smoky. One of the men who lived down here worked in the movie business and had set up his lights so that anyone driving up the canyon would have a hard time seeing. The lights were hot and smoke seemed to rise from them. A couple of men stood around, in the shadows, holding shotguns.

Terry stopped next to the lights, and one of the men said, "If I were you, I'd stay home."

"I got a sick man here," Terry said.

The man shrugged. "I don't know about that," he said. "You'd have to be pretty sick to want to go down there. It's spreading."

"Maybe we should just go back," said George.

"I want to get down to my hospital," Terry said.

"That's south of here, isn't it?" said the man.

"Yes," said Terry.

"There's trouble down that way," the man said.

"They didn't mention that on the radio," Terry said.

"So what?" said the man.

"OK," Terry said. "Thanks."

They turned downhill, into the warm, dark air of the canyon, where the scent of eucalyptus mixed with the odor of burning insulation and stucco, the combination suggesting both anxiety and the illusion of safety.

"Pull over," said George.

Terry did.

George opened the door. "There," he said. "I'm feeling better."

Mostly, it seemed like a good idea to stay away from the freeway. The radio said people had been shot there.

"Did anybody in your family ever have a heart attack?" Terry said.

"Just about everybody," George said. "You go along and you

don't think this moment's going to come. You always imagine it happening to someone else."

George closed the door and locked it. They drove on. Up ahead the intersection was bright, although the fire was unsteady and seemed to change in hue, from a yellow to a deep red, and the entire thing vanished as the smoke turned back on itself when the wind changed. The flames burned straight up in the shape of a maple leaf from a car that was in the street. Fifty or so people stood in the intersection, not milling around, but waiting for something to happen.

Terry stopped. George's breath seemed to come a little louder. Terry looked at the flames, thinking about the caress of morphine. Well, he'd listen to her voice again. Maybe he was wrong.

"What are you thinking about?" said George.

"Getting to the hospital. How you're breathing?" said Terry.

"I don't mean that," said George.

"I'm trying to make a decision," said Terry.

"About what?" said George.

"A woman," said Terry.

"And you don't know what to do?"

"No," said Terry.

"Well," said George, "when you get old, you think about the chances you had with women, but you didn't take. They're the ones that gnaw at you. Even when you're getting ready to die."

The door handle of the Subaru clicked repeatedly, and George said, "Someone's trying to get in." Another man appeared out of the smoke. He stood on the curb and coughed, then sat down, leaning forward on his knees. The door handle jerked again, and Terry heard other voices, not entire sentences, just words, exclamations, which seemed to rise with the same cadence of the insistent flames.

Someone hit the hood of the Subaru. The car started to rock from side to side as three or four men tried to overturn it. Someone swung an aluminum baseball bat, a new one still bearing its price tag, and the arc, in the sudden brightness as the smoke shifted, made a silvery streak, like light on a CD. The windshield crunched, although it didn't shatter. The intersection appeared through webbed cracks as George said, "Drive on. They'll get out of the way."

The car moved forward, as though through a car wash, in that the pounding on the hood seemed to sweep up to the roof and along the sides, and finally seemed to trail away, to exist only behind them. The voices receded into the smoke, and Terry and George were on a dark street with ordinary houses from which, here and there, came the gray-blue glow of a television set. In one of them, people were sitting down to dinner, but most of the houses were dark. It was probably a good idea to keep them that way.

George's breathing was a little more labored, but that might have been just because of the pounding on the car. Terry would probably have to get the thing painted. Or maybe he could sell it, but it had a hundred sixty thousand miles on it. There probably wasn't even a blue book for this make and model. Not anymore. He tried to think how many years back the blue books went, but he didn't know really. He guessed this car was in that no-man's-land between new and classic.

George looked at the spiderweb of cracks in the windshield, the edges of them silvery gold from the flames in the next intersection. "It's a good thing about safety glass," he said. "You have to hit it pretty hard to knock a hole in it."

"People still go through it," Terry said.

"Do they?"

"Uh-huh," Terry said. "Deep facial cuts come not from going

through a windshield, but from someone pulling their head back through."

"Well," said George. "That's a cheerful notion."

Let him think about someone else's trouble. There was glass on the street in front of a burning store, and the bits looked like sapphires and garnets, the liquid throb of them in the flames evoking uncertainty itself. Then Terry thought, Well, that's right. It's hard to know what's really happening with Virginia. Maybe she just needs a doctor. But then she could've called at the office.

"Maybe we should have taken the freeway," Terry said.

"What are we going to do?" said George.

"Wait for a minute," Terry said. "Then drive right through there. Maybe the intersection will clear out. People tend to move around in a riot."

George looked through the cracked windows. One hand was on his chest.

"You know," he said. "There's a lot I never told anyone."

You're not alone in that, thought Terry.

George swallowed and closed his eyes, shaking his head, seeming to resist not the bad taste of a heart attack, but the secrets he had been carrying around.

"It's going to be all right," Terry said.

"I bet you say that to everyone who's getting ready to die," he said.

"No," Terry said.

"Well, what do you say to someone who's getting ready to die?" he said.

"It depends. There isn't usually a lot of time for that. Mostly, you're pretty busy."

They were both quiet for a while. George said, "I worked for the U.S. government."

"Let me guess," Terry said. "You were a social worker."

"You could say that," he said.

"Well," Terry said. "What were you?"

"I was a professional prick," he said. "Now I'm a retired prick."

Four or five other cars in the intersection were on fire now, the flames red and yellow and topped by very black smoke, which rose with a dark curdling. George breathed heavily. The smoke, the air, the shapes of the people, all reminded Terry of the lack of morphine, which was one definite thing he could have done for George. Maybe some Lasix, too. He didn't have that either. Or a cardiac cocktail.

"You know something?" George said. "If this riot was happening on my watch, you know what I'd do? Let's say it was happening in North Africa. Maybe Lebanon."

He laughed now when he said the word *Lebanon,* although there wasn't anything funny in his voice.

"I can imagine that," Terry said.

George looked at Terry with some doubt. "Well, maybe," George said. "But if it was happening there, what do you think I'd do?"

"Send in some troops," Terry said.

"Naw," said George. He shook his head, in much the way a plumber looked at a job that had been botched by an amateur. "You don't want to do that. The best thing is to win without fighting. Or without fighting yourself."

"Is that right?"

"Sure," said George.

George sat there, looking through the cracks, thinking it over. He was breathing hard now, but when he glanced, expressionless, at Terry, the look was contradictory, at once almost completely bland, or even friendly, yet thoroughly malignant, too.

"It's beginning to feel like I'm being squeezed," said George.

More people entered the intersection, and as they did the wind changed, blowing smoke over them so that they looked like phantoms in front of the flames. The shapes that moved through the gloom were indistinguishable from one another, like men in bird costumes, or men wearing capes. There hadn't been many women out because the atmosphere, a mixture of gaiety and malice, was one that no one could trust for very long.

"Listen," George said. "Name a country. I'll tell you things that will curl your hair. Go on. Cuba. Russia. Even England."

"I've got enough trouble."

"Do you?" he said. "Well, in my business we never knew what we were getting into."

"We've got the same thing in medicine. There's even a saying about it," Terry said.

He looked at the intersection. It had to open up soon. Couldn't be too much longer. Then they'd get to the hospital and get George on Lasix, a good diuretic. Give him some morphine. Morphine.

"What's that?" George said.

"Well, if you're in southern California and you hear hoofbeats, you can usually be sure you're hearing a horse. But one time out of a hundred thousand, it's not a horse. It's a zebra."

"Zebras," he said. "I'll tell you about zebras. I'll tell you one about a woman."

"All right," Terry said. "Tell me."

"Like I said, there are chances, or what you thought was a chance, that you keep thinking about," said George.

"I understand," said Terry.

"No," said George. "You don't. Believe me, you don't."

"Are you going to tell me or not?" said Terry.

"Well, yeah. In the war I was a navigator on a bomber," said George.

"Which war?"

"World War Two," he said. "You weren't even alive."

"Well," Terry said. "I guess that's right."

"And let me tell you something," said George. "We were patriotic."

"I don't know about that," Terry said. "I just don't want people to die on me."

"You better get ready," said George. "I think you're going to have to get used to it." The smoke washed back over the intersection and George thought about things for a second. He said, "You wouldn't like it if I died on you, would you?"

"No," Terry said.

George started laughing, a short, gasping sound that came out of the dark.

"What's so funny?" Terry said.

"I was just thinking," George said. "If I died on you, you'd feel you'd done something wrong, wouldn't you?"

"Maybe," Terry said.

"There's no maybe about it," he said, looking at Terry.

"What was that about being a navigator?" Terry said. "You were telling me about World War Two."

The houses on this block were dark, although one could see a little flare in a room where someone lighted a cigarette.

"We got shot down over Germany. We belly flopped right into a field. Cold as hell. I thought the people who caught us were going to kill us right then. One skinny farmer came out with a pitchfork. Anyway, we ended up in a prison camp, not too far from Salzburg."

"Where do the zebras come in?" Terry said.

"Oh, don't worry," he said. "There's a zebra here. And love. Longing."

"Is that right?" said Terry.

"People of your generation don't have to worry about that. Free sex and everything."

"I don't know," said Terry. "I think that's over. People are pretty careful."

A pop sounded in the intersection, and fire spread across the street. Its movement reminded Terry of a flood.

"I'd been taught a code when I was training to be a navigator," said George. "You pick up all kinds of information in a prison camp, and I used the code to send back information in a letter."

"What kind of information?" Terry said.

"Like where to bomb," said George. "It was a book code. You know, everyone had these little bibles."

George looked through the windshield where the edges of the cracks pulsed with yellow and red, and beyond it there was the ominous smoke and the flicker that came from those shapes, like birds, that moved in front of the burning cars. He put his hand on his chest and closed his eyes for a moment.

"I started getting letters from someone called Flora," said George. "She was the one I was supposed to send the letters to with the code in them. Someplace in New York. Of course, I never knew any Flora. I guessed she was just working for the Defense Department. Anyway, she used to write these letters telling me what she was going to do when I got home, how she was going to caress me, things she was thinking about late at night, what she was going to do with the tip of her tongue. . . . Every letter ended with the same phrase. 'I love you, Monkey-Poo.' It was stupid, but I wanted to see it."

The thing about her, he said, was that in his longing he could imagine the touch of her skin, or a certain look in her eyes. His fantasies were blended with a sensation of how much he loved her. He told himself, in the beginning, that this was just longing gone a little wild, but after a while he wasn't so sure: instead, he began to think that someone's personality could be conveyed through the words she chose, and that the letters revealed the essence of the woman that he loved completely. She wrote a letter that said she had held the paper it was written on against her skin. George sat in the dark evenings of the camp, staring at the ceiling, able to hear her voice, which had a throaty quality that was at its best just above a whisper. His longing for her seemed to increase, and just when he thought that he had reached the top of what he could endure, he realized that he had been kidding himself, and that he would be able to take more. Friends died, and he was profoundly restless and confused, but he always came back to her letters, each one a little more salacious than the last, yet each seeming to be not so much about sex, but about love, the two combined like the fragrances of flowers. Terry thought about the wedding, of Virginia in the white cloud of her dress in the masses of wild roses as she stumbled toward him through the scented air.

George rested now, sitting in the car, trying to clear his throat. Terry didn't like that. His breathing was like the sound a bellows makes when it has a hole in it. Up ahead a small explosion revealed itself with a burst and pop and a shower of embers. A helicopter hovered in the distance, the steady whop whop whop making its way into the car with a slight, though constant, insistence.

Accuracy was important to George because what he said now might turn out to be all that remained of his story. No one else knew anything about it. So, he said, what did it feel like to love this woman? The details of her personality seemed as real to him as the texture of the blanket he pulled over his shoulders when he tried to sleep, or the dusty grit that was in the camp's dry winter air, although when he thought of her, he apprehended her as a sensation that was part physical and part mental, at once emotional and yet like a piece of silk being run across his chest and over his face. He concentrated on that feeling, although he found that when he tried too hard, it simply vanished, leaving him in the rank blanket in a hut filled with the sourness of sleeping, hungry men.

In the car, George's breathing had a wet sound, and his skin had a grayish cast, like the skin of a dead fish. He spoke in groups of words, four or five at a time.

Still, he said, when he had information he wrote as he had been instructed to do, using the code, although he wrote freely, too, because after all, he was writing a love letter. At these times, he found that he had no history to refer to, nothing that they had shared, and so it was impossible to ask her if she remembered that night on the sand dunes when the air had been so warm they had stretched out on their blanket under the stars, which were so keen and sharp that he was convinced he could feel them on his skin. Instead, he said that his health was good. He guessed he was getting a thousand calories a day. No fruit. Privately, he was afraid his teeth would fall out, and wondered how he would smile at her, hiding his mouth with his hand? He said that he hoped she was well, and that she should take care of herself. He told her that nutrition was important. He signed himself Your loving George.

The thing that was critical, though, was in that tactile, silky sensation of who and what she was, which, mixed with his admiration of her, allowed him to believe something else, too: that she forgave him everything he had ever done, and that she did this with the same understanding he would have liked to have given himself.

"So?" said George. "Do you think I loved her?"

"Yes," said Terry.

"Yeah. Sure," said George. "I guess that's right." He swallowed. "The war ended. I came home."

He looked over at Terry with that expression, partly bland, partly malignant. Terry looked at the cracks in the windshield, and he knew what it was they reminded him of: strands of Christmas tinsel.

"Well," said George. "I only weighed a hundred and twenty-five pounds. They wouldn't let me go. So I sat around in a hospital in New Jersey. I could see the marshes, you know, where the reeds grew."

His breathing was louder. Terry decided to go through the intersection. They could be stopped up there. There wouldn't be any time to explain, or to say, There's a sick man here.

George was quiet, as though trying to put his memories in the proper order. He said that he took the train to Washington, although he was upset that he didn't look very good. He hadn't gained that much weight, although he'd eaten as much as he could stomach. He was a little yellow with jaundice. He found a department store near the train station, and he went in, not wanting to show up empty-handed. He was sure that Flora could use some nylon stockings because they had been hard to get during the war, and he bought a pair and had them gift wrapped.

The office he was looking for was in one of those institutional, yellowish office buildings in Washington, which has since been torn down. He asked where he could find the section he was interested in and was told to go downstairs. The brownish linoleum in the hall had just been buffed to a sheen. How often had he associated a sheen with her, in her eyes or on her bare skin, or over her legs? The walls were made of poured concrete and overhead there were bulbs in little cages. The offices themselves had furniture like those at a small-town newspaper: functional, gray metal filing cabinets and desks, typewriters on metal stands.

George talked to an officer, a colonel, who told him what a good job he had done. The information had been good. A lot of raids had been conducted on the basis of it. Did George want to meet Flora?

"Yes," said George.

"Down there," said the officer. "In that door on the right."

The office George went into was like others he had passed. Two desks with green blotters, wire baskets, typewriters, a calendar, a corkboard on the wall. Outside in the hall he heard the glug glug of someone getting a drink from the watercooler. A man by the name of Garrity, who had been a classmate of George's at Princeton, sat at one of the desks. Garrity stood up, and said, "Hey, George. Gosh, I don't think I've seen you since we were at school together. Tell me, when we were at Princeton, did we ever think we'd end up like this?"

"No," said George. "At Princeton, I didn't think much at all, to tell the truth."

"Well, you know what?"

"What?" said George.

"I'm Flora."

George stood there, listening to the sound of the watercooler in the hall, and said, as he took the gift-wrapped nylon stockings from under his arm, "Well. Here. I guess these are for you."

Garrity reached out and took the package, and said, "Gee, thanks. What is it?"

"Oh," he said, "just a little something."

George went out into the hall and had a drink of water, concentrating on that glug glug glug while the water splashed into a little cup like an upside-down dunce's cap.

Now the helicopter came closer, its lights cutting through the smoke that rose from the intersection up ahead. If they were going to be stopped, Terry thought it would be a good idea if the helicopter was overhead. Maybe it could give them some help. He started the engine and swung into the street as the flames swept out from one side of the intersection as though someone had thrown a pop bottle filled with gasoline. The fluid movement of fire suggested all the aloofness of the workings of human affairs, the connections and hidden associations that lead to such things as a gift of nylon stockings, or Terry and George, sitting in this car, hoping that they had enough time. Or the voice on the answering machine in Terry's house. The critical thing seemed to be to get through the curtain of flames that stretched across as though, on the other side, they might discover a secret they needed to know. The car wasn't going fast enough to hit anyone, but certainly fast enough to convey the notion that Terry wasn't going to stop either. That was clear, wasn't it? No stopping.

George said, "Well, there's your goddamned zebra."

People emerged from the smoke, their faces turning toward the car. A lot of glass was on the sidewalk and in the street, each piece red or yellow, as though the sheets of flame had been frozen and shattered. The people in the intersection stood together. They looked mostly exhausted, and if they had trouble getting out of the way, it was because so much had already happened, rapes and broken bones, cuts and head injuries, the fires and the broken glass.

Most of the people started to get out of the way, but four or five men remained. They carried baseball bats and a tire iron and a two-by-four. A piece of concrete came out of the smoke and hit the car, and a brick landed on the hood and slid up toward the windshield. The car came very close to the flames, which bent

115

over it and filled the interior with a mixture of orange and yellow and an undulant shadow, too, from the curdling smoke. The odd thing was how quickly the fire slipped away, leaving Terry with the disorienting sense of moving from light into sudden darkness. The flames behind the car were presided over by that helicopter, which swung its light back and forth, back and forth, like an enormous pendulum or some brutal way of keeping time.

"Well, what are you going to do?" said George.

"About what?" said Terry.

George looked at him. "Don't be cute," he said. "I'm getting ready to die. I meant what are you going to do about the woman you're thinking about."

"I don't know," said Terry.

George shrugged. "God hates a coward," he said.

They arrived at the hospital. The guard in the parking booth had his pistol on the counter in front of him, and his eyes went over the car and Terry's face. Then the guard turned back to the street. At the triage desk, Terry paged a cardiologist. The morphine helped. The cardiologist said he was having a busy night. There was nothing like a riot, or an earthquake, to bring the cardiac cases in. Hurricanes did it too, but they didn't have any hurricanes in California. George closed his eyes when the morphine hit.

Terry went into his office and sat down. He got up and washed his hands at the sink in the corner, using the soap that smelled of iodine, and which always made him think of maternity wards. Then he sat down again and picked up the phone and called her. He held the phone in his hand and squeezed it pretty hard while he waited. Out of the darkness the phone connected. He heard that ring and stop, ring and stop.

VIRGINIA AND TERRY sat opposite each other in the hotel lounge. She looked at him when he said, "I've taken a room here. Let's have a bottle of champagne sent upstairs." He had no idea he was actually going to say this. In fact he didn't think of it as a possibility, not a real one, until he spoke, as though the making of a reservation, the registering, the acceptance of a key were all part of some figment of imagination, which didn't become real, with all its complications, until he actually spoke out loud. For an instant, he was convinced that he was more startled than she was.

He heard the sound of a piano, the murmur of conversation around him, the touch of a glass against a table, and a click of a knife or a spoon, all of it alarming to him, if only because he had often thought that an enormous disaster might first make itself apparent through such small, inconsequential details. The tinkle of ice, the almost inaudible sound as a woman slipped off her silk-lined jacket, the sigh of a plate being put on a white table-cloth, all left him confronting a kind of terror. He had no business doing this. The woman who sat opposite him was the newly married wife of a man who had been a friend of his. Such moments were alien to the heart of what he had always tried to be as a physician.

At the same time, he looked around the room: the lighting was a little subdued, although some places were bright, too, and from the arm of a chair or the top of a table, the shadows ran to the floor with an edge that was as straight as a yardstick. These reminded him of his house, when he had been wondering about the rate of absorption for Xanax while he hoped the speed at which it was absorbed was sufficient ammunition against those late-night shadows so infused with the effect of the dead child and its lightness in his hands.

The green and gold-flecked color of Virginia's eyes suggested fertility and power, like sunlight filtering through leaves in springtime. The thing that distinguished her glance, aside from its sharpness, was a hint of something else, and just as he was able to apprehend the possibility of forgiveness, she said, "Yes. Why not? I've always liked champagne."

They made finishing their drinks into a contest to see if each was up to the restraint of sitting there and smiling politely. She reached out for her glass, the tips of her fingers steady, although for a second she was distracted by the presence of a waiter, and then they started shaking. She smiled and looked down, as though dropping a weight.

"Have you paid?" she said.

"Yes," he said.

She stood up.

"The elevators are over there," he said.

"I know," she said.

They started walking, Virginia in front, both of them going

across that soft carpet and passing the dark furniture, the wing chairs next to small tables on which there were flowers, the petals of them pink, symmetrical, fragrant. In one chair there was a man who must have weighed three hundred pounds, his large fingers, perfectly manicured, holding a glass of beautifully colored brandy. He glanced at the two of them and had a sip, swallowing slowly. Terry walked in the wake of Virginia's scent, the odor of her hair reminding him of those occasions when he had unexpectedly come close to a woman in a crowded restaurant, or getting in and out of a car, and when, without any warning, the sudden, intimate fragrance had made itself apparent, its influence lasting far beyond the seeming importance of the moment. He thought of those occasions when this had happened, on an airplane, for instance, and, of course, with his patients. His women patients had always trusted him.

As he walked along, he wondered if he could stop things now, even if he wanted to. What would happen if he said, Well, don't you see, I was only kidding . . . all this was just a joke . . . I don't know what got into me . . . He imagined her expression. What would the colors of her eyes be then, when he had managed to get her to reveal a profound secret about herself, and, more, to get her to act on it, and then dismissed her as nothing more than the butt of a joke?

Virginia was wearing a green silk skirt. The light played across it with a liquefaction, the movement of her arms and back defined by the luster that came and went as the silk of her skirt formed elongated folds. The material was smoother over her hips and thighs, and the light lay across it in broad and undulant shimmers. Terry thought of how she had walked at the wedding, over the grass and through the arbor covered with white roses, her feet coming down hard enough to reveal a physical shock under her clothes. This giving of flesh was something Terry tried to deny. One day, for instance, when the elevator had been out of service in the hospital, he had walked up the stairs behind a woman whose hips had swayed before his face, giving and taking with a subdued and smooth movement, seemingly at odds with Terry as he went along in his white coat, as sterile as a paper towel. Well, just what was it exactly that had ruptured that safe, endless restraint?

They waited in front of the elevator. She wondered if he had had any doubts when they had crossed the room, or any notion that had left him less than certain. If he had, would he humiliate her now, after having gotten her to admit that she was . . . willing. He put out his hand, the fingers unsteady, the gesture seeming to suggest that it was impossible to stop. She looked at his hand and apprehended the gesture with an odd sensation of reassurance perfectly mixed with terror. She turned to stare at the descending floor numbers above the elevator door, 8, 7, 6, and stopping. Then 5, 4, 3, and stopping again. The piano was very faint. A woman behind Virginia rustled a bag. Virginia looked directly at the door, and said to Terry, "What's the weather going to be like?"

That she asked such a question, as though to demonstrate that she was totally in control, that she was able to make idle conversation in the midst of waiting, of watching the elevator start and stop, which seemed to make the time flow with a coldness, if not malice, such a question left him as shocked as he had been when he had spoken earlier, asking her if she would like some champagne. The control came to him with the same impact as if she had said, Well, do you want me to . . . you? What he wanted to convey was understanding: if restraint was required, if control was what she was asking for, he would be able to give it while he thought of . . . the color of . . . or the texture . . .

or the taste . . . or as she ran a finger along . . . Just as he would be able to stand up to what he was sure was coming, the abandonment of his previous ideas about himself in the face of the discovery of his flaws, and the fact that once he knew these flaws, he'd only be able to take comfort in the thing that had shown him these flaws in the first place: more meetings like this. Even standing at this threshold, he wanted to stand up to the implications of what he would discover about himself. So thinking, Would you like me to run my . . . across . . . would you, would you . . . sit this way, like this . . . , he said, "I hadn't heard a report."

"I guess there will be one on the radio later," she said.

"Or in the paper."

"Yes," she said. "There's always the paper."

"I've heard it's going to rain," said the woman with the package.

"Really?" said Virginia.

"Yes," said the woman.

The elevator arrived. The people on it looked like actors who, just as the curtain went up, had forgotten their lines. They straightened their expensive clothes and looked down and murmured, Excuse me, excuse me, as they walked into the lobby. Then the woman with the bag got on. Terry pushed the button for the number of the floor. The elevator had a mirror on one wall and a seat opposite it. Terry had the desire to look in the mirror to see how they had been affected, or for any visible signs of compulsion. Instead, he glanced at the display above the door, the floor numbers flickering on and off scientifically, as though measuring a new variety of time, one that flowed more slowly than usual.

The door opened, and the woman with the bag got off. "Sometimes the weather reports are wrong," said Virginia. "You can never trust them."

Terry turned to the mirror. Virginia looked pale, but still radiant, like apple blossoms in a frost. He stood next to her, his face set in the same expression, he realized, as when he knew something about a patient that he didn't want to know and, worse, knew he would have to explain. The door opened and they went out, into the silent hallway. Flowers stood in a vase on a table by the elevator, and Virginia stopped to touch one, looking at the petals and the green asparagus fern, doing this to slow everything down, if only so nothing embarrassing or haunting could happen at this instant.

The door to the room was heavy, and it swung open quietly. The windows were covered with a gauzy curtain. Virginia pulled the curtains back, letting the sunshine fall onto the bed, as though, as far as she was concerned, they would hide nothing, there would be no soft lighting, nothing to obscure the facts of what they were up to: here, at least, some dreadful honesty had to be at the center of what she was sure was going to be an almost infinite collection of lies (to her husband, or to anyone else who got in the way). She tried to imagine the lies, and what came to mind was trees in the fall, the leaves like the color of the tip of a soldering iron or yellow like a daffodil, each leaf falling, the lies accumulating on the ground, giving the afternoon a glow of deceit. Here, they would make it otherwise.

The champagne was in the room, in a silver bucket, which was covered with cold sweat, and over the top of it a white napkin was folded and wrapped around the foil of the bottle. Virginia sat down on the bed, her feet together on the floor. The pop of the bottle, subdued, allowing a wisp of vapor to escape from its mouth, like a thread of smoke, carried with it an association to other times. Terry remembered the afternoon when he had been accepted to medical school, the pop of the champagne cork then, the dry taste, all coming down through the years to this moment when he poured the bright liquid into a glass and held it out for her, bearing down now so that his hand was almost steady.

She looked at him over the rim of the glass. Then she closed her eyes and had a sip. She looked around the room. The light fell across her face, her features making shadows that fell across her cheek, and the sunlight made one eye bright with a dot the color of the champagne. There were times when Terry had driven through the vineyards in the north, the rows of grapes appearing as the spokes of a wheel as he drove past, and the constant bubbles in the champagne at the tip of his tongue reminded him of the repetitive passing of the rows. She took off her shoes.

She held the glass up and looked at the bubbles, miniature pearls. Terry tried to think about what had brought him here. Was it just an impulse, or had the impulse been the absolute tip of other matters that had been carefully arranging themselves for years? It seemed to him that if he was doing something wrong, it was out of strength rather than out of sloth or weakness, although as he thought this, as he watched the bubbles in her glass, rising so regularly and with a diminutive beauty, he thought, Yes, of course, does anyone ever say he is doing something attractive because he is weak?

Terry looked at the bubbles in his own glass and through them saw Virginia reaching under her skirt and then holding her underwear in her hand, then folding them, like someone going on a journey, a schoolgirl. She put them on the dresser. Virginia sat down again and picked up her glass, her glance inflammatory, as though they had started along a course that didn't lend itself to anything sweet and romantic, at least not now, but something more frank and consuming: in fact, as Terry sat there, he was reminded of a progression of events, one detail demanding the next, each new one more complicated and bigger than the previous one, the scale of the last demanding even more intensity from the next. Terry wondered if, under these circumstances, any dark contour of the heart could possibly remain hidden.

So she sat there, looking at him.

"Do you like champagne?" she said. "Can you remember your first glass?"

"I guess it was at a party," he said. "Up in the hills. I could see the city."

"It sounds romantic," she said.

She undid the white button on her blouse. It was a mother-of-pearl button, and the color of it, white and a little shiny, seemed to come from another era, and for a while Terry watched her fingers as they touched it. It was one of those details that stopped him for an instant. He guessed he had seen such a button when he had gone to an elegant party someplace, or when he had been in his early twenties and had seen an elegant woman far beyond his reach. Why he had remembered the button was a mystery, but he was sure the small and hazy object was a reminder of a youthful sense of exclusion when Terry had faced one of those walls that exist between young men and experienced, elegant women. Now, he watched Virginia's fingers, which seemed to hesitate, their slowness an attempt to remind him of just what they were doing.

He looked at her hands. One had many small scars from the times when she had been bitten at work. She was tan and this made the scars seem white, some shaped like new moons, and milky, too. She held her hands out for him to see, obviously trying to say, Here. Look. Here is where I have been marked. Look. These scars come from something everyone is terrified by, the bites of snakes, but I show them to you as scars of every terror, every bit of carelessness, every flaw that makes me human. Here.

124

I make you a present of them. They look like mother-of-pearl, don't they? Just like the buttons on my blouse.

"You don't mind the scars, do you?" she said. She put her hand out so he could see the scars more clearly.

"No," he said.

"They show more in the summer," she said.

Her finger went back to the next button.

"They're the only scars I have," she said.

He turned and looked out the window. In the distance the Pacific was a smear where the haze seemed to collect. He wondered what he had to give to her in return. Could he say that he was afraid that it was possible to be so compromised that he wouldn't be much of a physician anymore? After all, the first thing was to do no harm, the second to do no wrong. But was it a flaw that he couldn't take those moments alone anymore, such as when he tried to sing over a dead child? He hadn't any idea why he was convinced that she would be able to help, but from the first he had believed it, even when he had seen her in that ridiculous white cloud of a dress, in the scent of those white flowers, her face stricken. All she had to say was, I understand. I'm sorry. Her fingers undid the last button, and the quiet folding of her silk blouse, now just dropped on the floor, left him aware how soothing the silence of the room was. He tried to remember if there were any old stories in which men and women outraged the world around them in this way, and what the consequences were, but he couldn't think of any. He had studied medicine, not literature. But as he'd watched her fingers, he realized that possible consequences were part of what made the scent of her, the taste of the champagne, so powerful as to pull the two of them into a vacuum: consequences were what made this real. She started murmuring a little, looking beyond him, out the window over his shoulder, saying, This isn't just a cheap thrill for you, is it? You couldn't be that much of a monster, could you? You wouldn't come here just to say to yourself that you were able to get me to . . . Then she stopped and looked at him.

The light in the room seemed to him to be about as far away as possible from those shadows that can be seen only at three A.M., and which had left him with the impulse to come here, as though everything here was an antidote to that furious sense of longing that came from those times when he had tried to explain too much to himself. He supposed it wasn't only the child, but that the child had been the last detail that had made him aware of a hundred other times. There was the case, for instance . . . but he stopped, and watched as she stood and removed her skirt and folded it and put it on her chair and turned back to face him.

She said, There isn't anything I wouldn't do, nothing I wouldn't rip apart, nothing, if I thought it got between us and relief. Do you understand? Do you? I've made so many mistakes. So many. All I want is relief from them. Not forever. But just for a little while.

In the early fall in California, the air was the temperature of skin, and when Terry stood outside, it had been hard to tell where he ended and the air began, and now, as he lay down, against her, the warmth between them was the same as that September air. It was hard to tell where he ended and she began, although even then he waited for the world to reassert itself and to leave them wondering just what would be required of them after all.

VIRGINIA CALLED TERRY at the hospital. Could she come down to see him? Her husband was out, and no one at the hospital where Terry worked knew Rick anyway. Terry said that it was a slow night. She could come down, if she wanted. They could talk. She said she had been thinking things over. For instance, what were they really up against? How far were they willing to go? They hadn't ever really talked about it, she said. Is this the way real trouble began, the two of them spiraling down to . . . well, to anything? At the center of her fear was one thing: just what were they exposed to, or what power had seized them, and what was it capable of? She said she could be there in a half an hour or so.

Terry sat in his office behind the triage desk, trying to read a book, when a case came in off the street, no warning. The office had just a desk, a computer, book shelves, a sink. He put the book facedown on the desk and went out.

The man who had been brought through the door had been

stabbed. He was wearing brown pants and a blue shirt, both very bloody. He lay on the examination table, and under the lights he raised one hand languidly, like a sleepy man in a desert. The man had been stabbed in the chest with a long blade, maybe a bowie knife or even a bayonet. A nurse looked at Terry and made a motion with her hand across her neck, which meant, This one's finished. Forget it. The man still had a pulse. Not much blood pressure. The knife had cut into the heart. Terry called for the surgeon who was on duty, but he hadn't arrived yet. For all Terry knew, the surgeon was in the bathroom someplace, reading the stock market newsletter he subscribed to. The surgeon was always losing money, mostly in biotech stocks, which he was supposed to know something about. So Terry said to the nurse, "I'm going to need some help."

"Oh?" she said. She looked out the door. The nurse knew they weren't supposed to do any surgery. The medical staff didn't like it if the properly trained physician didn't do the procedure.

"Don't worry," said Terry. "I'll say I twisted your arm."

"I don't know," she said.

The first thing was to put a tube into the man so that he could breathe. It didn't go in easily. He had the notion, a couple of times, that the man had died. Terry kept swinging back and forth between the near hysteria of trying to get the tube in and the suspicion that he had failed. The nurse said, "I bet I know what happened. The surgeon's got another case like this one. That's why he's not here."

"Yes," said Terry. "That's probably it."

"He'll get here," said the nurse. "Don't you think?"

"Sure," said Terry. "It can't be long."

He followed the path of the wound, opening it up as he went. At one point he had to spread the ribs, and when he had a little exposure he saw that the pericardium, or the sack that the heart sits in, was filled with blood. He used his scissors to open the sack, and removed the clotted blood with his hand. He put his finger over the hole in the heart, and used the suture the nurse gave him, going over his finger and then underneath, remembering that the heart wasn't that tough and that he didn't want to tear it when he pulled the sutures tight. He did so just until the bleeding stopped.

The surgeon came in, and said, "Jesus. My God."

"I didn't tear it," said Terry.

"OK," said the surgeon. "That's good. We've got to move him."

Then they moved him down to the surgical suite, where the surgeon looked the man over and then closed the chest. When the surgeon came back to see Terry, he said the man who had been stabbed had a chance. It depended on infection. The surgeon said it wasn't like a gunshot wound, where the bullet isn't what's dirty so much as the pieces of clothing that the bullet drives into the wound. High-velocity rounds caused more infections than low ones. Terry went into his office and sat down, thinking about the color of the heart. Well, they had some good antibiotics these days, some really good ones. Terry thought, When will she get here?

Another case arrived.

A man who had been shot in the abdomen was brought in by two paramedics: they wore blue jumpsuits, like the ones that plumbers wear. One held a bag of fluid, a salt solution that temporarily restores blood volume. There hadn't been much warning here either because the man had been shot only a quarter of a mile from the hospital. His name was Billy Morgan. At least that's what the ID in his pocket said. Terry looked at the man's strangely peaceful face.

The two paramedics appeared relieved that they had managed to get Morgan off the street and here without him dying. They looked a little sick, and they were still sweating. Terry asked how much fluid they had given him. They told him.

The taller of the two, with dark hair and a mustache, said, "This guy got shot over a Chevy."

Morgan's pulse was over a hundred, and his blood pressure was low. Terry started to look for the holes in him. One hole (no exit wound) means there is still a bullet inside somewhere. Two holes, and a bullet has passed through. Three holes, the patient has been shot twice, with one bullet going through and one remaining inside. Although it's possible, too, that someone could be shot three times with three bullets left inside. Morgan had one hole, in the lower back, no exit wound. The nurse went down the hall to get the surgeon. Terry guessed he would be here faster than before.

"This guy's getting sour," said one of the paramedics.

The x-ray technician, a young woman, came in, wheeling her equipment in front of her, and Terry stepped back while she made two films, one at ninety degrees to the other.

"It was a goddamn Chevy that got this sucker whacked," said the tall paramedic. "That's what he was saying. He sold a Chevy that he'd fixed up with a bunch of stop leak . . . So the guy who bought the car is driving on the Santa Monica freeway, and it overheats. The buyer has a thirty-eight under the seat and he gets out and starts walking, carrying the pistol. You know what Morgan here says to me when I pick him up? 'That goddamned stop leak. It ain't worth a shit, you know that?'"

"Well," said the other one, "he could use some stop leak right now, I can tell you that."

Terry looked around, thinking that the heart can go on beating as long as there's fluid, although blood pressure is problematic in gunshot cases. Sometimes the bleeding stops when the pressure goes down, but it begins again when you get decent pressure.

Billy Morgan started to shiver. "I feel cold," he said.

The technician went to develop the films.

Two policeman had come into the room, each dressed in blue uniforms that were creased in three places across the back. They were heavyset, not quite gone to fat but getting there. For a second, Terry had the sensation of that hour in his house at three o'clock, when he wanted to call Virginia but knew that he couldn't.

One of the policeman said to Billy Morgan, "Who shot you?"

Morgan kept on staring at the overhead light. His blood pressure was falling and he had a very high pulse.

"Why don't you wait outside?" Terry said.

"He could just tell us who shot him," said one of the cops.

"Come on," said the other cop. "He looks like he can talk a little. We want to know who shot him."

"He isn't so bad," said the first cop. "Not yet."

"How do you know?" said Terry.

"Oh," said the cop, "I know."

"Look," Terry said. "When you're driving around giving tickets . . ."

"We're not working on traffic, Terry. Does this guy look like he was in a fender bender?"

"Well," Terry said. "When you're driving your car around, do you find me looking over your shoulder?"

The policemen stood there.

"He might tell us something," said one. "Then we go pick up the guy who shot him."

"I'll tell you about that," said the paramedic.

Now the surgeon came into the room. "What have we got here? A Harlem sunrise?"

"He's a white guy," said one of the paramedics. "It's a Glendale sunrise."

"Or Santa Monica," said the other paramedic. "A Santa Monica sunrise is more like it."

The films came back, and Terry and the surgeon looked at them. They were taken from two angles, one from the top and one to the side, and they showed two bullets. Terry went back to Billy Morgan and looked him over. He only had one hole.

"Jesus Christ," said the surgeon. "How did two bullets get in there? There's only one hole. You don't suppose someone put the pistol right up against him and shot him twice through the same hole?"

The x-ray showed a white shadow, which indicated some bleeding in the cavity, and also some air just under the diaphragm. Perforated bowel. That's what was creating the air pocket.

As they got him ready for surgery (putting a catheter into him), Morgan was still shivering. The surgeon looked at the films again. Terry stood there, hearing the cluttered movement, the sound of a sheet being pulled back, footsteps in the hall, the squeak of a curtain moving on its overhead runner as it was stripped back, the ripping noise of an IV needle being taken out of a cellophane package, each noise, each detail, existing as ordinary in the face of chaos. Terry thought of Virginia, and had the overwhelming desire to be precise. He looked at Billy Morgan, who stirred, moved a little, and opened his eye, staring into the overhead lights. He swallowed and licked his lips, and said, "That no good stop leak."

The overhead light, which was almost theatrical in its intensity, gave Morgan's skin a paraffin cast. Terry didn't know why he hadn't thought of it before. Maybe he was tired. The second bullet came from a previously untreated gunshot wound.

Terry told the surgeon about it.

"Yeah," he said. "I'll bet that's it. He must have been afraid to get treatment. Must have held up a liquor store and got shot."

Terry guessed Virginia was close now, maybe even pulling into the parking lot. He imagined the shape of her legs as she opened the door and got out of the car, walking over the broken glass. People were always throwing bottles over the fence into the parking lot.

A nurse from the triage desk came in. "There's someone here to see you," she said. "She said you were expecting her."

They wheeled Billy Morgan down the hall. The silence was pierced by the squeak rumble, squeak rumble, of the stretcher. Then a cool, medicine-scented silence seemed to flow into every corner of the place. Terry washed his hands, and said to the nurse, "OK. I'll be right out."

Virginia was standing up, looking at the magazines on a table when he came into the waiting room.

"Maybe we could go down to the cafeteria," said Terry. "You know, we could get a cup of coffee."

"OK," she said.

There was blood on his clothes, and when he saw it, he said, "Excuse me. I'll be right back. I've just got to change."

He went down the hall and put on some clean clothes and came back. A policeman had been talking to the nurse at the desk, a young man with aviator glasses. The policeman seemed to be carrying a lot of things on his belt, a gun, a walkie-talkie, and he wore a bright badge.

"Have you seen anyone wandering around in here?" he said to Terry. "Got a mustache. Short haircut. Little taller than me."

"No," Terry said.

The cop took off his hat and ran his hand through his hair. Everything about him, his clothes (even though they were starched), his hair, probably even his gun, smelled of smoke. Terry guessed it was left over from the riot. It was hard to get that stink out of clothing. Dry cleaning probably wouldn't do it.

"We got a real Apache loose in here," the cop said. "We brought him in here and left him alone with a doctor, and he took off." The policeman looked down the hall. "How come there aren't any more lights on?" he said.

He went down the hall. It really wasn't well lighted, and a man could easily disappear into shadows and doorways.

"What was that all about?" Virginia said.

"Some guy got away from the cops," Terry said.

Virginia turned and looked into the shadows. "You know," she said. "You hear stories about people who meet on trains and they start talking. They know they're never going to see one another again. They tell each other secrets that they wouldn't dream of telling friends. Or husbands. Or lovers."

Terry looked around: it was a long way from this corridor to a train like the Orient Express.

"Well, let's talk that way," he said.

"Is the coffee any good?"

"No," he said. "Everything tastes like medicine here. But what can you expect?"

The sounds of their feet on the linoleum were out of sync. The policeman came back up the hall, not quite running, just jogging along on the balls of his feet, the walkie-talkie and other equipment on his belt rising and falling like broken wings. He was still looking from side to side, and when he came up to Terry, he said, "You still haven't seen anything, have you? I didn't flush him this way?"

"No," Terry said.

"He's got to be here," he said. "But this place is filled with closets, you know that?"

He turned and started looking again, saying only, "This guy shouldn't be played around with. You understand what I'm saying?"

Virginia and Terry started walking. Both of them kept looking at the shadows, which now seemed alive, or at least filled with mystery. A mop handle fell in an alcove as they went by, the quick slap disturbing the silence of the building. They stopped, and Virginia waited, listening to the quiet that seemed to flow back around her after the sound of the falling mop, and as she waited, she wanted more than ever some understanding of what she had gotten into. Or, more importantly, as she looked into the shadows, she seemed to sense that here, just beyond her fingertips, was a delineation of forces that she faced.

"Maybe we should look around a little," Terry said.

She glanced from the shadows to Terry.

"I don't think the cop looked downstairs," Terry said.

"Oh?" she said. "All right. I guess we can talk while looking for . . . what is he, a rapist, a murderer?"

"I guess," said Terry.

The stairway was made of poured concrete, topped with metal plates and with a metal banister that had been painted crimson. The echoes of their steps blended with the sound of a closing door, which had all the resonance of anxiety.

"I want more time with you," she said.

"I know," he said.

"But maybe that's just a reflection of sneaking around. Could we be that shallow? Could we be trapped by anything that mundane?"

They came up to the lab. It was a room of medium size, with five or six long counters. A large machine that did basic tests, blood chemistry, for instance, and blood gases, stood against the wall. It was hard to keep it cool enough, and one of the lab technicians had set up a fan from home to blow air at the back of the machine. The place had an ominous quality, but that probably stemmed from their uneasiness about the man they were looking for. A telephone on the wall began to ring, and its jangle, the lonely shrillness of it, seemed to be a mixture of the familiar and the unexpected.

They went back to the stairway and up one floor. Virginia kept looking into the recesses of the hall. Terry had the sense that the possibilities between them changed from moment to moment, or that the entire time they spent together, which he had come to need, was dependent on saying the right thing. But what could he say?

"You didn't answer me," she said. "Are we so shallow as to be excited by the sneaking around?"

"No," he said. "We're not so bad as that."

"Are you sure?" she said. "Why can't we just go about our business. Why can't I just say, Thanks for the champagne. It was great. Good-bye?"

In the cafeteria they went down to the coffee and hot water urns, passing the glass shelves on which Jell-O or sandwiches wrapped in plastic usually sat. Virginia put her lips to the coffee. What it lacked in quality it made up in temperature. She jumped back and pursed her lips.

"All right, we'll talk. Like on a train," she said.

She held her coffee cup up, and the mist rose in front of her lips. Over her shoulder, a table stood by the wall. Along the far side of it some chairs sat in the darkness. Maybe the cafeteria lights were low in an effort to save money. In the shadows, a man sat at the end of the table by the kitchen door. He held a cup of coffee to his face. His hair was dark, and all that showed were the whites of his eyes and the white coffee cup in his hands. He sat there, looking at Terry.

A silvery mist hovered above the table in front of the man. Terry thought the table was pretty shiny, then realized the wedge-shaped haze was something else. In the kitchen knives with black handles usually hung in a magnetized rack on the wall.

"What are we really in the grips of?" she said.

"I want to know, too," he said.

She sat with the cup in front of her, her hands just touching it.

"Maybe we should think about being on a train," he said.

"Which one?" she said.

"The Trans-Siberian Express," Terry said. "Imagine that we've got a rye bread we've bought. It's wrapped in a newspaper printed with words we can't read. I've got a piece of cheese and an onion. A bottle of beer in a large brown bottle with a funny cap on it."

"Uh-huh," she said. "Have you got a knife?"

He looked into the shadows again. "Yes," he said. "Outside we can see hills covered with birch trees. It's springtime, and the light that comes into the train has a greenish tint to it. Like light that comes through a piece of light green silk."

"It sounds cool," she said.

"Maybe. I guess it's morning. It hasn't started to get hot yet."

"We've just met," she said. "Is that right?"

"Yes," he said.

"Well, then I'd tell you I was newly married and that I was betraying my husband."

"You'd use that word?" he said.

"Yes," she said.

Betrayal. He thought about the word, and the way it seemed to fall from her lips. Behind her the man took another drink of his coffee. He seemed to be listening, too, as though he had some notions about the subject of betrayal.

"Don't you think that something has simply walked into your life and taken over?" she said. "Do you like that?"

Just keep talking, he thought. That's good. The atmosphere at the table was confessional, or it had the small change in the air that goes along with the telling of a secret or the establishing of a confidence. Although, at the same time, he could see that at any moment she could simply get tired, and then they would be left, just two people sitting in a hospital cafeteria, drinking lousy coffee and wondering just what had gotten into them. Terry didn't know what he feared the most: the arrival of the mundane or the man at the other table.

The man sat half in the shadows, like a figure being sculpted from stone and only partially emerging from it. This, along with the stillness that weighed on him like a manifestation of fear, gave Terry the impression that the man was also trying to figure out what to do.

"You know the train makes a sound," Terry said.

"What sound?"

"Clickety-clack, clickety-clack," Terry said.

"Sure," she said. "That's right."

"And then there's that rye bread. The newspaper makes a crinkling sound as I unwrap it."

"Maybe some ink comes off on the bread," she said.

"No. It's old paper. Do you like the heel? I'll cut you a piece."

She had a sip of her coffee.

"They make tea on a stove in the corner of the train," he said.

"That green light is nice. In the distance you can see a river. The sun on it looks like a million nickels. Then there's the sound."

"The clickety-clack?" she said.

"Yes," Terry said.

At the other table, the man put down his coffee, right next to that hazy wedge. He looked at Terry, and said, raising his voice a little, "You know what it says?"

"What?" Terry said.

"That sound," he said. "You know what it says?"

"No," Terry said.

"Cut-your-head-off. Cut-your-head-off. Cut-your-head-off. That's what it says."

"Uh-huh," Terry said.

They sat for a second, looking at each other.

"Haven't I seen you around here?" Terry said.

"No," he said.

"Do you work here?"

"Me?" he said. He laughed a little. It wasn't very pleasant, but there was real mirth in it. "You could say that," he said. "In a way. Maybe I send you some business." He cocked his head toward the hall. He looked back at Terry. "You know how you get to know what that sound says? You got to ride under a boxcar. That way you can really hear it. Oh, you can hear it loud and clear."

Virginia sat there, looking at Terry. The man was behind her. She still held the coffee cup just by the tips of her fingers. The man went back to sitting quietly, saying nothing, simply existing in the shadows. She concentrated, as though the steady, abrupt words suggested the scale of what she confronted, if not the power of its grip, too.

"So," Terry said to her. "You can see the hills in the distance."

139

"Can I?" she said.

"Sure," Terry said. "Maybe you're hungry. So I cut into that onion. It's a sweet one. I put some on a slice of that bread. You've never tasted anything like it. In a station we buy a hot potato from a woman who sells them on the platform. She hands one up through the window. There's a piece of cheese in the potato that melts."

"What is this?" said the man at the next table. "Charades?"

"Maybe," Terry said.

"Maybe I should add something," he said.

"Like what?" I said.

"Maybe there's an angry son of a bitch on the train, too," he said. "Maybe he's going to be sent to prison or something. Maybe he's trying to get the fuck out of there."

"OK," Terry said. "Fine."

"So what's he thinking about?" said the man.

"I got a good idea," said Virginia.

"Do you?" said the man.

"Maybe he's trapped and he doesn't know what to do," she said.

"Well, maybe he's trying to figure that out."

"Maybe he just wants to do the right thing," said Virginia.

"The right thing. Don't make me laugh," he said.

"Maybe you should tell us what he wants," Terry said. He listened for a sound in the hall.

"Well," said the man. "He's probably thinking, like, if anybody's got any money on them. That's probably one thing. Then he's probably thinking he wishes he knew how to get out of the train. Yeah. Maybe he's afraid that if he gets caught he's going to get the shit beaten out of him. Maybe that's just for starters."

Virginia didn't turn to look over her shoulder. All she did was listen to that voice coming out of the darkness behind her. She held the coffee cup just on her fingers, not wanting to turn around, if only to avoid seeing the man, which she imagined would be like looking into the heart of malice. Why wouldn't he just get up and leave?

Terry sat there, looking at her. He could see that it would take almost nothing to push her one way or the other. Maybe she would simply get up and walk away. Maybe that would be her response to the horror of being in the same room with that man. Maybe she could see him as an expression of enough trouble, of enough things that were usually in the shadows, to decide that she had her answer after all.

"So tell her about the train," said the man. He was looking toward the hall, listening. All he wanted was to buy a little time to figure out what to do. Terry wondered where the man had been when the cop had come down here to look around. Maybe he had been in the kitchen or under a table.

"Well," Terry said. "It goes in and out of those stands of birches, and when the light isn't that green color, it's golden. You can see the bits of dust, just little bits, in those sections of light that come through the window on a slant, and there are lines, too, in that yellowish haze. The lines come from the corners of the window frame and the lines are parallel. Maybe we get sleepy after lunch."

"Is that right?" said the man.

"That sounds nice," Virginia said. She put a knuckle against her teeth.

"Everything's going to be all right," Terry said.

"Is it?" she said.

"I think so," Terry said. "Maybe on the train we buy a piece of smoked fish. We tear the pieces of it with our fingers and eat bread and onion. Wheat fields are outside. They ripple in the wind."

"That's fine," she said. "But that's just make-believe. What are we going to do?"

"Yeah?" said the man in the shadow. "Tell me."

"Don't sell make-believe short," Terry said.

"Yeah?" said the man. "What good has it ever done?"

Virginia sat there, just touching the coffee cup. The warmth of it reassured her. Terry looked at the man, who seemed to be running out of time. It was as though he had begun to make up his mind. Or that when he wasn't amused anymore with talk about a train in Russia, then he would do what he had decided.

"Go on," he said. "Tell me. Something about make-believe. Something practical. I'll bet you can't come up with anything."

"What are we betting?" said Terry.

"Oh, wouldn't you like to know?"

"Sure," said Terry.

"Do yourself a favor," he said. "It's something you care about. We'll leave it at that. Go on. Tell me."

"All right," Terry said. "I had a job once. When I was just out of medical school."

"What kind of job?" he said.

"For an insurance company," Terry said. "Doing physicals."

"Did that pay any kind of money?" the man said.

"No," Terry said. "Not much. But I was broke."

"You didn't tell us how much you got paid," he said.

"Thirty dollars apiece," Terry said.

"So," said the man. "Thirty iron soldiers doesn't sound like anything that was made up."

That wedge of silver appeared and disappeared, as though he was moving the blade. Virginia looked at Terry and swallowed.

"This isn't going to get out of hand, is it?" she said.

"No," Terry said.

"You're pretty certain, aren't you?" said the man.

"I'd like to think we're going to be OK," Terry said.

"You guys," said the man. "Always thinking. Thinking this. Thinking that."

Figuring the percentages. Trying to work the middle of the bell curve. Terry guessed he was right. "Maybe," Terry said.

"There's no maybe about it," said the man.

"OK," Terry said. "Fine."

"What about making the thirty dollars?" said the man.

"Well, one day I forgot my bag. I didn't have anything with me and I was way down in Manhattan Beach or Torrance or someplace and I was supposed to do a physical. Not even a tongue depressor or a stethoscope. So I knock on the door of the woman who had applied for a life insurance policy. I show her my ID. She's Ukrainian or something and doesn't speak English very well. I take her arm with my hand, and I give it a couple of squeezes, real fast, just like the collar for taking blood pressure. Then I say, 'Blood pressure's fine.'"

The man sat in the shadow, listening. "Didn't she think you were crazy?" he said.

"Well," Terry said, "she was Russian. Do you know anything about Russian medicine?"

"No," said the man. "Thank God."

"You know what they do with blood to sterilize it?" Terry said. "They strain it through a pig's bladder."

"No kidding," said the man.

"Yeah," Terry said. "Anyway, then I listen to the woman's chest."

"I bet that was all right, too," said the man.

"Uh-huh," Terry said.

"You know what you should have done?" said the man.

"What's that?" Terry said.

"You should have taken her in a closet and blinked at her and said her x-ray looked pretty good."

Terry took out his wallet and saw he had only ten dollars in it, but he took it out and pushed it toward the man at the other table.

"That's what I've got," he said.

The man sat there, thinking it over. A faint odor of generic vegetable soup that they made here sometimes filled the room. The man reached out and picked up the money. He picked up Terry's wallet, too, which he opened. He looked at the credit cards and the driver's license. He pushed it back.

"You're lucky," the man said. "You win the bet. You don't know how lucky you are."

Virginia put the coffee cup down. It made a little cluck.

"Hey," said the man. "Has she got any money?"

"No," she said. "I haven't got my wallet with me."

"Well, shit," he said.

He sat and waited. That piece of silver didn't move anymore, as though he had the blade pointed upward. Terry had seen some wounds, under the ribs, that were made by the upward motion of a blade. There were some others, too, that you don't forget, like one that was made in the hand of a man who had taken hold of a bare blade.

"Clickety-clack," said the man.

He stood up. Virginia kept her eyes on Terry. He was sure that if she heard another sound she was simply going to get up and start running, not from this man so much as an expression of things she couldn't control and didn't understand. What did the policeman mean by Apache anyway? Terry had heard some other, more insulting terms for men who were brought here, but not that one.

"I've got some advice for you," Terry said.

"Yeah?" he said. "Is that right?"

"Don't take the knife," Terry said. "If that cop finds you, it's going to give him a good excuse to shoot you. Leave it."

"I'll take my chances," he said.

Chances. Terry looked at Virginia as she sat there, her fingers just touching the cup.

"All right," Terry said. He shrugged. "Sure. You know best."

"And don't you forget it," said the man. He shifted his weight and looked around.

"What did they arrest you for?" Terry said.

The man thought about this for a while. The silence seemed to have a stink to it, but maybe that was just the mixture of medicine and that poor institutional cooking. Then he said, "Mayhem. That's the best way of putting it. You know, when you exist for a little without any restraints at all. None. You burn bright then, you know?"

"I guess so," Terry said.

"It beats being on some stupid train," he said. "How do I get out of here?"

"Down that way," Terry said. "You go to the end of the hall and turn left, and at the end you'll come to a door. When you open it, it's going to make a noise. There's an alarm on the door."

"OK. I can handle that. Everybody sit tight," said the man. "You just relax. Oh, you're lucky. Clickety-clack. Cut your head off."

He turned and went into the hall. Virginia put the coffee cup to her pursed lips, although her hands were shaking a little. "It's cold," she said.

"I'm going to have to go down the hall," Terry said.

"Why?" she asked, her voice close to despair.

"There are patients down there," Terry said. "I want to make sure he gets out the door."

"You're going to ask me to come along," she said, "aren't you? I'm coming."

Her hands were on the table. The fingers were long and the tendons in the backs of them were regular, making a kind of fan under her skin. "There's no going back, is there?"

They started walking down the hall. A film of light lay on the linoleum. Then they came to the end of the hall and turned toward the exit, where a sign said, ALARM. EMERGENCY EXIT ONLY. Out of a room next to the exit, a voice said, "Psssst. Hey, I'm still here."

Terry looked into the room. It had two beds, both newly made and both empty.

"I just thought I'd watch the parking lot for a minute," said the man.

"I don't see anyone out there," Terry said.

"I'll wait a minute," said the man. He kept looking out through the window in the door. "You know, I've got a rash on my skin. Itches something fierce."

"Let me look at it," Terry said.

"That's all right," he said. "What do you think it is?"

"I don't know," he said. "Could be anything. Syphilis makes a rash."

"No shit," he said. "Well, what if it's just like a rash that itches. I get it the most when I'm feeling nervous, you know."

"Get some hydrocortisone," Terry said. "Maybe some Valium might help."

"I can get that easy," he said. "Lot of that on the street. People feeling uptight."

He came out of the room and opened the door, saying, "Well, I'll be seeing you," and then, as the alarm sounded, he went outside. You could smell the burned air, or the smoke outside, which was left over from the riot. The lasting residue of it seemed to be the scent of the city now.

"All right," said Virginia. "All right. No stopping now."

OFTEN, SHE CAME to Terry's house in the morning to be there when he got back from the hospital, and he would find her in the kitchen, where she sat, sometimes nude, having a cup of coffee, waiting, looking out at the city. He found her this way one morning. He was tired. His hands still smelled of the soap with iodine, and he sat in the nook that was in the corner of the kitchen where she was having her coffee. She leaned forward to give him the sugar, her breasts just above the table. He turned and took a bottle of bourbon from the shelf behind him and poured some into his coffee. She drank her coffee a little sip at a time, and Terry took his in larger gulps, feeling the liquor in it, and saying, "Why don't you put on some clothes. There's something I've got to do."

"All right," she said.

She looked at him as if he had dared her. She put on her dress, wearing nothing aside from it. It was a way of daring him.

They got into his car, which still had a cracked windshield

and a dented hood. Terry had kept the car for years because it reminded him of being a medical student, and as his classmates had gone out and bought new cars, trading up, each new car a desire for validation, Terry had kept his old one, the accumulation of the miles seeming to be a measurement not of age, but of undaunted innocence. But now, when he looked at the car, at the cracked windshield, the dented hood, he saw the effect of time, as though he had glanced in a mirror and saw that he was aging after all.

They got into the car and started driving. It was a warm summer day, the air dry and slightly smoggy, but that faintly erotic odor of the Pacific lay just beyond the line of sight. The vents were open in the car, and from time to time Virginia's dress swelled with air. As she held it down, it looked like a collapsing parachute. They went down the canyon, the tires making a tearing sound as the car went over those sheets of water that lay across the pavement here and there. They turned onto Sunset and drove toward Beverly Hills and stopped in front of a car dealership.

They went in through the front door and looked at the cars that were parked on a carpet that one would expect to find in a good hotel. Terry liked a German car, and they got into it, Terry behind the wheel. Virginia sat in the passenger's seat, which was covered in pigskin, soft to the touch, and fragrant. For reasons she didn't understand, she wanted to give in to the luxury of the car. She sat there, and he thought of touching, of running his . . . but then stopped. She reached over and touched the dashboard, which was covered in leather, too, her hand sliding across it as though confirming something she already suspected. The gearshift lever was stainless steel, topped with a functional knob that emerged from a leather sleeve. The dials on the dashboard had a practical quality, not quite so severe as those on an airliner or a submarine, but with an aspect at odds with the domestic nature of most automobiles. Virginia took off her shoes and put her bare feet against the carpet, running them back and forth across it. She looked at him, and said, "How much do you think it costs?"

"I don't think we're worrying about costs right now," he said.

They got out and walked around it, seeing their elongated shapes in the blue finish, which seemed to reflect everything in a streaked, horizontal way, as though the car was moving at a high rate of speed and everything was streaming away from it. The hood and the windshield rose from the front of the car and also seemed to push themselves through the air. While they were looking at it, Virginia absently reached down and touched her calf, rubbing it where it had touched the smooth leather of the car.

The salesman, who was wearing a suit that had probably been made in London, or Rome, opened the hood, and Virginia and Terry looked at the engine, which had all the complexity of a piece of high-tech surgical apparatus, and which, even in repose called up the modern age's highest guarantee. Virginia moved along the side of the car with the light behind her, which showed her figure through her dress. The salesman politely closed the hood. He pointed out that the steering wheel was made of wood, laminated oak, and that it was covered with leather. The spokes of the steering wheel were stainless steel. Virginia leaned against the car and the salesman talked about the rate of acceleration, the brakes, transmission, steering, and when Terry glanced at her, she looked back. She still seemed to be daring him.

Terry sat down with the car salesman and took out his checkbook. He was sure that the bank would cover the check, but to make certain, he called and the manager agreed to do so. Terry signed the check. The salesman had two men, in clean overalls, come into the showroom, and with Virginia and Terry watching, they rolled out the car through glass doors that opened wide enough for it to pass. They put gas in it. Then they started it, and Terry got behind the wheel and Virginia got into the passenger's seat, and they turned into the stream of traffic of Sunset Boulevard. The entire operation took less than an hour.

They turned onto the San Diego Freeway, and Terry drove up the top of the ridge, Virginia letting the air blow in and lift her dress. They laughed as they felt the sure, hard acceleration, and noticed, too, the way in which the cars around them seemed to blow by not as solid objects, but as things that simply seemed to melt away.

Virginia drove for a while. She began to talk, saying, Would you like it if I . . . what I want, do you understand, what I want to do . . . then shifting, seeing those practical dials spring upward at an alarming rate, as though she were encouraging a living thing rather than commanding a machine. They went back down to Sunset and got off and drove through the traffic, up to Laurel Canyon and up onto a side street, into the warm, eucalyptus-scented air and the silence of the neighborhood in the early afternoon, which was punctuated only by the steady tip tip tip of a sprinkler and the ticking of the engine. They left the car at the curb, the two of them able to feel the caress of the acceleration as they went into the house.

TERRY WOKE in the doctors' lounge to the sound of a fly buzzing in a figure-eight pattern. It landed on his skin, and as he flinched the insect simply vanished, but then the sound began again with a perverse insistence. Then he sat up, and thought, Well, at least no one called me. Maybe the venom wasn't that bad. Maybe Virginia is all right.

He hadn't undressed, although he had taken off his shoes, and now he put them on, and went out into the hall. From there he could see the parking lot and the street beyond. His car was parked on the street, and a man had the door of Terry's car open and was working on the ignition. It was hard to see the man, who had his head under the steering wheel. He then closed the door and the car started, and he drove away.

Terry had heard that a lot of cars were being stolen in LA: mostly they ended up in chop shops, where they were stripped for parts. Terry thought for a moment of rumors he had heard, that with the demands for organ transplants, runaway teenagers

152

were being killed in the city and their organs sold, just like parts for cars.

Terry went farther down the hall until he came to the black sliding doors and entered Virginia's room. He talked to the nurses, who seemed to think everything was all right, at least for now. What Terry wanted was time alone with Virginia so that he could speak frankly. She hadn't always been conscious, and on those occasions when she had been other people had been in the room. He stood by the bed, hearing footsteps in the hall, shoes squeaking on the floor as a counterpoint to the rattling of stainless-steel carts, or the diminutive shriek of the wheels. Terry perceived these sounds as noise that accompanied trouble one could never stop.

He went down the hall to his office and picked up the phone and called the police. The dispatcher was a woman, and she said, "That's a nice car. You shouldn't leave something like that on the street. You got to have a garage for a car like that. It's probably being packed into boxes right now. You know, ready to ship to places that work on cars."

"Well, I guess that's right," said Terry.

When he got back to the room, Rick was there. Virginia looked around and stopped at Terry's face. She wrote on a piece of paper attached to a metal clipboard, in that odd loopy scrawl, one word, "Sugar."

Rick looked at it. "What does that mean?" he said.

"I don't know," said Terry.

"Does she want something sweet?" said Rick.

"Maybe," Terry said. "People get all kinds of cravings."

Rick went over to the head of the bed and asked Virginia if she wanted something sweet. An ice cream? She couldn't eat it, but at least it would be clear what she wanted.

She wrote "No" on the clipboard.

"What do you think this means?" said Rick.

"I don't know," said Terry.

Terry went out to check the results from the lab, which came on a little slip that looked like a cash register receipt: blood gases, electrolytes, trace elements. He wanted to see, too, how the lab had matched her blood, but he hadn't gotten these results and he went downstairs to find out what the trouble was. A young woman in the lab told him that she had never seen anything quite like Virginia's blood type. The lab technician couldn't match it at all. Was it possible that the venom interfered with the typing? Terry didn't know, but he called the local blood bank. They asked for a sample, and Terry had one sent over.

He went down the hall and gave a pint of blood. He thought that he could give her some of his own blood. It was reassuring to him that he would know, at least, where the blood was coming from: he wasn't sick, wasn't carrying anything, and while he was convinced that the blood supply was all right, there were nameless fears that he still wanted to allay, in spite of what he believed. He thought that he had done the right thing, and that if nothing else he had tried to anticipate the worst. Being a universal donor carried an odd sense of intimacy, the notion of being attached in some practical way to other people, although now that was enhanced, and he thought of his blood running through her veins. Then he dismissed such considerations as merely romantic. What he wanted to do was to think clearly, without any distractions.

Terry wrote orders for the antivenom. Before going back to the lounge, he looked in on his other patients. In the lounge, he put his hand in his pocket and found the telephone number of Angus

Bouton, the man in Australia. Terry looked at the clock. It was morning in Australia, and he picked up the phone and dialed the number. The man answered himself. Just like that.

His voice was Australian and cheerful. He asked some questions, and when Terry said that Virginia was allergic to horses, he heard an audible sound, or maybe just the absence of everything, a complete silence that was so palpable it seemed like sound. Bouton said that Virginia was probably more likely to die of allergy than the venom, but after a certain point it would be hard to distinguish one from the other. The treatment was straightforward, at least until things "came unglued." Bouton wished him luck in a somewhat saddened voice, and hung up.

Terry went down the hall and took the elevator, and walked into the office of the medical director. He was a man in his early forties with short brown hair, blue eyes, and a neatly trimmed brown mustache. The thing that distinguished him was an almost unnatural sense of cleanliness: his pants were always perfectly pressed, his white coat was always immaculate even by medical standards. He was stylish and precise, and he was a trauma surgeon with a specialty in gunshot wounds. Terry had learned a lot from him. They had worked together on a number of gunshot cases, many of which had been released to the Los Angeles Department of Corrections on the fiftieth or fifty-first or sixtieth day. The medical director's name was John Fox.

"Hey, Terry," he said, looking up. "What's this I hear about you wanting to hang onto a case? What's going on?"

Terry shrugged. "I think I know more about it than anyone else," he said.

"Do you?" said Fox. "Why's that?"

Terry explained his conversations with the man in Palo Alto and the man in Australia. He'd made some other calls, too. He knew something about critical care medicine. Fox knew that, didn't he?

Fox looked at him for a moment. "What we want," said Fox, "is to practice good medicine here. We agree about that, don't we?"

"Yes," said Terry.

"Well, the best thing is to give it to the critical care guys."

"I think I know more about it," said Terry.

"It's not cowardly to give up," said Fox.

"I don't think it's a matter of courage," said Terry.

"What the fuck," said Fox. "Let them have it."

Terry shook his head. Fox went on looking at him, and then he said, "OK. But any trouble, and I mean any, and you're gone. That's clear?"

"Yes," said Terry, although he was thinking, When the trouble comes, it will be too fast for anything like that. He wondered if Fox knew that, and he guessed that he did. Fox said that the critical care people would be watching, and Terry thought that was a good idea. Then he went down to the lounge.

In the morning he found a message from the LAPD on his voice mail. They had the car. He could pick it up at the LAPD car compound. That was in Downey.

In the afternoon, Rick came into Terry's office. For a while neither one of them said anything.

"I guess you're pretty tired," said Rick eventually.

Terry shrugged. "I don't know," he said. "Maybe."

"I never liked waiting," said Rick. "Time always seems to run the wrong way when you wait. Have you ever noticed that? You can tell how worried you are by the speed of time."

Terry nodded.

"I heard someone stole your car," said Rick.

"Yesterday," said Terry. "But you know what, they found it."

"No kidding?" said Rick.

"Yeah," said Terry. "I've got to go pick it up."

"How are you going to get there?"

"I don't know," said Terry.

"I'll drive you," said Rick.

"That's all right," said Terry.

"You got to have your car," said Rick. "All there is to do here is wait. I'll drive you. It will only take an hour. Come on."

"You don't have to," said Terry.

"I want to," said Rick. "There's something I want to talk to you about."

Terry looked at him now, thinking, Oh, no. He can't want to talk it over now. Not now. He can't know, can he? Was it because of that one word, *sugar*? It could have meant anything.

"All right," said Terry. "Thanks."

Rick's car was a big new Cadillac. At the exit of the parking lot, they both noticed the graffiti, the words that were sloppily painted, spelling out, "Yo gonna die soon." Rick asked Terry if he thought a Cadillac was the best car to have, based on what he saw in the emergency room. Was there a car that took the impact better? Terry hadn't made a study of it, but it seemed to him that the Cadillac took the impact better than some of the Japanese cars. He guessed it was pretty good. Rick said he thought Virginia was going to be all right. Wasn't that right?

"She's pretty sick," said Terry. His hands were shaking. He pressed them together. "I guess I'm tired," he said. "Maybe I'm not getting enough sleep."

"So you think she could die?"

"I didn't say that," he said.

"I don't know why she worked with those creatures," said Rick. "She liked to be in control of them, you know. She was right up against something that could hurt you, but if she did everything right, why, then, she'd be safe."

"Uh-huh," said Terry.

"You didn't answer me," said Rick.

"About what?" said Terry.

"What her chances are," said Rick.

Terry stared out the window. "She could die," he said.

Terry didn't say anything more as they drove along the Hollywood Freeway to the interchange, where they went out toward Downey.

"I don't want to pry into what you've done," said Rick. "I mean, if anything actually happened. I've got no right to pry anyway, do I?"

Terry thought, Please. Please. Not now.

"Oh, Christ," said Rick. "I don't know. I'm tired and worried. You think all kinds of things."

They drove along for a while in silence. Terry almost said that he had felt like praying. Then he thought about the impulse to do so. The few times he had prayed as an adult, he was surprised to find that it had made him feel a little better. Then he thought, How can I get control of the bleeding?

"Are you seeing a lot of gunshot wounds?" said Rick.

"More than before. A pretty fair number. I'm only doing this two nights a week. They're going to hire someone pretty soon."

"What do you do for a gunshot wound?"

"In the chest?" said Terry. "It depends. We've had good luck with just a tube and an antibiotic. Then it's different if the bullet hits a bone. It breaks down into powder. Like salt. A shotgun wound is a different thing, though."

"Uh-huh," said Rick. "I was thinking of getting a gun for the house. These days, you never know who's going to come through the door. Or what kind of trouble you might have. What do you think is a good thing to have?"

Terry shrugged. "I don't know," he said.

"Well, think about it," said Rick. "What kind of car did you have?"

Terry told him.

"That's funny," said Rick. "Virginia saw one of those on the street the other day and stopped to look at it. Do you think she wants one?"

"I don't know," said Terry. "How would I know?"

Rick shrugged. "Maybe she told you," he said.

The trees at the side of the road seemed to heave with the constant wind of passing cars.

"Yeah," Rick said. "I've really been thinking about a gun."

"We're seeing some accidental shootings," said Terry. "A lot of people are buying guns, and you know, they've never handled one before."

"Uh-huh," said Rick.

Terry stared straight ahead at the freeway, realizing the thing that he had grown to dislike about it: it was a road that promised a false escape. It seemed to imply that you could just get on it, going north or east, and could get away from this.

They passed a neighborhood where a car had been burned the night before and it was still smoldering. A thin, black ribbon of smoke wavered in the air. A woman walked along, coming back from the small store on the corner. She drifted past the car, holding a bag of chips and a carton of cigarettes.

"I wonder what Virginia's been doing the last few weeks," said Rick. "She's been going out to lunch a lot."

Terry nodded. "I guess so," he said. "I don't know."

Rick drove silently for a while.

"I bet they trashed your car," he said.

Terry was already thinking that maybe he would sell it. The people driving around them stared straight ahead. These days everyone drove with their eyes straight ahead. Probably a good idea, too. But as he sat there, he felt the sure, definite tug of terror. The thing about doubt and fear was that they seemed to taint the landscape. He tried to think of what he would say if Rick asked him directly.

"Are you seeing any unusual cases?" said Rick.

"I don't know," said Terry. "Some."

"Like what?" said Rick. "Tell me one."

"Well, a woman comes in and she's having abdominal pain. When I look her over she says she's been having some kinky sex with her boyfriend. You know what they're doing? They've got a compressor in the bedroom and they've got a rubber tube and . . . you know, they're sticking the thing in her rear end. The woman's got a perforated colon. She's giggling when I tell her, and she giggles some more. It wasn't the perforation that killed her so much as the lubricant they were using. That's how she got peritonitis. She got sour. Not a fucking thing I could do." Terry shrugged and looked out the window, wishing he hadn't mentioned this case. It was one of those that he thought about from time to time. Still, he wished he hadn't mentioned it.

Then he looked across the seat, and thought, Well, has he got what it takes just to ask me and be done with it?

"Well," said Rick. "People do strange things."

"I guess so," said Terry.

"It's hard to figure out my wife," said Rick. "Now, why is she spending so much time away from the house? We haven't been married long."

160

Terry shrugged. "Maybe you should ask her," he said.

"What kind of question is that?" said Rick.

"I don't know," said Terry.

"It doesn't sound very friendly," said Rick.

"Take it anyway you want," said Terry.

"Well," said Rick. "All I'm trying to do is to figure out what's going on." Rick swallowed. "A lot of things don't make sense."

The landscape of Downey looked like a country that lost a war and never really recovered. Burned cars and abandoned washing machines sat in the street, and beyond some fences was a collection of trash and grass, which was yellow because of the refineries here. A dog food factory was close to the exit of the freeway. On one side of it horses that had been bought on the hoof stood in a pen, and each of them wore a bright magenta halter made of heavy twine. They waited, heads down, some of them resting a hoof on its edge, most of them swayback, glancing up from time to time at the towers of the dog food factory. Terry stared straight ahead. He wanted to understand how troubled the man who sat next to him was and, he supposed, even to comfort him, but he didn't want anything to get in the way of making decisions.

Rick swallowed and blinked, gripping the wheel hard. "Well," he said. "At least you're going to get your car back. That's the place. Up there."

At the end of the side road, beyond some industrial lots, which were surrounded with cyclone fences topped with razor wire, there was a place that looked like a parking lot, that is, if there were parking lots for the damned. The cars had an air of disuse about them, and most of them sat against the fence, covered with dust, windshields dirty. Here and there a window had been knocked out, and the shattered glass, crystallized by the impact, still hung like ice along the window frames. Even from a distance the interiors of some of the cars could be seen, dashboards ripped out, seats removed, and some cars, too, had a cracked windshield, the spiderweb pattern appearing like the seal of finality.

"Yeah," said Rick. "I think I better get a gun. Maybe a nine-millimeter, don't you think? I want something that packs some wallop. If I find someone coming into my house at three in the morning, you know, I want some stopping power."

"Maybe," said Terry.

"It's funny how you get ideas," said Rick. "You know, when I was in medical school, I always thought there'd come this moment. I'd be living in a house, maybe down by the beach someplace, above Santa Monica someplace, or maybe in Westwood, someplace nice, maybe up in the hills. I'd be sitting there, looking at the city, and I'd have a nice car in the driveway, and my wife would be there, and everything would seem just right. Then you know what I'd say?"

"No," said Terry.

The car was down at the end of one of the rows. The scent of the ocean was in the air, although it smelled a little burned, as though someone had been dumping sludge in the Pacific.

"I'd say, 'Now, this is really living,'" said Rick.

An office like that of a small insurance agency stood beyond the gate of the lot, but instead of a sign for All-State or Farmer's, it said, LAPD AUTOMOTIVE CLAIMS.

They pulled up in front of it. Terry got out, and said, "Well, thanks for the lift."

"I'm not done yet," said Rick. "I want to talk to you."

"Isn't that what we've been doing?" said Terry.

Rick just stared across the seat. He said, "I'll help you find your car."

He pulled up and parked, the bright Cadillac out of place

among the other cars, which were covered, on closer inspection, not with a layer of dust so much as a fine, whitish layer of ash. The cars had something unmistakable about them, an aura so palpable that Terry stopped and stared at the lines of automobiles that stretched into the distance, where they came to the end of a barbed-wire fence. Terry guessed the atmosphere came from what had happened in and around these cars. They reminded him of clothes that ended up on an emergency room floor.

Inside the office, a uniformed officer, a woman, stood behind the counter. She was overweight, and she wore a blue, short-sleeved uniform. The badge on her shirt was very bright and shiny. Terry said hello and said that he had come to pick up his car.

"Let's see some ID," said the woman.

Terry took out his wallet and showed her his driver's license and his hospital identification card.

"You a doctor?" the woman said.

"Yes," said Terry.

"You one, too?" she said to Rick.

"Yes," said Rick.

The woman shrugged and began to look through some papers in a gray metal in and out box, and as she did so, she turned and said to someone in the private office behind her, "Hey, Kerjeski. Your man's here."

The woman went on looking through her papers, and as she did so a man came out of the back room. He was wearing a pair of dark brown pants, a lighter brown jacket, a Dacron shirt, and a green tie. He was about six feet tall, and he was wearing expensive running shoes. He had blue eyes and he was a little jowly. Terry guessed he was in his late thirties, even though he looked like he was in his forties.

"Mr. McKechnie?" he said. "I'm Detective Kerjeski."

Kerjeski was overweight, and his face seemed puffy, as though a slow, constant swelling was one of the disadvantages of being a cop. He didn't smile. Everything about the man suggested a chronic fatigue. Terry noticed that the man had some swelling in his neck, too: maybe he was having some thyroid problems. Kerjeski had a cup of coffee in a paper cup.

"We got your car for you," said Kerjeski.

"Good," said Terry. "Thanks."

"Is it out there?" said Rick.

"Yeah," said Kerjeski, looking at him briefly. Then he turned back to Terry. "It says in the report that you saw the man who stole the car."

"That's right," said Terry.

"Can you describe him?"

"Heavyset. Not flabby though. About thirty, I guess."

"Could you pick him out of a lineup?"

The policewoman looked at Terry now.

"I don't know," said Terry. "Look. I just want my car."

"Well," said Kerjeski, "We could hold it as material evidence."

"Why would you want to do that?" said Terry.

"To make sure you try to pick a man out of the lineup."

The woman had found the papers that went along with Terry's car, and, as she put them up on the counter, they reminded Terry of the papers that he signed when he picked up his car after it had been serviced.

"What did the guy do?" said Terry.

"It's complicated," said Kerjeski. "In fact, all you have to worry about is whether or not he stole your car. Everything else is a different matter."

"Is he a gang member?" said Rick.

"Listen," said Kerjeski, "I'm not talking to you." He had a sip of his coffee, and said to the woman, "Give me the papers."

"What are you doing with them?" said Terry.

"I'm thinking about that," he said. "Right now I'm trying to get a little cooperation. That's all I'm asking for. Is that any big deal?"

"No," said Terry.

"There are guys in this city," said Kerjeski. "You can't imagine what kinds of messes they leave around. You should see what they leave behind. You couldn't stomach it."

"Is that right?" said Terry.

"See, here's the thing," said Kerjeski. "The guy steals your car. Then he holds up a man in the Valley. A dry cleaner. Then he kidnaps a woman and rapes her in the car. All right? He keeps something over her head. She can't see him. He leaves her in the car. We pick up a guy near the car, walking around."

Terry looked out the window. "All right," he said. "I'll try."

"Is he a gang member?" said Rick.

"Who isn't a gang member?" said Kerjeski. "Anyway, what's all the worry about gang members?"

"It's a problem these days, isn't it?" said Rick.

Kerjeski shrugged. He signed the papers, held them out for Terry to sign, and after Terry had, the man gave him a copy, just like at the garage.

"Tomorrow afternoon," said Kerjeski. "Downtown. About three-thirty, all right? I'll write out the address for you."

"OK," said Terry. "Fine."

Terry and Rick went out of the small office and began to walk along the rows of cars. It was a hazy day now, the sky gray yellow, and the sun appeared in it as a yellow ball, as in some paintings. Terry went along, thinking, Monet. Those paintings along the river. Isn't there a sun in one of those? But even as he was trying to think about the painting, he was aware of Rick, walking beside him toward the car and the end of the row.

The crystalline bits of glass on the asphalt looked like something that kids could grow in a science kit. Terry began to think about Virginia. He remembered once . . . when she had looked down at him, and said, "I really like that . . . my husband never does that for me . . . it makes me feel you love me . . ."

They approached the car.

"Were you seeing my wife?" said Rick.

Terry got a good look at the car at the end of the row now. The windows weren't broken and nothing else was wrong, although just by the angle at which it was parked, it nevertheless suggested disorder. Terry hesitated for a second, as though just by reaching the car he would arrive at the chaos he was always trying to deny. And as he stood there, he considered his obligations to Virginia. What, under the circumstances, were they? More than anything else, what he wanted to say was, "Yeah. You might as well know. I met her regularly." This, he realized, even as he acknowledged the impulse to say it, was nothing more than self-indulgence.

"She called me," said Terry.

"What did she want?" said Rick.

"She wanted to talk," said Terry. "But there wasn't anything more than that."

They came up to the car. Rick stood there and looked around. The cars stretched out now, back toward the entrance, and behind him the fence and the razor wire were very bright.

"These days you don't know what to think," said Rick. "You know?"

Terry looked out toward the Pacific. He wished he could see it.

"All I ever did was try to do the right thing, go to school, become a doctor. What was so wrong with that?"

"Nothing," said Terry.

"I never did anything like what happened in your car. You're going to feel it in there, you know that?"

"Yeah," said Terry. "I never did anything like that either. The idea of it makes me pretty angry."

Rick nodded. He seemed to think that this was a bond between them. "All right," he said. "I'm going to believe you."

Terry turned and looked at the Pacific again, or where it would be if he could see it. He thought maybe he'd drive back along the coast. Somehow he found it comforting to drive along the coast and see that line where the sky and ocean were welded together.

"Listen," said Terry. "I want to thank you for driving me down here."

"Sure," said Rick. "Glad to help."

Terry had the keys, which were stapled to the piece of paper that Kerjeski had given him. He reached down and opened the door.

It was hot in the car, even though the sun wasn't shining, and Terry sat there as he pushed the button to roll down the window. He didn't look in the back seat. He started the car and backed out, saying to Rick, "Get in. I'll drive you up to your car."

"No," said Rick. "That's all right. I'd rather walk."

T ERRY GOT HOME LATE. Beyond the window he saw the grid
of city lights, a mixture of red, purple, and blue, along with
the ubiquitous yellows, which reminded him of dew clinging to a
spider's web. He took a shower, using the bar of soap she had
brought from home. The scent was very strong. He got out
and toweled off, rubbing himself hard, glad for the sensation of
the terry cloth, which was abrasive enough to make him feel a
little less tired. He checked the answering machine. Its red light
glowed steadily. He'd had no calls while he was in the shower.

He lay down and closed his eyes. The scent of her hair was on
the pillows, faint but still intimate. He tried to imagine her perfectly, a smile, a laugh, the occasions she had cried tears of rage
or frustration, but it was all as elusive as the scent of her hair.

He got up and looked out the window again. What he wanted
to do was to pray, but he resisted the impulse as mere supersti-
tion. After all, he was a man of science, a medical doctor, with
very definite ideas about the nature of death. Was it just vanity

that kept him from acknowledging the desire? He was almost glad of the fatigue, which acted on the terror a little, almost as a mild analgesic. He wondered if it was a bad thing, from a purely practical point of view, to be ambivalent toward praying. Then he closed his eyes and shook his head. He didn't want to let any doubt enter his mind now, and it seemed to him that praying was an admission of doubt, or at least an acknowledgment that he didn't know what to do.

He went back into the bedroom and stretched out again. The red glow of the digital clock gave the room a faint crimson cast, which made him think of the cockpit of an airplane at night. He thought, All right. How do I do it? What do I say? He thought the best thing was to give thanks, so he tried to think of how thankful he was for the time he'd had with her. He hoped that was the right thing to do. At least he knew it was sincere. It occurred to him that he should concentrate on things he had seen that he was thankful for, too. He thought of the Pacific in the morning, when the blue sheet of it was covered with silver scales, and the horizon seemed like an unknowable place, which haunted him now like the scent of her hair. In the mountains he had seen a stand of poplars, the leaves shimmering in the wind, the trunks tinted green, beguiling in their promise, as mysterious, too, as the horizon and the scent of hair. He thought about streams in which the current formed clear braids, just like hair. Then he thought that praying was all right, so he added, Please, no bleeding.

In the morning, he drove to the hospital. He tried to ignore the unpleasant odor in the car. The traffic was getting worse at this hour, and he noticed, too, that people were edgy for no apparent reason. It made for an atmosphere of general uneasiness, as though everyone was waiting for an earthquake to begin, or a bomb to go off, and at the same time, everyone was trying to pretend there was no possibility of an earthquake, and no bomb either. He parked behind the barbed wire and went into the hospital.

He went into Virginia's room, which had just one bed with a monitor above it. The tube that carried oxygen to her mouth was a transparent blue, and moisture had collected in it where it sagged. The moisture was as clear as distilled water. He watched carefully to see if she had a rash on her face, or any swelling, particularly around her lips. He thought that he would look her over completely to make sure. He leaned forward, and put his lips next to her ear. He could smell her hair, and as he began to speak, to whisper, just whatever came into his mind, he looked down and saw that she had begun to bleed.

At first, it was just around the puncture where the IV tube went into her arm, but there was a little pinkish froth at the top of the tube where the oxygen flowed in. He guessed there was a little bleeding in the lungs. He opened her gown and saw a bruise on her skin which was in the shape of his hand. The venom would make almost any firm touch begin to bleed. The last time they had been together, she had wanted him to pull her against him, when they had been lying together, spoon style. He stood there for a second, looking at the shape of his hand. The nurse came in, and they looked at her carefully, looking for swelling, although Terry was more concerned about the bleeding. The toxin would make someone bleed in any place she normally would, and in some places she never or almost never did. The nurse said that Virginia was having some vaginal bleeding.

Rick came in and stood at the foot of the bed.

"Maybe she had a sore of some kind," said the nurse. She turned to Rick. "Did she ever have pain when you had intercourse?"

"No, she never had any pain," said Rick. He looked at Terry. "Isn't that right?"

"I guess so," said Terry. "If that's what you say."

Virginia stirred a little. Terry looked up now.

Virginia couldn't talk because of the tube, but she looked at Terry, and wrote on her metal clipboard in large, sloppy letters, "Can you stop the bleeding?"

"Yes," said Terry.

"That's good," she wrote.

Yes. What else could he say? The venom made the blood lose its ability to clot. In fact, this happened because the venom tried to make all the blood clot at one time, and because of this, the clotting factors were used up so that it couldn't clot at all.

"What are we going to do?" said Rick.

Terry realized he was sweating. He had been taught always to shoot for the middle of the bell curve in the treatment of patients because the most likely occurrence was in the middle of the realm of possibilities. But this case didn't fall in the middle. He feared he was at the thinnest section of the end. Now he went out to the nurses' station and called the lab. Had they typed her blood?

"Well," said the lab technician, "yeah. They typed it."

"All right," said Terry. "What is it?"

"It's an odd type," said the lab technician.

"How odd?" said Terry.

"It's something called Bombay," said the technician. "Does that mean anything to you?"

"No," said Terry.

"Well, there it is," said the technician. "It's pretty rare."

The blood type, said the technician, was one that broke down any blood that was given to a patient. If you gave any blood but the type the patient had, you'd kill her.

"Even blood from a universal donor?" said Terry.

"Yes," said the technician. "A universal donor won't help your patient."

"Is that right?" said Terry. "Has the blood bank got any matches?"

"No," said the technician. "They're going to try to find some."

"How long is that going to take?" said Terry.

"I don't know," said the technician.

Terry hung up and turned to Rick and asked if he knew anything about a rare blood type, or if Virginia had ever mentioned anything to him about it. Rick had never heard of it. Usually, if someone knew she had a rare type, she'd register with a blood bank and donate blood so she could get it if she needed it. Virginia hadn't done that, and all Terry could think of was that she hadn't known anything about it. Had she ever been hospitalized? Rick didn't know.

Rick went out into the hall and sat down with his head in his hands. Terry went into Virginia's room and found that she was still bleeding. It wasn't bad, but it was steady. The best they could do was to keep the blood volume up with fluids, so he wrote the necessary orders. Her blood pressure was up, but not as much as he'd like. That left him contemplating something the man at Stanford told him he should do only if she was getting ready to die: use adrenaline to get her pressure up. This, of course, could raise the pressure in her brain. He thought he might be able to use something else, a similar drug, and that he could give it slowly, a drip at a time, to bring up the pressure slowly. Still, he wasn't sure about that, and didn't want to have to do it.

And he had to consider the effect of the venom on muscle tissue. It broke the tissue into toxic substances. The critical care physicians hadn't seen any cases like this one: they were as uncertain as he was, especially because of the possibility of allergic reactions. No one mentioned it, but everyone was thinking about shock lung.

He stood at the side of the bed. He couldn't tell if she was conscious, really, but her eyes were open and she looked into his, her glance at once demanding, even pleading, and elusively peaceful, which frightened him more than anything else. He leaned over and whispered into her ear, speaking freely, not caring if anyone heard.

He knew that the critical care people had heard it all before anyway. There wasn't much that hadn't been said here. From a certain perspective it could be argued that these words were the things that killed people. When people started talking about love, the patients died. He guessed he was right on the edge, thinking like that. He wrote the orders. Fluids. On her clipboard, she scrawled, "I'm scared and alone."

There was nothing to do but wait. He had a phone in the car, and he had a pager, too, so that anyone could reach him. He guessed it would be all right to go downtown. It wouldn't take long. The blood bank was contacting other banks to see if her blood type was available anywhere.

He drove downtown. When Terry had been a kid, downtown was composed of neighborhoods, hotels and rooming houses and small grocery stores, and the atmosphere in these places had always been mysterious, if not faintly sinister, and yet romantic too. People had gone there after having bad luck, or a dream that hadn't worked out. Now, though, these places were gone, and the rooming houses had been replaced by poured-concrete buildings whose architects hoped they would stand up to an earthquake, though they probably wouldn't. But even in the new landscape of concrete and glass, and especially in the sterile plazas around the criminal courts building, Terry still felt the presence of those old neighborhoods that had been razed but somehow not thoroughly eradicated from the atmosphere of downtown Los Angeles. He squeezed the wheel, thinking about Virginia in his house, wearing a T-shirt and nothing else, drinking beer from a bottle and laughing at something he'd said. He tried to concentrate on that laugh so he wouldn't feel quite so alone. He tried to console himself by thinking that though they had done something that was forbidden, they had done it together and were bound by it, which should make him feel close to her. But then he dismissed the thought as desperation. He just wanted to . . . well he just wanted a chance.

He found a place to park, a flat lot with a little booth and a fence around it, and he walked up the sidewalk, feeling the size of those large cement blocks that formed the bases of the buildings. A lot of pigeons flew around, the popping of their wings surprisingly vital.

In the lobby of the police building, streams of people went across the polished floor and in and out of the elevators and up and down the stairs, as though their movements had been choreographed: no one bumped into anyone else. At the desk he asked to see Detective Kerjeski.

Kerjeski was waiting for Terry upstairs, in the hall.

"Well," he said. "Thanks for coming."

They went into a room like a small theater, or maybe a screening room in eastern Europe, containing two rows of gray chairs with green padded seats.

"Sit down," said Kerjeski. "I'll be right back."

The odor in the room was a residue compounded of a million cigarettes, coffee, perfume, and sweat. Terry concentrated on the atmosphere of the room, and it reminded him of the room where he had worked, at a ski resort, where broken legs were treated. Then Terry thought about the bleeding.

Two other men stood behind Terry, one tall and thin with gray hair and blue eyes who wore a dark suit and a shirt with no tie. He leaned against the wall and drank coffee, bringing the cup up and blowing on it for a minute. The sound of it, that huff, huff and then the slurp, filled the room. The other man stood against the wall with his arms crossed. The room was quiet, although the absence of sound seemed to suggest the working of some other presence, like disease or injustice.

Terry heard some men walking slowly up three stairs and opening the door to the lineup and filing out in front of a wall that had lines on it, each marked off with a height, 5 feet 5, 6, 7, 8, 9, 10, 11, 6 feet, 1, 2, 3, 4, 5. There were seven men. For a moment Terry just sat there, looking at them not as individuals, but as an aggregate of possibilities.

"Take your time," said Kerjeski.

Mostly the men had dark skin, but two of them had fair complexions, one with blond hair and one with brown hair. Terry stared at them now, going from one to another, wondering how many of them, including the policeman in the lineup, had come into the hospital where he worked. Maybe he'd treated half of them. Maybe all, for all he knew. But, as he looked, he confronted the necessity to make a decision, to be right, to do the correct thing when the circumstances he faced were vague, or worse, misleading.

The goddamned bleeding. He worried that the blood could be pooling in her extremities. Then he'd be forced to try to raise the pressure. He thought, too, of the morning the car had been stolen. Why had he bought the thing anyway? Just what had he been trying to prove? The entire thing had been some impulse toward . . . the romantic, he guessed. He thought she needed romance.

The number-two man seemed familiar, especially in his expression, which combined boredom with fury to produce a palpable sense of danger. Terry went on staring at Number 2. The features seemed to change before Terry's eyes, at first friendly and then malignant. Maybe it was a gift the man had, a chameleonlike quality.

"Number 2," Terry said.

"You want to see him from the side?"

"Yes," Terry said. "You haven't got his medical records, do you?"

"No," said Kerjeski, "Why?"

"I was wondering if he's come to the hospital. A lot of these guys look familiar."

"Number 2," said Kerjeski, speaking into a microphone so that his voice could be heard in the lineup room. "Step forward. Turn sideways."

The man did so. He swaggered slightly, radiating malice mixed with a barely subdued impatience. He stepped forward, his hands behind his back, his chin up, as though daring someone to take a swipe at it. He seemed to think better of that and, with a rolling of one shoulder and a twist of his neck, he turned sideways. It appeared that he was drawn to his calling, whatever it may have been, if only because havoc or mayhem made sense to him and, from his point of view, actually brought order into the universe.

"Are you in good health?" said Kerjeski.

"I got a little cough," said the man. He coughed, politely putting one hand to his mouth. "Nothing comes up though."

"Do you take medicine for it?"

The man smiled. "Not right now."

"How long have you had the cough?"

"A couple of weeks," he said. "My diet isn't what it should be, you know."

"Any broken bones?" said Kerjeski.

"I broke my hand once," he said.

"Have you ever been to the emergency room at Cedars West?"

"Yeah," said the man. "Somebody cut me once. I got stitched up. They gave me a shot, too. Something *tet.* Tetanus. Didn't hurt much to speak of. I got a high pain threshold."

"Well?" said Kerjeski to Terry.

The man held up his hand to show where he had been cut. A purple scar, the color of a grape Popsicle, ran across the palm. It looked as though he had taken hold of the blade of a knife and that someone had jerked it away from him. He held it up matter-of-factly.

"When did he come to the hospital?" Terry said.

Kerjeski bent over the microphone, and said, "Number 2. When did you come to the hospital."

Number 2 shrugged. "I don't know," he said.

Terry thought about the cough: it could have been anything, bronchitis, lung cancer, an allergy. Terry was seeing a lot more allergy than ever before. In fact, he thought of a woman who had been in an automobile accident. They had tried to rebuild her face using a piece of rubber to support her eye. It turned out she was allergic to rubber. Then he went back, listening to that cough.

"Maybe a couple of years ago," said Number 2.

Terry put his head down.

"Well?" said Kerjeski.

"Have him say, 'Clickety-clack. Clickety-clack. Cut your head off, cut your head off.'"

"What?" said Kerjeski.

"Go on," Terry said.

Kerjeski asked the suspect to repeat the phrase.

Number 2 stood there, his eyes sweeping across the black space in which Terry sat. He smiled for a moment. "What's this?" he said. "Are we playing trains?"

"Just say it," said Kerjeski.

"Where we going?" Number 2 said. "Are we going on the Trans-Siberian Express?"

Kerjeski waited, looking through the glass. Number 2 seemed more alert now, like a man trying to see something on the horizon.

"Maybe there are some bad asses on the train, you understand?"

"Speak when spoken to," said Kerjeski. "Repeat the words."

"Clickety-clack, clickety-clack," said the man. He put his chin up. "Cut your head off, cut your head off."

Terry didn't think this was the man he had seen in the street, stealing his car. But it was hard to say for sure because Terry had seen him in the cafeteria. Did Terry want to accuse the man of stealing his car just because he had seen him in the cafeteria?

"It's possible," Terry said.

"What do you mean?" said Kerjeski.

"It might be him," Terry said. "I guess it could be."

"I don't like that *guess* word."

"What do you want me to do about it?" Terry said.

"I want you to be more certain," he said.

"Certain," Terry said.

"Yeah," said Kerjeski.

"Have you got any physical evidence?" Terry said.

"We're not talking about that," said Kerjeski. "We're talking about whether or not you can go into court, and say, 'That's the one. That guy right there. He stole my car.'"

Number 2 went on staring directly into that space in front of him. Then he said, his eyes filled with the overhead lights, "You done with that train business? You know, maybe there are some pissed-off guys on that train? You know, out there in Siberia. Siberia can be one lonely place."

"Speak when you're spoken to," said Kerjeski.

"I'm not certain," Terry said.

"That's not good enough," said Kerjeski.

"Sorry," Terry said.

"Look," he said. "You're a doctor, right?"

"Yes," Terry said.

"Well, say you send some blood to a lab and they tell you, it could be like, appendicitis, but we don't know, what would you say about that?"

"Well," Terry said, "I can tell you one thing. I wouldn't throw some son of the bitch to the wolves when I wasn't sure, I can tell you that."

"Ah, shit," said Kerjeski. "Either you can make up your mind or you can't."

"It's not a matter of making up my mind," Terry said. "It's a matter of being right."

"Ah, Jesus," said Kerjeski. "Can't you do better than that?"

"Cut your head off," said Number 2. "Cut your head off."

"Are you threatening someone?" said Kerjeski.

"Me?" said Number 2. "Isn't that what you wanted me to say? Didn't you ask for that? You know, I'm looking out the window of the train. The rivers look like you threw a handful of nickels in them, where the sun hits the water. Siberia's a lonely place to be. Isn't that right?"

"Quiet," said Kerjeski.

Number 2 coughed. He said, "Yeah, I'm not feeling too good. Maybe I got to see the doctor."

Kerjeski got up and went to the back of the room and spoke to the men. They mumbled steadily, as though going over a contract they had all agreed was right. Number 2 stood there, his eyes sharp, waiting. Kerjeski came back, and said, "What's the big deal? They've all done something. I guarantee it."

"I'm not sure, beyond what I told you," Terry said.

"Step back, Number 2," said Kerjeski.

The man stepped back. He didn't smile or change his expression. He coughed again, covering his mouth, looking a little troubled about that cough.

Terry went out into the long hall. The floor was worn, although it had been polished recently and it had a bluish luster from the window down at the end. The atmosphere was a little gritty.

A woman stood in the hall. She was in her middle thirties and she was dressed in a pair of blue jeans, a sweater, and a white shirt. She carried a small handbag which she brought up to her mouth as she sipped coffee out of a Styrofoam cup. She had a bruise on her face, and when she blew on the surface of the coffee she made it quiver. It was as though she were staring through the wall, and without looking at Terry, she said, "Did you own the car?"

"Yes," he said. "I owned the car."

"It's a nice car," she said, looking at him now.

"Well," Terry said. "I don't know."

The woman swallowed. "It's not so nice because of what happened in it? Is that what you're saying?"

"I didn't say that," he said.

"But that's what you were thinking, isn't it?"

"Yes," he said.

"You know what?" she said. "That's the first truthful thing anyone has said to me in the last two days." She looked right at him. "But let me tell you, a lot of things aren't so nice anymore," she said. The coffee was trembling now.

"It's a stupid car," Terry said.

"Why did you buy it?" she said.

"Romance," he said. "I had some romantic idea."

"Romance," she said, and went on looking at him. "I always wanted a car like that," she said.

He waited while she had another sip.

"It's got leather seats. Tinted glass," she said. "A CD player. Good sound. But what is good sound, anyway, when push comes to shove?" Now she hesitated, not wanting to walk into that room where the men were lined up. "Did you see anyone you recognized?" she said.

"I wasn't sure," Terry said. "I don't know. Maybe."

"That's too bad," she said. "I'm not going to be able to do much better. I never got a good look at him."

"Me neither," Terry said.

"Well," she said. "That's a shame."

She turned into the room. The door had a pneumatic arm on the top, which pulled it shut with a sucking sound. Then Terry stood there as Kerjeski said through the microphone, "Number 3, step forward, turn to the right." Down the hall someone started coughing, a steady, dry cough. The man who was coughing lighted a cigarette, blowing plumes of smoke into the air, while from the lineup room there was no sound at all. The silence had a weight to it, as though the air was explosive, and all it needed was one good spark.

At eight o'clock, Kerjeski called and said that the woman couldn't identify Number 2 either. Maybe she was just too tired to go through with it. Certainly no one was giving her any help, right? Anyway, Kerjeski had let Number 2 go. How did Terry like that? All they had on him was driving a stolen car, and Number 2 had posted bond and was gone. So, there it is, said Kerjeski, he's loose out there. How do you feel about that? Then he hung up.

T ERRY STOOD at the foot of her bed. She wasn't awake now, although earlier she had written on her clipboard that she was seeing double. It made her feel sick. The venom also prevented her from moving her eyes very much: when she was awake she stared into the distance as though trying to make out some small, important detail on the horizon. Terry looked at her lips. She didn't have any swelling. Or a rash. Sooner or later, though, they were going to need to find some blood. Terry guessed they had forty-eight hours. They could probably wait that long.

When he came into the hall, a woman said to him, "Can I speak to you for a minute?"

She was about five two, a little heavy, and she had bleached her hair blond. Her eyes were blue, and she was wearing a lab coat. Terry guessed she was one of the technicians from downstairs. She just stood there, in the busy hall, her arms hanging by her sides. She looked tired and a little scared.

"Sure," said Terry.

"I've got something to tell you," said the woman.

"Haven't we met?" said Terry.

"Yes," she said. "We met downstairs. My name is Claire. Claire Nickolson."

"Sure, of course. I remember."

"The other night I saw something like the blood you're trying to match. A couple of weeks ago. A man was brought in here by the cops and he got away. A cop came downstairs into the lab, thinking maybe the guy had come down there. Anyway, I think his blood matched the type you're looking for. I don't know because we never finished the matching, but I think it's the same. The guy ran away, and we had other things to do for patients who were still here."

"You didn't get an address for him, did you?"

"No," said the lab technician. "The cops had him. Maybe they know. It all happened pretty fast. Anyway, I think it was the same type. Something called Bombay."

Terry went back into Virginia's room. No one in there, not the nurse, or the critical care physician who came in to look at her, too, talked about it, but they were all thinking the same thing. They didn't talk about it because there wasn't anything to be done. The lab said the blood gases were falling a little. Terry increased the percentage of oxygen she was getting, from fifty to sixty. There were cases of wounded patients, or those with bad infections, or heart trouble, who developed a systemic inflammation, and then a cascade of organ failure. It often started in the lung, and the level of oxygen in the blood gases would fall. This was, as Terry had often thought, a reflection of the fact that the mysteries of medicine kept receding before the advances, right down to the molecular level. But despite the available treatments, supported breathing, maybe even dialysis, usually the patient died. So that's what he would be facing, watching her die, doing one thing and then another and having her slip away. Some of the items that set off the inflammatory response were toxins. Like venom, Terry supposed. He stood there, thinking about the mysteries of medicine receding ever further, and he tried to imagine them, but couldn't really. All that came to mind was a notion of galactic space, of spirals, the Horse Nebula, all of which were distant and mysterious and cold. Anyway, no one mentioned this possibility. He wrote the orders. They'd give her some fluids. There was nothing to do but wait. Nothing. He guessed he'd go home for a while.

He went down the hall to his office. It was quiet there. He tried to calculate the chances of two people with the same rare type of blood coming into this hospital in the same month. How to figure it? Multiply the odds of finding a donor by the number of days you were looking for one? He thought of the cases that had a life of their own, an intricacy and maliciousness that sought out their own path. He'd seen it before, and mostly the thing to do was to get out, to turn the case over to someone else, but he knew that he wasn't going to do that. He came up against the moment in which cowardice seemed to match good sense perfectly, leaving him at an abyss: no matter what he did, he'd think that it was the wrong approach, either by asking for help because he was in over his head, or by staying with it because he knew more about what was happening in the case than anyone else.

In his office he called the police and asked to speak to Detective Kerjeski. Kerjeski said he didn't know where Number 2 was, and, he guessed, Number 2 wasn't staying around. These guys were good at slipping away, said Kerjeski. After all, it's what they had devoted their lives to doing. Kerjeski said that Number 2 would turn up after a while because they always did. It was just a matter of time.

"I haven't got a lot of time," said Terry.

"Well," said Kerjeski. "That's a shame. Maybe we should have hung onto him when we had him."

Outside, in the hall, there were only the sounds of people pacing, but then Terry thought of Virginia when she had come into his house a few weeks before. She came through the door and stood in front of him, a look of curiosity on her face, as though she were puzzled. She said, "Well, I've come back. Even though I said I wouldn't. I'm condemned to this. So I might as well enjoy it. I've never been more alive and more scared." Then she dropped her handbag on the floor. "Well, are you glad to see me?"

"Yes," he said. "You know that."

"Did you think I was gone forever?"

"It crossed my mind," he said.

She went into the bathroom and ran a shower. "I worked hard today," she said. "There are some new creatures at work. Bad ones from New Guinea."

She said she would like to get drunk with him sometime. She wanted to wake up in the morning, quivering with a hangover, the two of them unable to move, just under the sheets, barely touching. Maybe that way she would be able to know exactly what he was thinking. She'd pressed his hand against her. Just as she was doing now. Then, hung over, lying next to him, she'd say, See? You feel that? Have you ever felt a woman that wet?

Rick came into the office. He didn't say anything for a while, but after a minute he sat down in the chair where patients usually sat.

"What are you thinking about?" Rick said.

"Virginia," Terry said. "Do you want some coffee?"

"No," said Rick. "I'm going to go have a drink."

"That's probably a good idea," said Terry. "We'll call you if anything happens."

"Sure," said Rick. "It's nice to be told. If anything happens. Tell me, when Virginia called you, what did she want to talk about?"

"It wasn't important," he said.

"Is that right?"

"She just wanted to talk. It wasn't any big thing," said Terry. "Maybe we can talk about it some other time."

"Some other time," said Rick.

"We don't have to talk this way," said Terry.

"No?" said Rick.

"We could find something else to talk about," said Terry.

Rick looked around the office. "You know," said Rick. "Someone once said there is no such thing as a mistake."

"Yeah," said Terry. "It was Freud, but he didn't use the word *mistake*. He said *accident*. There's no such thing as an accident."

"Is that right?" said Rick. "Well, these days Freud has fallen out of favor, hasn't he?"

"That's not my specialty," said Terry.

"Yeah, I guess that's right," said Rick. "Anyway, that's what I was trying to say. There's no such thing as an accident."

"Do you really want to talk this way?"

"Well, I'm pretty pissed off. So we'll talk the way I want," said Rick.

"Maybe I'm pissed off, too," said Terry.

"You?" said Rick.

Terry sat there, thinking about the atmosphere of the hospital, about the endless number of details that conspired to bring someone here, or the number of details that had gone into his sitting in this room at this moment. What was he most angry about, that he had made a mistake, or that he had managed to betray something that he hadn't wanted to betray? That he suspected he had managed to cut away something of himself that he had always liked, and now he felt its absence, like an amputated limb that still itched? But who was to blame for that? In his heart, he was infuriated about what was happening to Virginia.

And what was the cause of that, what principle or element was at work there? How many times had he come up against it as a physician, in the presence of clever diseases that had perfected themselves over millions of years? It didn't matter to him whether it was something as simple as the infinite sensitivity of natural selection in being able to produce the toxins in venom, or a thousand other aspects of living creatures. What eluded him, what seemed to recede forever beyond the tips of his fingers, was the malignant principle behind such a mechanism. He couldn't even really define it, or put a word on it. He just knew it was there, waiting for a chance to use any tool that came along.

"Well?" said Rick. "What have you got to be angry about?"

"It's hard to explain," said Terry.

"Uh-huh," said Rick. "Well. Here's something for you to think about."

"What's that?" said Terry.

"That business about accidents?" said Rick. "Maybe Virginia was feeling so bad about you that she got careless on purpose. Maybe that's why she's in there now. Maybe you were the one behind it. Maybe she wouldn't be in there if you'd just left her alone."

Terry looked directly back at him. "Don't be an asshole," said Terry.

"What?" said Rick.

"Listen," said Terry. "Do you want to get someone else to look after Virginia?"

"No," said Rick. "You know more about it than anyone else. No. It's better this way." Rick leaned forward and put his head in his hands.

Oh, no, thought Terry. No.

When Rick looked up, there were tears on his face. He seemed to think that Terry should feel sorry for him, or that his wet face was a weapon of some kind. In the hall, a physician was being paged, and the amplified voice was cool, womanly, and oddly erotic. Terry looked across the desk.

"I'm not going to get a gun," said Rick. "What the fuck would I do with a gun? I'm kidding myself. No, I'm not going to buy a gun."

Terry apprehended fatigue as a gas that seeped into everything in the room.

"That's best," said Terry. "There's a paper towel behind you."

"Thanks," said Rick. He reached around and took one, which made a dry sound as he pulled it out of the dispenser. "I'm sorry about this."

Terry thought, Please, don't make it worse.

"Have you ever thought that in one minute you could fuck everything up? You know, you'd do the wrong thing and then you'd have to live with it?"

"Sure," said Terry. "All the time."

"Ah, shit," said Rick.

He went into the corner and ran the water in the sink, and then he went out the door, into the hall and the scent of medicine, coffee, and stale soup. It was evening now. Upstairs, the patients were getting their dinner. Terry thought of the racks of trays, on wheels, going down the halls, the food under plastic covers, not quite warm. Little packages of juice. A small paper cup filled with pills. Terry thought that what he needed was a little time, just to think things over.

NUMBER 2 was leaning against Terry's car in the parking lot. In the evening, the razor wire that went around the top of the fence showed against the reddish sky, and the glass in the cars all seemed slick and pool-like. Number 2 was wearing a shiny nylon jacket, a pair of dark pants, and boots. He had his hands in his pockets. Terry looked at him, and as he came across the parking lot, he thought, even then, I didn't press charges, didn't identify him, so maybe there's a chance. I could threaten him, though. That's a possibility.

But, of course, what Terry wanted to do was to shoot for the middle of the bell curve: what was the best way to go about it? Certainly, being panicky wasn't going to help. Begging, pleading, what would that get him? Terry waited, feeling in the thrill of recognition of Number 2 something else, which was another understanding, another tug, which Terry apprehended as another aspect of his love for Virginia. What wouldn't he do now?

"Hey, doc," he said. "How's it going?"

"I've been better," Terry said.

"Well, you know," he said. "You got to take care of yourself."

"Is that right?" Terry said.

"Sure," he said. "You got to get all them vitamins. You getting any C?"

"No," Terry said.

"You got to have C," he said. "And all that other stuff."

"Well, I'll do that," Terry said. Terry opened the door of the car.

"Hey," said Number 2. "Not so fast. I think we should have a little talk."

"About what?"

"One thing and another," said Number 2.

He was on one side of the car and Terry was on the other, and the reflection of the lights lay on the top of the car between them. Both of their shapes were smeared in it, the polished roof holding them like figures in the film of a pond.

"You're not looking so good," said Number 2.

"As I told you, I've been better," said Terry.

"Haven't we all?" he said. "Open the door."

Number 2 stood there with defiance mixed with lightheartedness, the two combining with a charm that had, at its heart, a sense of something concealed and just barely controlled. Maybe it was a good idea to leave it that way. Sure. Maybe they could talk. Maybe that was the way to begin.

Terry got in and reached across and opened the door.

"Hey," said Number 2. "This is nice. Maybe I should get some of that medical education, you know? I remember in school we had to memorize the bones, you know. Hipbone connected to the leg bone. What's that thighbone called?"

"Femur," Terry said.

"Yeah, that's it, like one of those little animals."

"You mean a lemur?" Terry said.

"Yeah. One of those little furry things."

They pulled out into the street. Of course, he had other things to be concerned about. Was Number 2 carrying anything, hepatitis, say, or drug-resistant tuberculosis?

"You talked to the cops again?" Number 2 said.

"No," Terry said.

"Well, they been poking around me again, you know? They just won't leave me alone. Always been that way."

He sat there, hands together, looking out through the windshield.

"Up there," he said. "We can stop there. You got any money?"

"Yes," said Terry.

Number 2 pointed to a bar. Its yellow and green neon palm tree sign jutted into the street. It was somehow upbeat and suggested romance, although a low-key one, to be sure. Terry parked and they went in. They got two beers in long slender bottles that had come out of an ice chest, and rivulets of water ran off them like sweat. Terry held his bottle to his head. Number 2 watched. The bar had a collection of lighted advertising, bright yellow and red and blue, which gave the place a commercial cheer, like a Christmas tree in a store window. Beneath it all, though, was the glance of Number 2.

"What are you worried about?" said Number 2.

Terry took a sip of his beer, tasting the hops, the tingle of the carbonation, all of which were distractions from his attempt to find words. He wondered if he was caught in one of those moments in which a kind of eddy opens up and sucks you in because you're human. Could he have been more moral in his actions and less human? Would he have been complete if he hadn't been so tempted by Virginia? How could one be a perfect human being without a flaw? He guessed these were questions a physician didn't put himself in a position to ask. That's what the rules were all about. They kept you from moments like this one. He looked at Number 2.

"I guess there are times when someone's life really does hang by a thread," said Terry. "I guess I'm worried about that."

"You're telling me?" said Number 2. "I was in a convenience store once, you know? I needed some money. The guy behind the counter is scared. And he's the only one around. The only one who's seen me or the car I was driving. Tell me about that hanging by a thread stuff."

Number 2 took out a cigarette and lighted it, letting a puff of smoke out while the cigarette was still between his lips, and slowly shaking the match, a wisp rising from it, the undulant smoke suggesting the consideration of delicate matters. "You've got your own temptations, don't you?" said Number 2. He watched Terry's face. He took a drag on his cigarette, and said "temptations" again, this time making the syllables come out in puffs of smoke.

"What's it to you?" said Terry.

"What's it to me?" said Number 2. "It's everything to me. You know, he who is free of sin, let him cast the first stone . . ." Number 2 took another drag on the cigarette, making the tip very red. "Like today. I bet today, downtown, you were thinking that you could say you saw me stealing your car just because you think I've done something wrong anyway, and what the hell, let's let him have it."

"I was trying to be more exact than that," said Terry.

He looked around the room. Then he thought of the venom breaking down the blood, the slow, steady beginning of the inflammatory response.

"But you were thinking about it," said Number 2.

"Yeah," said Terry. "I was thinking about it." He looked at the festive colors of the beer advertisements.

"You see," said Number 2, "the only way I can get a fair shake is to make sure you remember your shit stinks, too."

"Did you steal my car?"

"Oh," said Number 2. "You want to know about that, do you? You think that means something. You're clinging to facts."

"There's nothing wrong with facts," said Terry.

"You tell me a fact, and I can make it disappear," said Number 2. "Was I in your car? Well, I can say that whether I was or whether I wasn't had a lot to do with other things. Maybe things have happened to me that only happen to people in another world from yours. So? Where's your fact? How can we agree on anything?"

Terry shrugged. You didn't answer me, he thought.

"You know what real evil is?" said Number 2.

"Yeah," said Terry. "Yeah. I've got a good idea about it."

"Like what?" said Number 2. He stuck his chin out, his expression a dare, or part something else: the vanity of hard knocks.

"It's what gets into you in such a way as to make it impossible for you to tell what evil is. That's the genuine article," said Terry.

"Well," said Number 2. "Maybe. I'll have to think about it."

"You didn't answer me about the car," said Terry.

"You want to know, do you?" said Number 2. "That's why you're sitting here talking to me. You think I'm going to tell you?" He sipped his beer, puckering his lips on the bottle. "Have you got anything to calm me down, something good from that hospital?"

Terry had a couple of samples of Xanax in his pocket. He took them out now and pushed them across the table. Number 2 looked at them and picked them up and put them into his jacket. "You have trouble sleeping, I'll bet."

"Yeah," said Terry.

"But you don't think I can be bought off with a couple of hits of some downer, do you?" said Number 2.

"No," said Terry. "Look. Do you know what your blood type is?"

"You mean like A and AB and stuff?"

"Yeah," said Terry.

"I've got a rare type. Hardly anyone's got it. The blood bank asked me once if I'd sell it. They've got to be kidding."

"Let's go back up to the hospital," said Terry.

"Oh," said Number 2. "So that's it? You think if you get something on me about the car, I'll give you some of the blood. Jesus, and I thought we're just being friendly."

"We're friendly," said Terry.

"Let's build a little trust first. Before we go back up to the hospital," said Number 2.

"All right," said Terry,

"Tell me what you're tempted by," said Number 2.

Terry shrugged. He didn't want to go home and think about those times when Virginia had come in. "There's not much to say," said Terry.

"Uh-huh," said Number 2. "Are you stealing something out of the hospital? Typewriters or something, computers maybe? Or drugs, something like that?"

"No," said Terry.

"Of course not," said Number 2. "What am I thinking of? That's not it. No." He looked at his cigarette, at the coal that looked like orange foil under the layer of ash. "No," said Number 2. "For you it's something different from that. You're paying your taxes, all right. No. It's got to be a woman you're not supposed to be interested in, right? Something like that." He stared right at Terry now, momentarily dropping the mask of that spirited friendliness, just looking at him.

"What about you?" said Terry.

"Me?" he said.

"Sure," said Terry.

"I don't know," said Number 2. He shrugged.

"Isn't this a two-way street?" said Terry.

"I'm thinking about that," said Number 2.

"Maybe a little whiskey is what we need," said Terry.

"Sure," he said. "I know what you mean. This beer is for kids."

They went up to the bar and got two small glasses of whiskey, its color reassuring as they carried the glasses back to the table. The warmth of the whiskey began to affect the coldness of Terry's fear, not cutting into it or piercing it but just wrapping it up, like someone in a blanket. Maybe, thought Terry, the fear would go to sleep for a while. Give me a little rest. Then he thought of a moment when Virginia came into his house and sat down at the kitchen table. She'd looked at him, and said, "I've been thinking of going to church. Is there a church close by? Maybe we'll get out of bed, and we won't take a shower. We'll still have each other's smell on us. We'll take the smell of life with us. In the dark place, with the smell of incense, we'll be able to grasp what's happened to us. I'll be able to whisper to you there, to tell you that I love you."

"What are you thinking about?" said Number 2.

"A case," he said.

"You're always thinking. I can see that's your problem."

"I'm a physician," he said. "That's what I do."

"Have you ever lived when you were just alert? No thinking. None of that kind of thinking stuff."

Terry thought of Virginia.

"You ever felt that way?" said Number 2. "I mean just alert. Terror on your skin like some greasy cold thing."

"I've seen some bad cases," said Terry.

"But that doesn't have anything to do with you," said Number 2. "You're not bleeding. Nothing's happening to you. You're not risking anything."

"You'd be surprised," said Terry. "Maybe it builds up over time."

"You know, that's a difference between us," said Number 2. "When you think about time, you're thinking months, years, decades. I'm thinking about the next couple of hours."

Terry tried to imagine where the whiskey had been distilled, where the water that had gone into it had come from, the time it had spent in a barrel, and as he tried to imagine these things, he thought, Careful. Careful. "What tempts you?" said Terry.

"Me?" said Number 2. He looked across the table. It was a glance of fury perfectly imbued with sadness.

Terry looked back, trying to imagine what was behind it, or where it came from.

"I don't know what to say," Number 2 said.

"Were you in my car?" said Terry.

"You keep asking that," said Number 2. "I keep telling you, that's a fact that doesn't matter. Can't you understand?" Number 2 finished his drink and put down the glass with a bang. "I want you to come with me."

"Where?" said Terry.

"It's not far from here." Number 2 smiled.

"What are we going to do?" said Terry.

"Understand each other," he said. "Yeah. That's right. Enough of this talk talk talk. You want to know what I'm tempted by? People like you. I see you around, driving your cars. Going home.

Going to the bank. Making decisions. There's something in it, something I can't quite get my hands on. It drives me crazy. What the fuck are you doing?" Number 2 watched him for a while. "What's all this decent shit, all this morality crap, what the fuck is it?"

Terry finished his drink, feeling the warmth of it. "I've made some mistakes along those lines," said Terry.

"Yeah," said Number 2. "And you see them as mistakes. I don't get it. Why don't you just take what the fuck you can get?"

"Maybe if you do that, you start shrinking. You get smaller and smaller until you're nothing," said Terry. "So where are we going?"

"Not far," said Number 2. "You come along and maybe I'll tell you about the car."

"Is that right?" said Terry.

"Yeah," said Number 2. "Maybe I will."

"What about the blood?" said Terry. "If I come along will you —"

"Stop that," said Number 2. "Just come along. No deals. Just trust. Come on. Will you trust me or not?"

They got up and went outside, into the warm night air.

"You know, the black death was in LA," Terry said.

"Is that a rock group?"

"No," Terry said. "It was a long time ago."

"Oh," he said. "You mean like the plague? Probably down in San Pedro. That's where everything comes in."

They got on the freeway. Number 2 said they'd go only one exit. Terry thought the freeways at night had their own beauty: the lights on the other side of the road approached in a steady flow, as in a beam of yellow particles, and ahead there were the lines of red taillights, all bright and suggesting the heart of something, like light in a foundry, or the glow of the depths of chemistry, as if some genes in strands of DNA had an aura to them, like fox fire.

"Tell me," said Number 2. "What's the best weight for a piece?"

"You mean caliber?" said Terry.

"Yeah," said Number 2. "What really stops them."

Terry went on driving. The orange needles in the car's gauges shone dimly: oil pressure, alternator, manifold temperature.

"A lot of people ask that question these days," Terry said.

"That's LA for you," said Number 2.

"A forty-four Magnum. It makes a mess. Especially when the bullets start tumbling end over end through organs."

The exit from the freeway curved down in a faintly shiny ribbon. At the bottom, at the stop signal, Terry saw the glow of a small shopping center, a place that probably had a dry cleaner, maybe a liquor store. Terry recognized it. Sure. A big liquor store, almost a supermarket.

A car went along through the darkness with the illusion of levitation, and as it came, Terry began to think that he really had done something that one shouldn't do, no matter how you decided these things, and that this evening wasn't only an attempt to save someone's life, and the life of someone he loved at that, but punishment for his errors. Number 2 was very still, and Terry had the impression that Number 2's concentration filled the car with an airy presence, which Terry could feel on his face and hands as a chill.

"Turn right," said Number 2.

Up ahead, the shopping center glowed more brightly. A woman in the lane next to them was accompanied by an inflatable dummy. Number 2 looked at her and turned back to Terry, saying, "Well, there's hope for you. She thinks she can face this town with nothing but a big, blown-up balloon. Well, well." Number 2 was quiet for a few moments. Then he said to Terry, "Say, how much do you make a year?"

"About ninety thousand dollars."

"That all?"

"There are doctors who make more money than that," Terry said. "Surgeons. Orthopedic surgeons."

Each time a car went by in the opposite direction, a scrim of illumination swept over Terry and Number 2. The ebb and flow of light mimicked the constant change of Terry's intentions, which moved from the impulse to do anything to get the blood to an impulse to give in to numbness, or the desire to sleep, just for a few minutes, so that he could be better prepared for whatever he was facing. Then Terry thought about the woman he had seen downtown at the lineup. He didn't know why he thought of her, aside from the fact that she left him at once infuriated and unable to fix what had happened. He seemed to swing back and forth along this arc, from light to darkness, from being able to take action to a state that would have been panic if he'd had enough energy.

"You know," said Number 2. "I bet that train stuff is right. I'll bet people do meet on a train and tell each other all kinds of things they wouldn't even tell people they're close to. Like in Siberia. Tell me about Siberia."

"I've never been there," Terry said.

"You've got a good idea about it for someone who's never been there," he said. "I heard you the other night. Tell me. Are there fish in those rivers?"

"Salmon," Terry said.

"You mean like what comes in a can?"

"They're not in a can yet," said Terry. "The water is made

green by the trees on the bank, and the fish are silver. They look like their sides are made out of small silver coins."

"Yeah," Number 2 said. "I guess that's right." He thought some more. "And you get dark tea and rye bread?" Number 2 took a pistol out of the pocket of his windbreaker and put it in his lap. It was a revolver with a wooden grip, and a blue barrel, which looked as if it had been scratched and knocked around some, just as the cylinder looked as if it had been knocked around, too, left in a glove box or a toolbox or maybe even in a woman's handbag. Terry glanced down at the thing. He thought of the gunshot cases he had seen. Usually, they were shivering.

"My old three-eight," he said. "There it is. It's not a forty-four, but what can I say? Tell me, where's the best place to shoot someone. I mean, if you want to fucking kill them?"

"Behind the ear," Terry said, "back of the head."

Number 2 put the barrel of the pistol up to the back of Terry's head and tapped him. The hard touch of it, which he felt in the bones of his head, seemed to penetrate everything around him with urgency.

"There?" he said.

"Yeah," Terry said.

"Right there?" he said.

"Yeah," he said. "Right there. Why don't you put that thing down?"

Number 2 took the pistol away and put it back into his pocket. He just put it in his pocket and sat there, looking at the cars. "Stop here," said Number 2.

Terry pulled into the liquor store parking lot and stopped. The place behind his ear still buzzed as though something had been pressing on it for a long time.

Terry used to stop here after work sometimes when he'd had a night of bad cases: then he'd walk in and get a cart and go up and down the aisles, taking down a bottle of Macallan single-malt scotch, or a Margaux (at fifty-four dollars a bottle), or a case of champagne. Now, he thought of Virginia as she had sat in his house, blue-green veins showing in the white places left by her bathing suit. She had spilled champagne on her thigh, saying, Oh, I can feel the bubbles.

That place behind Terry's ear still buzzed, and he touched it to make sure the gun wasn't there anymore. He thought about the head wounds he'd seen in which the bone had been hit so hard as to look like pulverized crystal, and yet, at the same time, these cases had a mundane quality to them that was alarming because they made death seem so much like something that was just broken.

Terry suspected, as he sat there, that the solution to the difficulties he faced right now had to do with making a decision and sticking with it. Still, he wondered, with horror, whether it was a mistake to think that order came out of one's own intermittent and yet hard-won convictions. Anyway, it was all he had.

A bluish light came through the windows of the liquor store and fell into the parking lot with the hint of an arctic dawn. Terry wondered about the scent of venom. Did it have a whiff of the arctic to it, like the scent of dry ice? He told himself that this was no way to think: he was going to have to make decisions, and what kind of decision would he make if he gave in to speculation? Just imaginative conceit? That never saved anyone, did it?

"You didn't tell me if you were in love?" said Number 2. "What about that?"

"What's there to say?" Terry said.

"Oh, come on," he said. "You've got whole libraries around here filled with books about love. And all you got to say is 'What's there to say?'"

Terry shrugged. He looked out at the empty parking lot. For

an instant, he could see what the world might look like if she died. The moment of realization carried with it a hint of being forever separated, of being forever incapable of intimacy. Now, as a variety of ballast, as something that made him feel unafraid, he was desperate to do the right thing. For instance, just who had stolen his car?

"So?" said Number 2.

"Maybe it's like this," said Terry. "You get to be someone you can only be when you're with the woman you love. And you like being whoever that is. Maybe the person you get to be is a little scary, too, because he's so different from who you normally are."

"Sure," said Number 2. "I like the scary part."

"I didn't mean violent," said Terry.

"What's the difference?" said Number 2.

"Maybe I don't mean scary," said Terry. "Maybe I just mean exciting."

Number 2 brought the pistol out of his pocket and sat with it in his lap. He handled it gracefully, as a surgeon handled instruments. He put the pistol on his thighs, thinking things over, glancing at those rows of bottles behind the glass in the liquor store. Finally, he said, "We're going in there."

Terry looked into the liquor store. "If I go in there," said Terry. "Will you help me?"

"I thought we were building trust," said Number 2. "Is trust made up of a bunch of promises?"

Terry had picked up a little fever. Flu probably. He felt the beads of perspiration on his forehead and along his upper lip, and under his clothes. Along his sides, he felt a quick, sudden rivulet.

Another car pulled into the parking lot, and a woman in slacks and high-heeled shoes got out of an old Mercedes that needed new tires. She walked up to the door, her shoes clicking on the concrete of the parking lot. She went right through the door and without missing a beat went directly to a shelf that sold large bottles of vodka. She picked two of them up.

"Let's wait for that bitch to get out of there. She looks like a screamer," said Number 2.

The woman stood at the counter now. She teased two bills out of her wallet and shoved them over with a lack of ceremony, as though the clerk were a machine. He put the bottles into a bag and stuck in a piece of cardboard so the bottles wouldn't bang together.

Cars went up and down the avenue. Any one of them could pull into the parking lot.

"Now," said Number 2. "Come on."

The woman came out to her car and opened the door and put the bag in first, giving it a shove, as though she'd been having an argument with it for a long time.

Number 2 got out of the car and left the door just leaning against its frame. "Leave your door like this," he said.

Terry got out of the car. Maybe some aspirin would help the fever.

"That's it," Number 2 said when he saw how Terry left the door.

They walked in. Only one clerk was in the liquor store, a man who was wearing a blue cotton jacket, something like a lab coat, with Sunset Liquors sewed into it with red thread. The counter and cash register were to the left of the door, and the clerk sat there, on a stool, looking into the rows of shelves that confronted him. The shadows at the bottom of the shelves, along the counter, next to the pile of cardboard boxes, were all a dark blue. No one else was in the store right now, and the cashier's expression revealed his struggle between alertness and boredom.

Terry wondered how many times the place had been held up, and whether the clerk had an alarm switch he could work with his foot.

Terry stood in the air-conditioned air, sweating. He thought of his grandfather with a scalpel in his hand, saying, "Hold it like this. See?" The chrome of the shelves seemed to blend perfectly with the memory of the stainless steel blade, the present and the past combining in such a way as to seem almost visible. The elusiveness of the memory left him straining a little, wanting to talk to his grandfather. Hadn't that been an easier age, when the decisions were clearer? The door swung shut behind them. It was quiet in the store.

Number 2 walked slowly down the aisles. There was nothing in the cashier's gestures, nothing in his movement, not even a change in his expression, but through nothing more than the slightest shift in posture, the atmosphere in the store changed from boredom to fear. Just like that, thought Terry.

Terry thought of Virginia as she stood in front of the icebox reaching for some milk, drinking right from the carton, letting it run out of the sides of her mouth, across her breasts, along her stomach, down her thigh.

Terry felt the fever again. He went over to a cooler and took out a bottle of water. The cashier turned slightly now. He had a paperback book on the counter next to the cash register, but he didn't seem to be reading it. Then he abandoned pretense and just put the book down. Number 2 put his hand in his pocket. The cashier hesitated and seemed to move his hand closer to the book and to the shelf below. The room seemed to be getting a little brighter, and Terry noticed the odor here, a faint, almost chemical scent, which he supposed was from the accumulation of broken bottles of liquor or wine, and which had, underneath it, a faint whiff of the erotic, of celebrations and late evenings.

"Nice night," said the cashier.

"Yeah," Terry said. "A little warm, though."

"You call this warm?" said the cashier. He looked from Terry to Number 2 and back again. "It's nothing compared to those days when that dry wind starts blowing out of Riverside. Or out in the Valley in August. It gets to be a hundred and one, maybe two."

"Is that right?" said Number 2. "I hadn't noticed."

"It's funny how you don't notice things," said the cashier.

"Yeah," said Number 2. "Busy tonight?"

"No," said the cashier. "Kind of slow."

"You hear that," Number 2 said to Terry. "Everybody's getting squeezed these days."

The cashier didn't move much, although his hand was a little closer to the shelf. Terry turned and looked at one of the coolers, the glass door of which was streaked with condensation. He needed to do something about the fever.

"Have you got any aspirin?" he said.

"Sure," said the cashier. "On that shelf."

As he pointed, he seemed to bend over a little more, and his hand disappeared beneath the counter. He didn't look comfortable that way, but not totally unnatural either. He could have been leaning on his hand. Terry turned and walked over to the plastic rack that held over-the-counter junk: antacid, breath spray, mouthwash, Preparation H, and some aspirin, too. He picked up a bottle and looked at it. Five dollars. There couldn't have been more than twenty-five in the bottle.

"There's a lot of flu around," said the cashier. "My sister had a case that you wouldn't believe."

"What was wrong?" Terry said.

"Oh," the cashier said. "You know. She said it was like pissing out her asshole. Couldn't stop."

"You've got to worry about dehydration," Terry said.

"You're telling me?" said the cashier. He looked over at Number 2 again.

Terry held the aspirin bottle up, as though he could stop everything by standing there like a traffic cop. Number 2 looked back at Terry now, and Terry could feel a gulf growing between them.

"Hey," said Number 2. "Look at that."

"What?" said the cashier.

"The price tag on the aspirin," he said. "Five bucks."

"So what?" said the cashier.

"I never thought I'd see the day when aspirin was five dollars for a bottle," he said.

"We got expenses here," said the cashier. "We're open late. Two o'clock in the morning."

"Yeah," said Number 2. "Well, that's great. You hear that?"

"Look," said the cashier. "If you got a headache, buy the aspirin. If you don't, put them back in the rack."

Number 2 looked at Terry, and then he put his hand back into his pocket. Terry thought, What happens if he gets killed, right here? What am I going to do about the blood? What if it seeps out, right through my fingers? He had that feeling of swinging along that arc, of a changing perspective, that left him suspended between faith and doubt. At the bottom of the arc, he thought about the woman outside the lineup room who had validated his worst suspicions about the nature of possibility.

"Five dollars," said Number 2. "There aren't more than twenty in there."

"Twenty-five," said the cashier. "It says so right on the bottle."

"I guess other people have complained," said Number 2.

The cashier shrugged. The air conditioner's compressor went on, and the throb of it came into the store.

"All right," said the cashier. "So some people complained about the aspirin? But you know what people come in here at two o'clock in the morning? It's like a spaceship from Mars landed. Or maybe some other place further away than Mars. The other night a guy was in here buying beer and talking about taking a taxi back to some place in Andromeda. Had an orange sky, he said, and twenty-eight moons. Nothing but peckerheads."

"I come in here late," said Number 2.

"I didn't mean anything personal," said the cashier.

Number 2 moved his hand in his pocket.

A car pulled into the parking lot, its lights swinging over the windows, and for an instant all of their shadows, Terry's, the cashier's, and Number 2's, lingered on the shelf behind them. Terry thought that the shadows were like those left on the walls in Hiroshima. After the bomb. Then he realized he wasn't thinking clearly. He was distracted. But as he stood there, sweating, he realized that when he was with Virginia she brought out the liveliest, most unfrightened part of him. What was scary, and what he confronted now, was how remote from his own desires he had been before he had met her. In fact, until he met her, he hadn't even known what his desires really were. How long had he been living that way? He had always wanted to be a physician, and to think the way a good physician thought, but what did he know about beyond that?

A man and a woman came into the store. The woman was in her late twenties and wearing a pair of cut-off blue jeans and a sleeveless blue-jean shirt. She was drunk and she squinted. Her boyfriend was wearing blue jeans and some sandals, and he said, "You sell cigs?"

"Yeah," said the cashier.

The woman went over to the cooler and took out some beer

and brought it back, swinging it down on the counter. She turned back and looked at the rack where the aspirin was and took out a bottle, saying, "I got a headache."

She put the aspirin on the counter, and her boyfriend said, "Jesus, it's five bucks," and she looked at the bottle and said, "Jesus, what a gyp." She put it back on the shelf as the boy reached into the front pocket of his jeans, with a high-shouldered, long-armed gesture.

Number 2 stood there and waited, looking out the window. He seemed to watch something on the other side of the street while he was aware of everything that was going on in the store.

The air conditioner came on again.

"I always like a cold beer after balling," said the woman.

"Yeah?" said the cashier.

She nodded.

"It's, like, Miller time," she said. "The pause that refreshes."

"That's Coke, not beer," said her boyfriend. "Don't you know anything?"

The man paid for the beer, and they went out into the parking lot.

"See," said the cashier. "What did I tell you?"

Number 2 looked out at the parking lot, which was empty now. The clerk had started to sweat. He swallowed when he looked again from Terry to Number 2 and back.

Number 2 walked along the shelf in front of the cash register, the one that held the mouthwash and chewing gum and Band-Aids, and then he stepped behind Terry a little bit.

"Yeah," said the cashier. "My sister sure was sick. They said it was a flu from Asia. The Bangkok strain. That's what they called it."

Number 2 took his hand out of his pocket.

"Oh shit," said the cashier.

Number 2 moved Terry around the end of the counter. He told him to pick up a bag. Number 2 told the cashier to open the drawer. Terry picked up the money and put it in the bag, doing so as quickly as he could. The cashier didn't say anything. He just stood back and licked his lips.

"Come on," said Number 2, gesturing to the cashier. "I saw a storage room back there. Come on."

"Why do we have to go back there?" he said.

"Wouldn't you like to know?" said Number 2.

"Yeah," he said. "Yeah. I would."

Terry held the sack by its top, which was bunched together. There seemed to be a lot of bills, but they weren't large, fives and tens mostly, along with some twenties and even a couple of fifties. A few rolls of coins. Quarters and pennies and dimes.

The cashier walked past the aspirin shelf, still licking his lips. He wasn't as tall as Terry thought he was. He wore his blue coat open and it flapped at his sides. From the back Terry could see his bald spot.

"I've got a wife and a kid," he said.

"What's your wife's name?" said Number 2.

"Michele," said the cashier.

"How much does she weigh?"

"Oh, come on," said the cashier. "What does that have to do with anything?"

"How much does she weigh?"

"I don't know," said the cashier. "Maybe she's a little over-weight."

"Uh-huh," said Number 2. "Give me a number."

"A hundred and seventy. Maybe one seventy-five," said the cashier.

"In here," said Number 2.

Boxes of liquor were piled against the walls of the storage

room, which smelled of cardboard and had the same chemical stink as the selling floor, only more so. The floor was stained, although it looked pretty clean.

"Get down there," said Number 2.

"Please," said the cashier.

Number 2 looked at Terry. Terry was shivering a little, still holding the bag.

"You know," said Number 2 to Terry. "I could really put you in deep shit, you know that? The laws in the state of California don't distinguish between being present at a murder and actually doing it."

"Oh, come on," said the cashier. "What do you want me to say? All right, she probably weighs a hundred and eighty-five." He started crying, blubbering against the cement floor.

"Here," Terry said. "Here's your money." He held the bag out to Number 2. "We're getting out of here," said Terry.

"Are you pulling rank on me?" said Number 2.

Number 2 looked like a man who is reading a piece of music he knows well and is about to begin to play it. Terry glanced at the walls of the room, at the boxes and their logos, although the names and labels, which usually seemed familiar if not dependable, now had an air of malice. The fever seemed to roll a little.

"Please," said the cashier. "Please."

"Please what?" said Number 2.

"Please don't," he said.

"Come on," said Terry.

"You're ordering me?" said Number 2.

"How could I order you? All I can do is to tell you what makes sense. That's all. Let's go. There's no point in waiting around."

"Sense?" said Number 2. "What the fuck makes sense?"

"Please," said the clerk.

"Stop saying that, if you know what's good for you."

They all waited. Terry had that sensation of swaying back and forth again, although now it was from the disorientation caused by thinking this was a dream to realizing it was not. Number 2 said, "Maybe some other time," and as though bored or impatient, and with an air of infinite dismissal, he walked straight along the shelves of liquor, the bottles filled with honey-colored or molasses-colored or clear liquid, and Terry walked behind him. The fever made the colors in the room more vibrant. The reds in particular shimmered, although the yellows were vivid, too, and reminded Terry of parrot feathers.

In the parking lot, they got into the car, the chrome shining brightly. Terry started the engine, turned around, and went out to the avenue. Number 2 looked in the bag, and said, "Isn't much. The guy was right. It was a slow night."

On the avenue, away from the store, lighted houses broke up the darkness. They drove on back streets toward the hospital. Terry thought he might be able to get him to come in right now. That was the important thing. Number 2 stared through the windshield, thinking things over. He looked at Terry and his entire aspect revealed a man who is giving in to something he wants but which appalls him. He said, "Yeah. I took your car."

Number 2 rolled down the window and threw out the empty bag. It fluttered away in the dark like some black, erratically flying bird. Terry got out his handkerchief and wiped his face. When he put it back in his pocket, he could feel the dampness through the fabric.

They drove along a little farther.

"Let me out up here," said Number 2.

"Wait," said Terry.

"No," said Number 2. "I'm getting out."

"I thought we had a deal," said Terry. "I went in there with you, didn't I?"

"So what?" said Number 2. "Pull over."

Terry pulled over and Number 2 got out.

"You know why I told you about the car, don't you?" said Number 2.

"Because you're going to disappear, right?" said Terry.

"That's right," said Number 2. "I'm going to start over someplace. Fresh as a daisy."

"I need your help," said Terry.

"Well, pal," said Number 2. "That's a shame." He slammed the door and turned into the night.

T HE SLIP from the laboratory showed Terry that Virginia's blood gases were getting lower. He could increase the flow of oxygen, but oxygen was toxic at high levels. He didn't want to, but he began to run it at seventy-five percent, which was pretty high, and as he did, he thought of something he had read, a theory of how life had begun as an attempt to resolve the toxicity of oxygen. He examined Virginia, pulling back her gown, looking for signs of a rash or swelling: all he found were the finger-shaped bruises where he had touched her before she had been bitten, which showed more now because of the bleeding. It looked as though he'd had purple ink on his hands when he'd touched her white skin. He looked at her lips, too. They were full, but not swollen. That was something.

He called his contacts at the blood bank again. They told him they weren't having much luck. They had located a donor, but he had gone on a canoe trip in the Arctic. Terry tried to imagine the man in a canoe on a river that went through a landscape that was without trees, just rocks and lichen. The donor could have been anywhere along hundreds of miles of river, but the blood bank said that maybe it could get a pilot in a float plane to look for him. It had done such things before. Would Virginia's insurance company pay for the plane? Terry didn't know. Well, who was going to pay for it? It could be a hundred and fifty dollars an hour, and then they might not find the donor anyway. What insurance company was going to pay for that these days? Terry said he'd pay for the plane. The blood bank wanted to know how much time they had.

Twelve hours, Terry thought. Maybe more. But not much. Her bleeding was slow, but constant. Sooner or later she wouldn't be able to get enough oxygen.

At ten o'clock in the evening, he went outside and got into his car. The car telephone was working all right. He checked it twice. He drove north into the hills near his house, but instead of turning into the canyon, he went up to the top of the ridge and out Mulholland Drive. Below, in the city, the lights seemed to fill the flat land like some sea that was composed of glowing bits, yellow, red, and green, a radiant ocean that washed up against the s-shaped bases of the hills. Then he pulled over and got out. Terry had come here to look at this sight on many occasions: the first time he had kissed a girl, his acceptance at medical school, the deaths of his mother and father. Every event that had required him to think, to understand, left him facing this collection of colors, this grid of luminescence, a beguiling suggestion of order. He wasn't sure why he came here. Now he stood on the hillside, crossed his arms, and tried to resist a sense of the approach of obliteration, as though physical effort would do the trick. He looked up at the stars, which were hard to make out. Only the brightest showed through the red mist over the city. He thought about trying to sum things up in the face of a scale so large that it defied imagination.

There wasn't time to go on at any length: what did he have to say, in a few words, in the face of extinction? He hoped he had done his best. Was there anything he had forgotten? Any clue that he hadn't pursued? He honestly didn't think so. Then he tried to remember a few dependable moments. As an intern he had worked on a maternity ward, and even now he could recall the reassurance that came from the fact that everything had turned out all right: the ward seemed bathed, after a birth, in the cool peacefulness and steadiness of life going about its business. He tried to think of something that would help him now, anything majestic or reassuring, icebergs like snowy mountain peaks, the taste of strawberries or the sight of them in the shadows under green leaves, or apple orchards in the springtime, so filled with blossoms the trees looked like indistinct puffs. He tried to remember the odor of the blossoms. He guessed he was grasping at anything that would slow things down, but these were all he had. He didn't think he could afford the luxury of remembering the scent of her hair, or the sound of her voice as she whispered exactly what he had wanted to hear.

At the same time, he thought about what a difficult time it was to be alive. The age was composed of nothing but doubt. There were no absolutes: all he had, like everyone else, was the attempt to try to stand up to chaos, although at times, like this one, when he was almost too tired for that, the only thing that kept him from giving up was the fear of what would replace fatigue.

He got back in his car, feeling a little better, and drove back along the boulevard and into the canyon, finally pulling up in front of his house. The hospital would call him if anything happened. Terry guessed that would be in the morning, and he wanted to get a little sleep before then. He went up to the door of his house, went in, and smelled the scent of tobacco.

217

"It's me," said Number 2.

As he moved his hand, the point of a cigarette made a path that looked like an orange neon tube.

"How did you get in?" said Terry.

"I got my ways," he said. "But I got to tell you, this place wouldn't keep anyone out. Your back door can be opened with a credit card or a piece of cardboard. You want to get a bolt, a dead bolt."

"I've been meaning to get one," said Terry.

"Close the door," said Number 2.

Terry closed it, and in the dark the smell of tobacco smoke was very strong.

"I'm having a drink," said Number 2. "You don't mind, do you?"

"No," said Terry. "Make yourself comfortable."

"I'm drinking something I can't pronounce. Smells like something's burning. Laga something. Comes from Scotland."

"Lagavulin," said Terry.

"Yeah," said Number 2. "I guess that's it. Tastes good after you get by that stink. What makes it smell that way?"

"Peat," he said. "Burning sod."

"No kidding," said Number 2.

Terry went over to the cabinet and poured himself a drink, too. He wanted to be calm enough not to do anything stupid. He guessed patience was what he needed most, but it was in the shortest supply.

"I thought you'd be long gone by now," said Terry. "Seattle. Vancouver. Mexico."

"I don't like Mexicans," said Number 2. "They've all got gas. You know, their diet isn't so good. Did you ever see a Mexican eat an orange?"

"No," said Terry.

"Well, there you have it," said Number 2. "Anyway, I got to thinking before I left. Maybe I made a mistake. Maybe it wasn't a good idea to talk to you about what I did. You can imagine how someone might get to thinking about that."

"What do you plan to do about it?" said Terry.

"Oh," said Number 2. "I'm thinking that over."

"I haven't told anybody. At least, not yet."

"That's good. Yeah. That's what I was hoping to hear."

"Uh-huh," said Terry. "I see."

"Do you?" said Number 2. "Well, that's got its advantages and disadvantages, doesn't it?"

Terry had a sip. He was thinking too far ahead, and he knew it, but it was reassuring. It gave him something to do. Mostly blood wasn't transfused off the street. That was the kind of thing that was done on a battlefield. He wondered if he could trust Number 2 if he asked him about AIDS or syphilis, or tuberculosis, or hepatitis. But then he thought, Not now. What can I offer?

"I guess there are times when you've got to take a chance," said Terry.

"You're telling me?" said Number 2.

Number 2 leaned forward, and Terry tried to see his other hand. Was the pistol in it? It was difficult to see.

"Ah, Christ," said Number 2. "I've got to get out of here. I don't know why I came back anyway."

"Maybe you want something," said Terry. "Maybe I can offer something. How about money? Maybe I can get some cash. We can go to an all-night cash machine."

Number 2 looked at Terry. "I didn't come here for money," he said. His voice was tired. "I thought maybe if I came up here I could stop thinking for a little bit. I just want to stop thinking.

Thinking this, thinking that. All the goddamned time. It drives you crazy."

Terry looked through the darkened room. He saw a luster on the edge of the glasses, on the coffee table, the molding around the door, on the stand of a floor lamp. Then he thought, Careful.

"People take all kinds of chances," said Terry.

"Do they? Tell me about one."

"Well," said Terry. "They go crazy places."

"Like where?" said Number 2. "Tell me about a place I never heard of before. A place I've never been."

Terry sat there, thinking about the hospital, and seemed to hear, with an almost hallucinatory quality, the voice of Frank Sims. "I knew a guy who went to some pretty strange places."

"Oh yeah?" said Number 2. "Like where?"

"A long ways from here," said Terry.

"Like an astronaut? I didn't think they went to doctors who weren't in, you know, the army or something. Are you treating one of those guys?"

"You could say that," said Terry.

"Where did he go? The moon?" said Number 2.

"No. It was different from that. Farther away. It had a double moon, you know, two of them revolving around each other."

"Why did he want to go to a place like that?"

"Maybe he had to," said Terry. "Maybe people have to take chances. Maybe they've got a conscience."

"That's not a good thing to have in my line of work," said Number 2. "Because you start thinking. You think this. You think that. Shit."

Terry had another sip. He tasted the peat. It was very strong. He tried to concentrate on it. Even if he got the blood, he'd have to treat Virginia for serum sickness, but he could do that all right.

That was still too far ahead. What could you do for yourself if you had a sucking chest wound?

"What happened to your pal?" said Number 2. "You know, the astronaut?"

"He's dead," said Terry.

"Well, that's great," said Number 2. "He took a chance and look what happened to him."

"Maybe he didn't have much choice," said Terry.

"I got a choice," said Number 2. "How about I just waste you and walk the fuck out of here and forget I ever saw you."

Terry swallowed. He didn't know what scared him the most, the possibility that Number 2 would do what he said, or that if he did, Virginia would be alone. The two were related anyway, and there wasn't time to split hairs. He looked down at the glass in his hands, where the shiny liquor swung back and forth.

"Maybe I'm asking you for something," said Number 2. "Maybe I'm asking you if I can trust you. I'd like to trust you. I'd feel a little better if I could trust you."

"Well," said Terry. "What can I say? Would you believe me if I said you could?"

"I don't know," said Number 2.

"So there we are. I can't say anything because you won't believe me. I guess I'm stuck with having to say I won't lie to you."

"That's a pretty goddamned thin reed," said Number 2. "Can I trust you?"

Terry looked down. "Not really," he said.

They sat there for a while. Number 2 lighted a cigarette, the flare making a small, flower-shaped glow in the dark.

"Well, well," said Number 2. He blew some smoke. "Tell me about that place your pal went to."

"The astronaut?" said Terry.

221

"Uh-huh," said Number 2.

"There were odd plants growing there, flowers as big as rowboats, and birds as small as paper clips. No snakes. Nothing like that. The air was filled with vitamins."

Number 2 smoked his cigarette.

"Go on," he said. "I'm thinking it over."

"You could taste the clouds, he said, it was like putting your tongue against a Popsicle."

"Could you get laid up there?" said Number 2.

"I don't know," said Terry. "My friend was in love with a woman here."

"That's tough luck," said Number 2.

"Sometimes," said Terry. "Not always."

"Not with me. With me it was always tough luck. Being broke a lot of the time didn't help, but what can you do?"

Terry wanted to say, There are things. But he said, "I don't know. Let's go down to the hospital. All right?"

"If I go with you, what are we going to do about my problem? You know, about what I told you? Are you going to forget that?"

Terry looked across the darkness between them. "We'll cross that bridge when we get there," said Terry. He stood up. "There's not a lot of time," he said.

"You're telling me?" said Number 2. He finished his drink. "If you had told me a lie, I probably would have fucking killed you." He put the glass down. "Flowers like rowboats. Jesus. Let's go down to the hospital. I guess I'm just like your astronaut friend. That's what I feel like, sitting on a rocket that's getting ready to blow. So let's get in the car before I change my mind."

They drove downhill, and Terry could feel gravity's tug as they went around curves, crossing those places where water ran in a black sheet, like oil. It was a comforting sensation, although it was filled with risk. It felt like giving in.

"There's some things we've got to talk about," said Terry.

"Like what?"

"Do you use a needle? Do you shoot drugs?"

"Oh," said Number 2. "So it's a two-way street after all? Well, well. So you're going to have to trust what I say, too."

"I guess so," said Terry

"There's no guessing here," said Number 2.

"All right," said Terry. "Yeah. I'm going to have to trust you. Are you using a needle? What do you do sexually?"

Number 2 sat quietly, thinking it over. They came down to the avenue.

"Say I told you I was using drugs with a needle, and that I was hanging around in gay bars. What would that do for you?"

Terry shook his head, thinking that the moment he had wanted to put off might be coming after all, which is the occasion when every decision is bad, and some are worse than others.

"I don't want to think about that," said Terry. "I'd probably have to use the blood anyway."

"Uh-huh," said Number 2. "But you wouldn't feel good about it?"

Terry shook his head. "No," he said. "Have you ever been in love?"

"I don't like to talk about it," said Number 2. "But, yeah. A couple of times."

"How would you feel if you killed the woman you were in love with?"

Number 2 looked out the window. The signal changed and they went through it, turning toward the freeway.

"Is that what we're talking about? Your patient is a woman you care about?"

"Uh-huh," said Terry.

"You're telling me the truth, aren't you?"

"Yes," said Terry.

"Jesus," said Number 2. "I wish things were different. You can't believe how I wish things were other than they are. . . ."

They passed a liquor store, a market, and some apartment houses.

"I don't hang around in gay bars or use needles. I'm in good health, as far as I know."

Terry looked over, trying to decide whether this was true. Wouldn't the worst thing be seduction by what you imagined were someone else's best impulses, when in fact they weren't anything more than a trap? They got on the freeway and drove south, until the exit came. When they swung into the hospital, they saw the words that said, "Yo gonna die soon."

The two of them went in through the main entrance and back to Terry's office, where Terry took a blood sample. Then he went into Virginia's room and took some of hers and mixed the two together on a slide. There was no reaction. The blood was all right, at least as far as a transfusion was concerned. Terry asked Number 2 to lie down, and he went into the lab and brought back the necessary equipment. He started drawing the blood. Number 2 stared at the ceiling.

The phone rang and Terry answered.

"How are you doing?" said Kerjeski. "Police work never seems to end, you know. Sometimes I think I never sleep. Is this a bad time?"

"No," said Terry. "Not really."

"Well, that's good," said Kerjeski. "That's great. I just thought I'd call to see how're you doing. Or if you've been thinking about what you saw or didn't see?"

"I've been thinking about it," said Terry.

"Well," said Kerjeski. "I'm glad to hear that. Sometimes if you think about something from a new perspective it will do wonders for you. I've noticed that."

"I guess that's true."

The bag of blood was almost full.

"So have you got anything to say?" said Kerjeski.

"Yeah," said Terry.

The color of the blood wasn't bright, like a fire engine, but much darker, almost purple. Number 2 went right on staring at the ceiling.

"Well, tell me. I'm all ears," said Kerjeski. "Can you identify him?"

Terry squeezed the telephone.

"I don't hear you," said Kerjeski.

"Yes," said Terry.

"Yes, what?" said Kerjeski.

"I saw him," said Terry.

"You don't sound too happy about it," said Kerjeski.

A nurse came in and took the blood and carried it up to Virginia's room.

"Yeah, well, it's complicated," said Terry. "He's here now."

"No shit," said Kerjeski. "We'll be right over."

Terry hung up. The hall was silent, although in the distance a siren whined. It got louder as it approached. Heart attack. Or automobile accident. The heart attacks usually came in the morning: the cardiac hour. Some guy gets up and goes into the bathroom and that's it.

"I'm feeling a little tired," said Number 2.

"That will go away. Maybe tomorrow."

"Uh-huh. That was a cop, wasn't it?"

"Yes," said Terry.

"I knew it," said Number 2. "I just knew it."

"What are you going to do?"

"Nothing," said Number 2. "I'm feeling a little tired. I guess I'll just rest here for a minute. I never liked Seattle anyway. But I'll tell you one thing."

"What's that?" said Terry.

"If you're going to be bad, stay bad. If you're good, stay good. It's that middle that's going to eat you alive." Number 2 started crying. He lay there on his back, the tears coming out of the corners of his eyes, his chin pitted. He shook a little. "Jesus. I wish things were different than they are. We could have been pals."

"That's right," said Terry. "Maybe we could have been. You never know."

"Tell me about that place," said Number 2. "You know where your astronaut friend went. Where was it?"

"Way out. Orion. Light years away."

"A double moon?"

"Yes," said Terry.

"Isn't that something?" said Number 2.

T ERRY WATCHED as the blood was given to her. The room was quiet, not so much that he could hear the drip drip drip of it, but enough so that he could imagine it, not the actual sound, but an ominous implication of what he was doing, as though fear could be broken down into discrete, drop-sized units. To distract himself, he tried to imagine the precise color of the blood. He thought it was like a redwood stain he had seen once in a jar, but even that didn't seem quite accurate. He guessed nothing was exactly like it, although the color of iodine was close. He looked at the blood. A transfusion like this wasn't done often, and he didn't like things that weren't done often. It was the way blood was given on a battlefield, and for an instant he thought he could sense a whiff of something, a scent usually associated with disorder (the stink of gunpowder, for instance) that probably went along with such transfusions. Terry realized he had accepted something on faith, and that he had taken a chance on infectious diseases, such as HIV-1, but there were others, too, such as hepatitis B or C, and the possibility of chronic disease, even cancer. As he waited, he thought about faith: mostly it was something that a physician didn't want to have to rely upon, but he stood there, so definitely in its realm. It was something like discovering a long-lost relative who turned out to be both more scary and reassuring than anyone had supposed possible. He tried to imagine what such a person might be like. A bank robber with a Ph.D. in astrophysics.

The crash started with the blood gases falling. The oxygen had been running high already, but even so, Virginia wasn't getting enough. A nurse watched the monitor and turned to Terry, and said, "Do you see that?"

"Yes," said Terry.

"Why is that happening?"

"I don't know," said Terry.

"What's wrong?" said Rick, who had come into the room.

"I don't know," said Terry.

"How come the oxygen is falling?" said Rick.

Terry shook his head, not because he had an answer, but to shake off anything that would get in the way. He opened Virginia's gown. It was odd to see her here, so clinically defined, so much a patient. He put a stethoscope against her chest and listened, and said, "The tube has slipped. That's the problem."

"What?" said Rick.

Terry adjusted the plastic pipe that ran into her lungs. It had slipped past the branches of the bronchial tubes and had gone into one lung. Then he turned down the oxygen, and they got another blood gas report. It was better, although Terry wasn't convinced that her lungs wouldn't begin to fill with fluid now anyway.

The crash began in earnest a little later. She began to swell, and the swelling came on quickly. Her hands became so smooth and puffy that they reminded Terry of a child's Mylar balloon. There is not a great deal of difference between an allergic heart and a traumatic one: the pulse elevates and the blood pressure begins to fall, and they did so quickly.

Terry had the odd sensation of keeping an appointment, that what he had been trying to avoid had come after all, and that it had waited until he was tired and most likely to make a mistake. Or maybe he had come to that moment in which, no matter what he did, he would be wrong. As he stood there listening to hallway noise, he had a feeling that a series of inevitable events had led to this moment, and that if he went back to try to find the beginning, he would only be lost. And, along with that, he suspected that Virginia's condition revealed his moral flaws, as though if he had resisted his own romantic impulses, he wouldn't be standing here trying to decide which bad decision to make. The venom had a tendency to weaken the vessels in the brain. What Virginia needed was epinephrine, a synthetic adrenaline, but that would also increase the pressure in the brain. A fair number of people who died of snakebite had bleeding in the brain. Of course, if he did nothing she would die, anyway.

He asked for the epinephrine, and while the nurse went to get it, someone shouted in the hall. Then Number 2 appeared in the doorway. He was wearing handcuffs, but he had obviously gotten away from the police just as he had gotten away before. Now, though, he hadn't looked for a way out, but had started looking for Terry. He stood in the door, holding his hands up so that Terry could see that he was chained. In the hall, people stayed away from him. The nurse, though, pushed past him and gave Terry the syringe.

"Well, did you get everything you wanted?" said Number 2. "Did you?"

Terry used the syringe. "No," he said to Number 2. "No. No one ever gets everything he wants. Get out of here."

"You're through with me now?" said Number 2.

Terry started to watch the monitor. "What?" said Terry. "Not now."

A policeman caught up to Number 2 and took him by the arm. Number 2 turned away, then looked over his shoulder, back at the doorway, screaming, "Not now! Not now! Not now! You son of a bitch. If I get a chance, I'll settle things all right. That's right. You remember. I'll be waiting. Oh, yes. I won't forget. I got a memory like an elephant. You hear that? Like an elephant."

The nurse and Terry watched the monitor. He wanted to see the blood pressure rise. That's all he wanted.

"What do we do?" said Rick.

"Wait," said Terry.

"That's it?" said Rick.

"Yes," said Terry.

I T WAS PART GILT and part sunlight, but while the sun was impossible to look at, the reverse was also true. Instead of making her turn away, the light was attractive. It sparkled, reminding her of being in bed with a man she loved, and of getting so close, so incredibly close, that if she just let go, if she just took a deep breath, if she just abandoned herself to it, then she would go over the top into that warm, buzzing light, the flecks washing over her. It would be like rising into the center of a welder's torch as it cut steel, where the bits of light fell over her in a shower. Although now, as she went over the top, there was a difference: it didn't end. She kept right on going. She didn't hit the bed again in a mundane room with bills to pay and the freeway to face and a check that might bounce at the bank. Instead, she hovered in the shower of welder's sparks, too distracted to murmur, or even to realize the words she'd use if she had a moment, which were *my God, my God.*

She couldn't really tell whether she had given in, although

she had a hazy notion, morphinelike and warm, that she couldn't be sure because she didn't want to know. She put her hand up and saw the flecks of light around it. They could have been from a sparkler or they could have been galaxies. It was hard to distinguish, and made no difference at all. With the notion of leave-taking, almost as though gathering a momento, as though leaving a room where she had worked hard and alone, she remembered a few details from a darker realm. She remembered being bitten. The creature had been so fast, light showing on its back as it struck, and she had started for the hospital. Even the freeway and the reflection of the sun, which made some of the cars seem like molten shapes, all seemed dull now.

She remembered two pillows against the wall in Terry's bedroom, and how she leaned on them, her legs out before her, the sunlight washing over them. It must have been around one o'clock or so in the afternoon. Terry had sat down next to her. He didn't say anything. He was wearing a pair of white pants and a white shirt. The shirt had come from the laundry, and she could smell the starch. In the sunlight, the shirt expressed what existed between them, an attachment that she perceived as heat and light and warmth. When she tried to use a word, like *passion* or *love* or *devotion,* she was certain something had been unsaid, or egregiously ignored. Nothing seemed intimate enough to suggest this nameless connection, although she prayed that she could discover an act that in its appalling intimacy would demonstrate just how far she was willing to go.

He sat there. She had never seen him cry, but she supposed his tears were pretty ordinary. She knew that he had come from the hospital. She didn't have to ask. By now it was obvious: A young man had died, drowning in his own blood, lung shot, or a child had died in some accident that was as ridiculous as it was appalling. Or another patient, a thirty-nine-year-old woman, had died of cancer, leaving a child. No one had been able to do anything.

She had never seen anyone cry out of anger before. He said, "Well, I've got to stop this. I really do. Maybe I should get undressed. There isn't much time, is there? I don't mean to spoil an afternoon." He pulled his shirt open, snapping the buttons off with a pop, pop, pop. One button flew through the sunlit air. It made an arc, flying from the front of his shirt toward the rug. It was a Persian rug, with a pattern of yellow shapes on a blue background, and she realized that the button traced a path that also resembled the spark from a welder's torch, a fleck whose trajectory described an equation.

The button landed with a slight *tup*. He sat there, his head in his hands now. She guessed that he was showing her how much he trusted her. But what could she do? If she said the wrong thing, what would happen? He'd turn and look at her with that polite expression that showed she had failed. If she said the wrong thing, he'd listen to her, and say, "I guess that's right." Then something wouldn't be the same anymore. They'd end up just two people sitting on a bed in the afternoon, unequal to each other or the moment.

She saw the button on the floor. It seemed a long way off. She sat up, moving through the sunshine, feeling it on her stomach and thigh and on her back as she leaned over and picked up the button, pinching it off the floor with her fingertips. She turned back to him, saying, "Here. I'll sew it back on."

"Will you?"

"Yes," she said. "I'll thread a needle. White thread, and I'll push the tip of the needle into the cloth." She flicked the tip of her tongue against his neck. "Would you like that?"

"Yes," he said.

"I can fix it," she said.

"That's nice," he said.

"All right," she said. "That's what I'll do. Maybe I can do something else, too."

"Like what?"

"Oh," she said. "It'll be a surprise. But you'll like it."

"I've had enough surprises for a while," he said. "Tell me. What else can you do."

"It'll be something innocent," she said.

"Uh-huh," he said.

"Have you ever sunbathed nude?"

"No."

"Well, we'll do that sometime. We'll find a private place. All right? We'll feel the heat and light."

She realized that she still held the button, and now it was whiter, at once blinding and attractive. It seemed to expand, to become somehow larger and infinitely small at the same time, as though she could look into the heart of one of those flecks that washed over her skin to see just how things were connected after all. Well, it was all right. She was reminded of the time she had seen Terry in the light, against the gold and silver scales on the Pacific behind him: it was all mixed up with giving in to him and in to a general warmth that beckoned.

She opened her eyes. Now, in the hospital room, she saw him. He hadn't shaved and his beard had highlights in it, reddish and gold ones that looked like wire. He stood very still. She heard the insistent and mindless beeping of an alarm. It didn't sound like her alarm clock, although maybe she had bought a new one. He held her hand and looked down at her. He said, "Don't. Please."

T HE BLEEDING STOPPED. Terry knew that it would eventually, although there had been moments in the last few days
when he wasn't so sure he would be able to buy enough time. He
had been waiting for the clotting factors, either from the blood
transfusion or her own ability to produce them, which would
come with time. Conditions such as this one usually responded to
time — that is, if the patient could wait.

Now that she was better he came to her room at night when
she was sleeping, and as he stood there he tried to apprehend the
change that had taken place in the room. The silence now was a
lack of sound rather than the presence of something else, which,
while impossible to hear, had still been palpable as a pressure, as
the existence of a turmoil in the room. He knew that she was
going to have serum sickness, but that was treatable. It would
be all right. The hush of the air conditioner seemed like order
itself. The paralysis had passed. She was weak, but that would
pass. No sequelae, or lasting consequences. He stood there, in the

shadows, allowing himself to wonder about where they would go from here.

On the day Virginia was scheduled to go home, Terry visited her room. It was just an ordinary room now. No monitors, no respirator, no sliding door that opened when someone approached it. Outside the window, some shaggy trees stood, not quite green, even a little gray, in the light.

"Well," said Terry. "This is it."

"Uh-huh," she said.

"Where are you going to go?"

She looked out the window. "I don't know," she said.

"Have you talked to Rick?" he said.

"Not really," she said.

"Well," said Terry again. He looked out the window and thought of the marks on her skin, the purple bruises in the shape of his fingertips, which had faded as she had gotten better. They had turned green and yellow, and finally just yellow, fading a little more each day. He had been glad to see them go, indicating that the bleeding had stopped and that she was getting better, but as they had disappeared, they left him increasingly disoriented. The marks had been a sure, palpable sign of something between him and Virginia, and now that they were vanishing, he wasn't sure whether the attachment wasn't going, too.

Rick came into the room and stood at the foot of the bed. Virginia looked at him for a moment. They didn't smile at one another. He was carrying a shopping bag.

"I brought some of your clothes," he said.

"Thanks," she said.

"We can go home, I guess," said Rick.

"I suppose so," said Virginia. "I'm feeling a little tired."

"That will go away soon," said Terry.

"Will it?" said Virginia. "I'm glad to hear that."

"Sure," said Rick. "You'll be feeling great soon."

"Ummmm," said Virginia.

Rick and Terry went out into the hall while she dressed. Lunch trays were being distributed. The trays were gray and the covers for the food were different colors, green, blue, red, very cheerful, although now Terry couldn't stand to look at them. He could smell the pale soup. Here and there a plate of trembling Jell-O went by.

"I never liked that stuff," said Rick. "Not even as a kid."

Terry nodded, and felt idiotic for doing so. What was so bad about agreeing that Jell-O wasn't the most appetizing thing in the world? He wanted to say, I hate the stuff, too, but this seemed like a confession. He watched the stainless steel carts, like contraptions in someplace where souls were bought and sold and carried away. Then he thought, After all, they're married. Didn't Virginia have obligations to see what was left? Wasn't that the decent thing to do?

"I never liked it either," he said.

"Well, I guess some things you just have to accept," said Rick.

"Yes," said Terry.

"There're lots of things like that," said Rick. "What can you do about it?" He shrugged.

"Not much," said Terry.

"Sure," said Rick. "Like lima beans. God."

They stood there in the hall. Terry wondered if any of the patients were getting lima beans. He thought he might be shaking but then decided that he probably wasn't, at least not visibly.

"I wanted to say thanks," said Rick.

"There's nothing to thank me for," said Terry.

"Well," said Rick. "You know what I mean. I was scared there for a while."

I still am, thought Terry. He looked back toward the door, which was open just a crack, and he could see some movement, like silk, as Virginia took off a robe and began to pick up the things she was going to wear. It was a flicker that reminded Terry of an echo, or a scent that was disappearing from a pillow. He thought again of the marks of his fingerprints as they had disappeared from her skin. He could have wished they were still there so that when she stood in front of the mirror, after a bath, she'd see the proof of his existence. He shook his head.

"Is anything wrong?" said Rick.

"Not really," said Terry.

Virginia opened the door. She had brushed her hair and washed her face and looked brisk, if a little tired. The three of them walked up to the elevator and got in. It made a humming sound and an occasional creak as it descended. Rick took the shopping bag from her, and they went out to the office, where they signed some papers. That's where Terry left them.

He went home and sat in his house, looking at the answering machine. He had a drink and tried to go to sleep, but he couldn't. He had ordered some articles from medical journals about toxins and snakebite, and now he sat down to read them. One of the articles described a bite in Germany. A man had kept an exotic snake in the house where he lived with his parents. Terry guessed he must have been unemployed. The man got drunk one night and took a hammer and smashed the terrarium in which the snake lived, and when it slithered out, onto the floor, the man grabbed it and it bit him. His father came in and began to fight his son for the snake. The father grabbed the tail and the son had the head, and they pulled on it until the snake ripped in two.

Terry turned to the other articles and read about the effects of various venoms. Mortality rates seemed to depend on how quickly someone got to the hospital. He said, All right, that's enough, but in the morning he got up and started again. He read an account of a pregnant woman who had been bitten by a brown snake in Australia. The paralytic toxins seemed to work in an identifiable way, and as he read the chemistry, getting closer and closer to the impersonal quality of its attack, he found that he was forever being pulled forward into some endlessly receding mystery. He stood up and walked around the room, saying, All right. Enough.

The building was made of institutional brick, and it was distinguished, even from the outside, by an inevitability, as though in the stained brick, in the film of dust that lay over the glass, in the fast food wrappers on the steps, one could see the grubbiness associated with folly. Terry stood in front of it, looking at the windows of the county jail. Inside it had the smell that all jails have, a mixture of unwashed clothes, marginal plumbing, the sweat that comes from men who have discovered their own worst fears, and the odor of the cheap disinfectant that had been used, with only partial success, to cover up the stink. Terry went up to the desk and asked to have a visit with Number 2. He was told to wait, have a seat over there.

As he sat in the waiting room on a plastic chair with a curved seat and no cushion, he kept his eyes on the wall opposite him to give other visitors in the room some privacy, but mostly this was unnecessary because the others already seemed to have accepted being in this room as a chore to be done on the way to the dry cleaner or the liquor store. He tried to imagine the medical problems of a prison: communicable diseases and trauma, skin diseases, ringworm.

A guard called his name and Terry stood up and walked down the corridor, counting the number of times a steel door slammed shut behind him. He sat down in a small cubicle with a telephone. A piece of Plexiglas separated him from Number 2. The plastic was scratched and made objects on the other side appear whitish and distortedly hazy. Number 2 was pale, but his complexion seemed a matter of mood, or of some unrelieved discontent, as much as a lack of sun. He looked at Terry through the glass.

"Pick up the phone," said Terry.

Number 2 went on staring through the plastic. It occurred to Terry that Number 2 could just stare at him until he got up and left, without a word being said. Surely that was the kind of cheap dramatics that appealed to Number 2. As Terry sat there, he thought of the young man who had been brought to the hospital after huffing butane: even now he felt the gulf that had opened between the two of them as the boy had slipped away.

Number 2 picked up the phone.

"What are you doing here?" he said.

"I thought I'd come by," said Terry.

"No shit?" said Number 2.

Terry hadn't thought about what he would say, and so he was left wondering if he had come here for the two of them to discuss the mundane.

"How's the food?" said Terry.

"Great," said Number 2. "If you like garbage."

"Have you got a lawyer?" said Terry.

"Yeah," said Number 2. "Public defender. I'm going to kill him when I get out."

"He's that bad?" said Terry.

Number 2 looked through the plastic. "You know something? When I was hanging around with you, I must have been crazy. It's like some guy who thinks because he puts on a suit, you know, he can hide the fact that he comes from East LA. But everyone always knows." He looked down.

"Maybe you can change your lawyer," said Terry.

"Naw," said Number 2. "It's not my lawyer. It's me. I see what I've been doing wrong. They won't catch me next time."

In the next cubicle someone laughed. It wasn't exactly a pleasant laugh.

"Can I send you something?" said Terry.

"Sure," said Number 2. "A hacksaw and a gun."

"Isn't someone listening to this?" said Terry.

"The screws know that's a joke," said Number 2. "It's like saying, sure, send in a blonde with long legs. That's a joke. You hear me?" He looked down to the end of the room, where the guards were listening in.

Screws. It was the first time Terry had ever heard the word used in earnest.

"Why don't you get out of here?" said Number 2. "Can't you see that just looking at your face is hideous for me? You didn't think I knew words like that, did you?"

"I just thought I'd tell you that I appreciated what you did . . ."

"Fuck that," said Number 2. "I made a mistake. I got fucking weak for a moment. That's all. Everything's great if you don't weaken."

"Uh-huh," said Terry.

"Sure," said Number 2. "Like you weakened coming down here. You should have gone on about your business without giving it another thought."

"Maybe that's right," said Terry. "But I don't think so."

They looked at each other.

"Maybe I'll see you when I get out," said Number 2. "Some night when you think the world is going along by all the rules and principles that you learned in school. Everything's going to look beautiful. Einstein's going to be working. Yeah. And then I'll show you something."

"Are you threatening me?" said Terry.

"Me?" said Number 2. He put his face closer to the glass.

"Look," said Terry. "I came down here to see how you were doing. Let it go at that."

"Why would you want to do that?" said Number 2. "Well, tell me. Have you got the guts to tell me?"

Terry looked into the room beyond Number 2, but all he could see through the plastic haze was someone walking by a green, two-tone wall. He held the warm and greasy handset. "If someone does something unexpectedly decent, you feel an obligation. The decency obligates you. It's got nothing to do with law, or anything, just an obligation that runs from one human being to another. That's why I'm here," he said.

He stood up.

"That's right," said Number 2. "That's what you can do. Leave."

Terry hung up the phone and started to turn. A constant murmur of conversation filled the room, some of it loud because the telephones weren't all working and people had to shout. The voices were saying, What's the lawyer's plan? Should I take the plea? How are the kids? Don't bring them here. I couldn't stand to have them here. Please. Are you seeing him regularly?

Terry took a step from the booth when he heard a knocking on the plastic.

Number 2 motioned. Terry came back and stood next to the plastic. Number 2 mouthed some words so that the guards wouldn't be able to hear. Terry couldn't make them out immediately, but he went on staring, and as he did he thought of some politician saying, Read my lips. Number 2 repeated what he had to say. Terry said one word. Number 2 looked at him and then turned back into the jail. Terry went back through the doors, not counting this time, and as he emerged into the hazy sunshine, he heard the question that Number 2 had mouthed. *Did she live?*

Rick's house was on Sunset Boulevard, out toward the beach. It was a place with a large lawn and a circular driveway, and the front of it was covered with stones that suggested a building in some other part of the world. England, perhaps, or maybe the house that an Englishman might build in some godforsaken place that didn't provide the same materials he could have found at home. It had a pitched roof, and in the back some palm trees stood, shaggy-looking and a little idiotic.

In the evening, Rick and Virginia had dinner, and they did so with all the formality of people who think that if they just ignore something long enough, it will disappear. Virginia could feel it, almost as though some cement for a plastic model had been smeared on her skin and hardened. She cooked for him, shrimp in wine and garlic served over a little angel-hair pasta, and they sat opposite one another, eating slowly, although Virginia wanted to bolt it down and get up and start doing the dishes. He insisted on doing them, as an acknowledgment of the fact that she was still weak and that he had failed somehow previously, and with the hope that by rinsing off a few pieces of china and a couple of glasses, everything could be put back where it had been. And just where was that?

"Do you like the shrimp?" she said.

"Oh, yes," he said. "It's good. Wonderful."

"Do you think so?"

"Yes," he said. "Maybe I can cook something tomorrow. Kind of a cook-off."

"Uh-huh," she said.

The table was a small one in the dining room. Outside they could see the fountain in the backyard, a pile of stones that had been designed and installed by a lesbian with a tattoo and her two assistants, young women with shaved heads. The stones almost matched those that were used for the facade of the house. Virginia and Rick ate quietly for a while. The grass had been mowed in the afternoon and they could smell it.

"I never told you about the architecture of this house, did I?" said Rick.

"Not really," said Virginia.

"Well, a few years ago I wanted to build a place that was totally safe. Everyone was talking about the Big One, you know. The Big Quake. Well, I wanted to be ready for that, so when I built this house, I had the engineers put the entire thing on a concrete slab. I mean a slab. Eight feet thick and reinforced with steel rods. You know, the ground could open right beneath us, and the house would be all right."

"Would it?"

"Yes," said Rick. "Almost anything could happen. Right at our feet. Isn't that something?"

"Yes," said Virginia.

"And you know something?" said Rick. "It cost a damned fortune, too."

Before they went to bed, Rick suggested that they take a sauna. It was one of those things that he thought of as stylish, and he was proud of it. Everyone who came to the house got a look at it, and some even had to sit in it, no matter what the season or what the occasion. They both got into it and sat in the cedar-scented heat, feeling it against their skin. Then the tickle of perspiration came, and Virginia sighed. He did too.

"All right," he said. "OK. I think we better have a talk."

"Who?" said Virginia.

"All of us," he said. "We're not going to get anywhere this way. Are you strong enough to take a little walk?"

"Yes," she said.

"All right," he said. "I know a place."

He got out of the sauna, and, still wet, with a towel wrapped around him, he called Terry.

"Tell me," said Virginia. "Did you ever buy a handgun?"

"No," said Rick.

They met the next morning, in a small town off the Pacific Coast Highway. The grassy hills here were all brown with the occasional green and shaggy puff of an isolated tree. A stone ridge stood beyond the grass. It looked more like Africa than California, and Terry half expected to see a zebra. The sky was hazy blue, marked here and there by the long trails of jets on their way to some impossibly distant place, China, Japan, Australia.

They walked through the grass and beyond the trees, where they stopped for a little while. They looked perfectly innocent.

"You know," said Rick. "I guess we can be adult about this, don't you think?"

"What does that mean?" said Virginia.

"Well," said Rick. "That we all feel that we get what's coming to us."

"I don't know," said Virginia.

"Sure," said Rick. "Isn't vengeance part of being adult?"

"I think we should just be thankful," said Terry.

"For what?" said Rick. "Having my life ripped up?"

"Everyone's sorry about that," said Virginia.

"Well," said Rick. "That's great. You know what? I'm sorry in one hand and I shit in the other, and you tell me which gets full first?"

"Please," said Virginia. "Please."

They walked along a little more, gaining altitude.

"Look," said Terry. "You can see the Pacific from here."

He had stopped to look back. Below them, beyond the savanna grass, he saw the Pacific, which was placid in the afternoon sun. It was the color of green tea.

"Let's go farther up. Maybe we need some privacy," said Rick.

"What do you mean?" said Virginia.

"To talk things over. That's what we came up here to do," said Rick.

Around them the grass heaved with the slight afternoon breeze, which carried a sudden coolness to their damp skin. They kept climbing, going up toward the first ledges of rock, which looked like some ruins that had finally collapsed into a heap.

"All right," said Terry. "Let's talk."

"In a little," said Rick.

"Virginia's tired," said Terry.

"I'm tired of a lot of things, too," said Rick.

"I'm all right," said Virginia. "Believe me, I'd rather be walking, out here, than a lot of other places."

"Maybe this wasn't a good idea," said Terry. "I think we should go back."

They came to the first layers of rock, gray and crumbled, and dappled with shadows. It was in one of the shadows that they heard the rattling of a snake. All of them stopped and waited, listening to the sound.

"Do you see it?" said Rick.

"No," said Terry.

"I think it's over there," said Virginia. "They don't like direct sunlight. It will kill them."

"No kidding," said Rick.

"It's over there," said Terry.

"Oh, God," said Virginia. "I don't know. I don't like that sound."

The snake was in the shadows, its coils looped over each other in a sloppy way, like a rope that had been thrown into a corner. It was hard to see all of it, but it seemed to be thick, dusty-colored, with diamond-shaped markings on its back. The rattle was like steam escaping from a pipe. The sound seemed to fill the air and the scent of dry grass.

"Do you think there's another one around?" said Terry.

"That's a reassuring thought," said Rick.

"I don't know," said Virginia. "It's possible."

"Maybe we should kill the thing," said Rick. "We could drag it out here and . . ."

"You want to drag it out?" said Terry.

"Maybe it will go away," said Rick.

They all stood there.

"Oh, God," said Virginia.

The rattling stopped. The silence was almost worse.

"Where is the thing?" said Rick. "Is it moving?"

"It wants to be left alone," said Virginia. "Just give it a chance to go and it will leave."

The snake started making that sound again, filling the air with what seemed like dry, dusty fear.

"What are we going to do?" said Terry.

"I don't know," said Rick. "I don't know."

"Let's get away from here," said Virginia.

"OK," said Rick.

They looked around.

"I'll bet when you were really scared," said Rick to Terry, "I'll bet you prayed, didn't you?"

"What difference does that make?" said Terry.

"Tell me," said Rick.

"I don't know what to call it," said Terry. "I was just scared. I didn't know what to do after a certain point."

Rick nodded. "Even as a physician you did that?"

"Yes," said Terry.

"Well, you know something?" said Rick. "I never came to that point. Not really." He looked back down, where they had come from. "So I guess that settles it, doesn't it?" Rick said.

"Settles what?" said Virginia.

"Do you want to go with him?" said Rick.

"I want to get away from here," said Virginia.

They turned now and started walking downhill. The sound receded and stopped, and it was replaced with the warm hush of the wind and the sound of it in the grass. As they went, they saw the Pacific, and the film of sunlight on it.

"Yes," said Virginia.

"Yes, what?" said Rick.

"Yes. I want to go with him."

Virginia brought over some of her things in the evening. They were in cardboard boxes and in a suitcase, and she pulled up in front of the house with the air of someone who has been through an earthquake and who has managed to escape with what she could carry. They brought the boxes in and hung her things up and cleared a place for her in the bathroom. Then they had dinner. They stayed up all night, waiting until they could see the sun rise. It came through the trees outside, making the edges of the leaves as bright as gilt pages in a book. The sky turned from deep blue to gray to a silver-white in the east.

The light came into her room with a fuzzy luminescence, and the rays were more direct as the sun rose, almost lines that were defined by the edges of the windows. Virginia watched as it moved along the sheets, up to her legs. She was very still as it moved over her skin. Her eyes were closed for a moment or two.

"I was thinking," she said. "I'd like to get away for a while. Maybe we could go up the coast."

"All right," he said.

She ran her fingers along his chest, into the warmth of the light.

"We could take a lunch," she said. "I could make a little something. We could bring some grapes. Not those purple ones. I don't like those."

"Well," he said. "Fine. We'll have the green ones."

"You can see a little dust on them," she said. "Have you ever noticed?"

"Yes," he said.

The light lay across her stomach. She waited, her eyes closed, concentrating.

"Sure," she said. "We'd put it in a basket. Have you got a small towel? We'd line it with the towel, and put the things in, some cheese, a loaf of bread, the fruit, some napkins." She swallowed. "That feels so warm." She shifted her weight a little.

"Yes," he said.

"We could just drive. There wouldn't be any traffic," she said.

"Well, I don't know about that."

"There might not be any. You can never tell."

"Maybe," he said.

"No cops around, either. We go just as far as we want."

"You can drive, then," said Terry.

"That's what I thought," she said. "Don't move. Just wait."

"All right."

She waited until the light moved over her breasts and up to her neck, and then she moved her hand so that she could feel the light even under her arms. She waited longer, both of them concentrating. The light fell over her face and left her features warm and very clear. When she opened her eyes to look at him, he saw two bright points, a sun in each dark pupil.

Available in Norton Paperback Fiction